Apuleius

The Golden Ass

Translated by William Adlington

Revised by S. Gaselee

With an Introduction by James Morwood

WORDSWORTH CLASSICS
OF WORLD LITERATURE

This edition published 1996 by Wordsworth Editions Limited
Cumberland House, Crib Street, Ware, Hertfordshire SG12 9ET

ISBN 1 85326 460 1

Typeset in Great Britain by Antony Gray
Printed and bound in Denmark by Nørhaven

The paper in this book is produced from pure wood
pulp, without the use of chlorine or any other substance
harmful to the environment. The energy used in its
production consists almost entirely of hydroelectricity
and heat generated from waste material, thereby
conserving fossil fuels and contributing little
to the greenhouse effect.

CONTENTS

INTRODUCTION

Apuleius was born into a prosperous family at Madaura in the Roman province of North Africa in about AD 125. He studied at Carthage, the capital of the province, and later at Athens, and he travelled to Samos, to Phrygia and to Rome where he practised as a rhetorician. Subsequently he married a rich widow called Pudentilla at Oea in Tripoli and was prosecuted by some of her relatives for (among other things) having won her by magic. His brilliant *Apology*, his speech in his defence, earned his acquittal. After his return to Carthage, he became a highly respected citizen. He was still a public figure in that city in the 160s, but we do not know when he died. A statue of him was set up in his honour and he was made the chief priest of the province. Travelling, rhetoric, sex, magic and religion were thus woven into the fabric of his life.

It may be that his first language was Punic, the native African tongue, and that therefore his Latin had to be learnt. Gwynn Griffiths (1975) has suggested that 'an acquired language, when used by a virtuoso, tends to be more richly treated'. This may go some way to accounting for the extraordinary flamboyance of Apuleius's Latin, a flamboyance well captured in the Elizabethan translation we have used in this edition.

Alternatively entitled *Metamorphoses, The Golden Ass* – so called because the Latin word for 'golden' is a term of high approval and thus Apuleius's book is 'the best of the ass stories' – is based on a lost Greek book, described as *Various tales of Metamorphosis by Lucius of Patrae,* and was probably written after he came to Carthage. It tells of the fortunes of a Greek called Lucius who near the start arrives at Hypata, a town in Thessaly, a Northern province of Greece 'where, by the common report of all the world, is the birthplace of all sorceries and enchantments'. Here he stays with the wealthy but inordinately stingy Milo, whose wife Pamphile is a witch. Lucius, as he repeatedly reminds us in the course of the book, suffers from an uncontrollable and self-destructive – and not merely self-destructive: see pp. 160–1 – curiosity and, wishing to discover more about the magical skills of his host's wife, he seduces their maidservant Fotis. However, while she aims to change him into a bird in imitation of Pamphile, he is transformed instead into an ass, and before he can regain his human shape through the necessary remedy of eating some roses, he is appropriated by a gang of robbers who need him to transport their booty to their den.

While Lucius in the form of an ass is trapped in the brigands' cave, they haul in the virtuous Charite, whom, in the hope of extorting a ransom, they have kidnapped just as she was about to be married. The girl tells her story to the crazy and drunken old hag who looks after the robbers (though their gratitude for her services seems non-existent: later, when they discover her body hanging from a tree, they simply throw it away, noose and all), and she, an unexpected teller, one may think, of so charming a tale, recounts to the wretched girl the romance of Cupid and Psyche. In due course Charite is rescued by her bridegroom and they are married, but he is soon murdered and she commits suicide after avenging his death. Charite's story is a grim one, and suicide is one response of the few virtuous characters in *The Golden Ass* to the intolerable cruelty of their fortune.

Lucius has found himself trapped not only in an ass's body but in a world of fearsome moral depravity. Here brigandage, violence, cruelty, greed and sexual lust are rife, and all is under the sway of a malevolent fortune. Nothing is predictable. As Tatum (1979) observes, 'the essence of *The Golden Ass* is that no event or character in it can be trusted to remain what it may at first seem to be. Nothing that is said – even by the narrator – can be taken at face-value.' The characters that Lucius encounters plumb increasingly horrific depths of viciousness in a world ever more replete with horrors. The bestiality described with so lingering a relish when Lucius-as-ass copulates with a noble and rich matron in Book 10 soon becomes a source of shame even to our hero when he is intended to repeat the performance in public with a multiple murderess. She is but one of a gallery of monstrous female gargoyles that haunt the narrative and provide so great a contrast with the lovely Psyche and the goddess Isis. Then there is the famous description of the mill, truly a glimpse into hell:

> O good Lord, what a sort of poor slaves were there; some had their skin bruised all over black and blue, some had their backs striped with lashes and were but covered rather than clothed with torn rags, some had their members only hidden by a narrow cloth, all wore such ragged clouts that you might perceive through them all their naked bodies, some were marked and burned in the forehead with hot irons, some had their hair half clipped, some had shackles on their legs, ugly and evil-favoured, some could scarce see, their eyes and faces were so black and dim with smoke, their eyelids all cankered with the darkness of that reeking place, half blind and sprinkled black and white with dirty flour like boxers which fight together befouled with mud . . . [The horses] had their necks all wounded and worn away with old sores, they rattled their nostrils with a continual cough, their sides were bare with continued rubbing of their harness and great travail, their ribs were broken and the bones did show with perpetual beating, their hoofs were battered very broad with endless walking, and their whole skin ragged by reason of mange and their great age [pp. 143-4].

Lucius certainly suffers greatly on his travels and gains much experience 'wherefore I now give thanks to my assy form' – but he learns nothing from that experience – 'I was then very little wise' (p. 144). Finally he is restored to his proper shape by the intervention of the mother of all the gods, Isis, into whose mysteries he is initiated and at last he learns the virtue of patience.

The Golden Ass is frequently funny – one of the best episodes is the Festival of Laughter at Hypata at the start of Book 3 – and frequently bawdy, but the humour is often black and the tone can be grim and grave. With the *Satyricon* of Petronius (written in about AD 65), it stands near the head of the great tradition of picaresque novels, books such as Cervantes' *Don Quixote* and Fielding's *Tom Jones* which describe the travels through a generally hostile environment of a character who seems in some sense ill-cast in the role of hero *(picaro* is the Spanish for 'rogue'). In its largely humorous presentation of a cruel and violent world, full of magic, and riddled with human selfishness, cupidity and female lust, *The Golden Ass* is a highly characteristic and influential representative of the genre.

The book is packed with stories, and by far the longest of these is that of Cupid and Psyche, for which Apuleius drew on a number of sources. In this tale of the girl who achieves happiness despite the machinations of her sisters, the ordeals imposed by Venus and her own human weakness, we find the writer for much of the time abandoning the racy, if always elaborate idiom he uses elsewhere, and writing in a more ornate and dignified style. The unbuttoned descriptions given of the sexual act in other parts of the novel are here muted: 'then came her unknown husband to her bed, and after that he had made her his very wife, he rose in the morning before day and departed' (p. 69). Even so, he keeps his sense of humour and comes entertainingly down to earth in the scenes where Venus is portrayed as a bitchy Roman matron. Yet overall this story, with its folk-tale elements and happy ending, seems designed to provide romantic escape, not only for Charite, the kidnapped girl, from her sad plight, but for Apuleius's readers from the savage, though comic world which most of the book presents to us. However, it is not completely self-contained: Psyche resembles Charite in her devotion to her bridegroom, while the sisters are very like many of the appalling women we meet elsewhere in the novel.

There are two further ways in which the story fits into the larger context of *The Golden Ass*: Charite has been separated from her bridegroom but will eventually be reunited with him, and thus her experience parallels that of Psyche; and, more significantly, Lucius, after being transformed into an ass owing to his curiosity and then undergoing various ordeals (from which he appears to learn little), is eventually restored to his proper shape and raised to a higher level of experience both in life and after death by the goddess Isis. Thus the story of Lucius is reflected in that of the over-curious, humbled, tormented and in the end immortalised Psyche.

How serious a work is *The Golden Ass*? At the outset the author seems to wish us to take it all with supreme levity. He kicks off with the words, 'In this Milesian tale . . . ', bringing to mind Aristides of Miletus who lived at the turn of the second to the first century BC. Copies of his collection of stories, the *Milesiaca,* which were found in the baggage of Roman officers after Crassus's disastrous defeat by the

Parthians at Carrhae in 53 BC led the victors to assume the worst
about the moral character of the Roman army. The element of
bawdy in so many of the stories in *The Golden Ass* certainly makes it
seem a likely Milesian tale.

Yet, as Book 11 makes plain, there is an allegory at work here, an
earnest intent beneath the playful surface. This perhaps becomes most
clear in the story of Cupid and Psyche which it would surely be
disingenuous to take at face value as a delightful romance without any
hidden significance. Rather it has a profoundly serious subtext. *Psyche*
is the Greek word for 'soul'; *Cupido* (Cupid) is the Latin for 'love'.
Thus, according to the allegorical interpretation, this tale shows the
soul being educated into the right approach to love. Psyche (the soul)
must be led out of her rash, impulsive and untrusting state of mind
before she can attain divine bliss and find the true reality. For
Apuleius, this cannot be finally discovered without external aid, and
the rescue of Psyche by Cupid and her subsequent attainment of
immortality symbolise the salvation of the human soul through the
intervention of divine grace. Once this has been encompassed,
Pleasure (as Psyche's child is called) can be born.

From the fifth century onwards, a Platonic interpretation of this
kind has been viewed as perfectly natural. In the seventeenth century
Milton, in his masque *Comus,* puts into the mouth of the Attendant
Spirit a description of a luscious garden to which only the virtuous
can gain admittance. Here,

> Sadly sits th'Assyrian Queen [Venus].
> But far above in spangled sheen
> Celestial Cupid, her fam'd son, advanc'd,
> Holds his dear Psyche sweet entranc'd
> After his wand'ring labours long,
> Till free consent the gods among
> Make her his eternal Bride,
> And from her fair unspotted side
> Two blissful twins are to be born,
> Youth and Joy; so Jove hath sworn.

About to fly up to the garden, the Spirit acknowledges human
weakness when, a few lines later, he concludes the masque with an
exhortation which surely refers to Cupid's rescue of the stricken

Psyche in the underworld:

> Mortals that would follow me,
> Love virtue; she alone is free.
> She can teach you how to climb
> Higher than the Sphery chime;
> Or, if Virtue feeble were,
> Heav'n itself would stoop to her.

Just as Cupid saves Psyche, so in the main story Lucius in his ass disguise eats his roses not on his own initiative but on the instructions of the goddess, whose priest reaches them out to him. Like Psyche, Lucius is basically good at heart. His faults of indiscretion, over-addiction to sex, credulity and above all curiosity do not seem very deep-dyed in sinfulness in the context of *The Golden Ass,* though the worshippers of Isis are surely ludicrously optimistic about him when they say: 'verily he is blessed and most blessed that by the innocency of his former life hath merited so great a grace from heaven' (p. 193). Like Psyche, he, in the process of his initiation, goes down to hell (p. 199). Just as she joins the company of the gods, so he is admitted to the worship of Isis and Osiris. We might expect the message of both stories to be one of learning through experience, but as we have seen, Apuleius does not follow that path. It is the intervention of the divine that makes Psyche immortal and grants to Lucius an enriched life both on earth and after death.

And there is a strong sense in which Lucius is Apuleius. Indeed he actually becomes him in the last chapter of all. After the confused wanderings of his life, Apuleius has found salvation in his priesthood.

JAMES MORWOOD
Head of Classics
Harrow School

SUGGESTIONS FOR FURTHER READING

J. Gwynn Griffiths, *Apuleius of Madauros. The Isis-Book (Metamorphoses, Book XI)*, Leiden 1975

E. J. Kenney (ed.), *Cupid and Psyche*, Cambridge 1990

J. Tatum, *Apuleius and 'The Golden Ass'*, Ithaca and London 1979

P. G. Walsh, *The Roman Novel*, Cambridge 1970

Kingsley Amis, *Lucky Jim*

Miguel de Cervantes, *Don Quixote*

Henry Fielding, *Tom Jones*

Thomas Nashe, *The Unfortunate Traveller*

Philip Sidney, *Arcadia*

THE TRANSLATION

The Golden Ass is printed in the Elizabethan translation of William Adlington, published in 1566. This was revised by S. Gaselee, fellow and librarian of Magdalene College, Cambridge, who published his version in 1922. I have left Gaselee's revision unchanged save that I have restored the passages expurgated by Adlington. Writing of the episode on p. 174, Gaselee comments, 'In a note referring to the whole of this passage Adlington writes, "Here I have left out certain lines *propter honestatem*", in which his modesty is much to be commended, and will here be followed.' This modesty bridged more than three centuries but is now inappropriate.

Gaselee writes in his Introduction, 'Of William Adlington we know nothing except that he dedicated his translation to the Earl of Sussex, writing from University College, Oxford, 18 September 1566; and that he was possibly the author of a little verse tract, *A Speciall Remedie against the furious force of Lawlesse Love,* published thirteen years later. . . I [Gaselee] have not only modernised the spelling and completely rearranged the punctuation . . . but I have altered it to bring it into greater harmony with the Latin according to modern ideas of translation . . . The result is, I hope, a rendering which, while not by any means a word-for-word representation of the original, is yet sufficiently accurate, without being literal, for all ordinary purpose, and at the same time preserves the charm of the sixteenth-century English version.'

THE GOLDEN ASS

The.xi.Bookes of
the Golden Affe,

Conteininge the Metamorphofie
of Lucius Apuleius, enterlaced
**with fondrie pleafaunt and delecta-
ble Tales, with an excellent
Narration of the Mari-
age of Cupide and
Pfiches, set out
in the iiij.
v. and vj. Bookes.**

*Tranflated out of Latine into Englifhe
by VVilliam Adlington.*

*Imprinted at London in Fleetftreate,
at the figne of the Oliphante,
by Henry VVykes.*

Anno. 1566.

BOOK ONE

In this Milesian tale I shall string together divers stories, and delight your kindly ears with a pleasant history, if you will not scorn to look upon this Egyptian paper written with a ready pen of Nile reeds – stories of men's forms and fortunes transformed into different shapes, and then restored again in due sequence back into their selves – a true subject for wonder. Who is the author? In a few words you shall understand. Hymettus of Athens, the Isthmus of Corinth, Taenarus of Sparta, being famous lands (as I pray you give credit to the books of more everlasting fame), be places where mine ancient progeny and lineage did sometime flourish: there when I was young I went first to school and learned the Attic speech. Soon after (as a stranger) I achieved at Rome, where by great industry, and without instruction of any schoolmaster, I arrived at the full perfection of the Latin tongue: behold, I first crave and beg your pardon, lest I should happen to displease or offend any of you by the rude and rustic utterance of this strange and foreign language. And verily this change of speech doth correspond to the enterprise and matter whereof I purpose to treat, like a rider leaping from horse to horse; I set forth unto you a Grecian story: whereto, gentle reader, if thou attend and give ear, thou shalt be well contented withal.

I fortuned to travel into Thessaly, about certain affairs which I had to do (for there, my ancestry by my mother's side inhabiteth, descended of the line of that most excellent person Plutarch, and of Sextus the philosopher his nephew, which is to us a great worship and honour); and after that by much travel and great pain, I had passed over the high mountains and slippery valleys, and had ridden through the dewy grass and fallowed fields, perceiving that my horse, a white thoroughbred of that country, did wear somewhat slow, and to the intent likewise I might repose and strengthen myself (being weary of long sitting) I lighted off my horse on to my feet, and wiping carefully away the sweat from his head, and stroking his ears, I unbridled him, and walked him on to a gentle slope, to the end that he might by nature's relief ease himself of his weariness; and while he went taking his morning graze in the field (casting his head sometimes aside as a token of rejoicing and gladness) I perceived a little before me two companions riding, and so I overtaking them made a third. And while I listened to hear their conversation, one of them laughed, and mocked his fellow, saying: 'Leave off, I pray thee, and speak no more, for I cannot abide to hear thee tell such absurd incredible lies.' Which when I heard I desired to hear some news, and said: 'I pray you, masters, make me partaker of your talk, that am not so curious as desirous to know all you say, or most of it. So shall the difficulty of this high hill before us be lightened by merry and pleasant talk.'

But he that had laughed first, said: 'Verily this tale is as true as if a man would say that by sorcery and enchantment the swift rivers might be forced to run against their courses; the sea to be bound immovable; the winds to lose their force and die; the sun to be restrained from his natural journey; the moon to drop her foam upon the earth; the stars to be pulled down from heaven; the day to be darkened; and the night be made to continue for ever.'

Then I, speaking more confidently, said: 'I pray you, you that began to tell your tale even now, leave not off so, but tell the residue.' And turning to the other, I said: 'You perhaps, that are of gross ears and an obstinate mind, mock and contemn those things which are perchance really the truth; know you not, i' faith, that those things are accounted untrue by the false opinion of men, which are either seldom heard or rarely seen, or are so high that they pass the capacity of man's reason? The which if you scan them more narrowly, you shall not only find them evident to the understanding, but even very easy to be brought to pass. Look you: the other night, being at supper with my fellows, while I did greedily put in my mouth a great morsel of barley fried with cheese, it stuck so fast, being soft and doughy, in the passage of my throat and my windpipe, that I was well nigh choked. And yet lately at Athens, before the porch there called the Poecile, I saw with these two eyes of mine a juggler that swallowed up a knight's sword with a very keen edge, and by and by, for a little money that we that looked on gave him, he devoured a hunting spear with the point downward, and over the blade of the spear, where the haft of the spear turned down rose through the throat towards his pate, there appeared on it (which caused us all who were present to marvel) a fair boy pleasant and nimble, winding and turning himself in such sort that you would suppose that he had neither bone nor gristle, and verily think he was the natural serpent, creeping and sliding where the twigs are cut off on the knotted staff of rough wood which the god of medicine is wont to bear. But do you, I pray you, that began, repeat your tale again, and I alone, in place of your fellow, will give credit unto you, and for your pains, will pay your charges for your supper at the next inn we come unto.

To this he answered: 'Certes, sir, I thank you for your gentle offer, and, at your request, I will proceed in my tale; but first I will swear unto you by the light of this Sun, the God that seeth all, that those things which I shall tell be true; nor, when you come to the next city, which is of Thessaly, will you doubt anything of it, for it is rife in the mouths of every person which was done before the face of all men. And that I may first make relation to you, what and who I am, and whither I go, and for what livelihood; know ye, that I am of Aegina, travelling these countries about from Thessaly to Aetolia, and from Aetolia to Boeotia, to provide for honey, cheese, and other victuals to sell again. And understanding that at Hypata (which is the principal city of all Thessaly) are sold fresh cheeses of exceeding good taste and relish, I fortuned on a day to go thither to make my market there of the whole. But (as it often happens) I came in an evil hour, for one Lupus, a wholesale purveyor, had bought up all the day before, and so I was deceived of my profit. Wherefore towards night (being greatly wearied by my hurrying, though it had been of none effect) I went to the baths to refresh myself, and behold, I fortuned to espy my companion Socrates. He was sitting upon the ground, covered with a torn and coarse mantle, so meagre and of so sallow and miserable a countenance that I scantly knew him: for fortune had brought him into such estate that he verily seemed as a common beggar that stands in the streets to crave the benevolence of the passers-by. Towards whom (howbeit he was my singular friend and familiar acquaintance) yet half in doubt, I drew nigh and said: "Alas! my Socrates, what meaneth this, how dost thou so appear? What crime hast thou committed? Verily there is great lamentation and weeping made for thee at home: thy children are in ward by decree of the provincial judge: thy wife (having ended her mourning time in lamentable wise with her face and visage blubbered with tears in such sort that she hath well nigh wept out both her eyes) is constrained by her parents to put out of remembrance the unfortunate loss and lack of thee at home, by taking (against her will) a new husband. And dost thou live here as a ghost or beggar to our great shame and ignominy?" Then answered he to me, and said: "O my friend Aristomenes, now perceive I well that you are ignorant of the whirling changes, the unstable forces, and slippery inconstancy of fortune": and therewithal he covered his face (even then blushing for very shame) with his ragged mantle, so that the centrique part of his body appeared all naked. But I, not willing to see him any longer in such great misery and calamity, took him by the hand to lift him up from the ground: who (having his face covered in such sort) "Let fortune" (quoth he) "Triumph yet more, let her have her sway, and finish that which she hath begun."

Then did I force him to follow and put off one of my garments, and clothed, nay, rather covered him, and immediately I brought him to the bath; with my own hands I served him with what he needed for anointing and wiping. I diligently rubbed away the filthy scurf of his body; which done, although I was very weary myself, and hardly held him up, yet I led the poor wretch to my inn, where I bade him repose his body upon a bed, and brought him meat and drink, and refreshed him with talking together. Then we grew free and merry, laughed and joked wittily, now he talked without any fear, until such time as he (fetching a pitiful sigh from the bottom of his heart, and beating his face in miserable sort) began to say:

' "Alas, poor wretch that I am, that only for the desire to see a game, famous enough, of trial of weapons, am fallen into these miseries and misfortunes. For, having set out, as thou knowest, for Macedonia, on my business, and returning the richer after the space of ten months, a little before that I came to Larissa I turned out of the way to view those games, and behold, in the bottom of a pathless and hollow valley, I was suddenly environed with a wild company of thieves, who robbed and spoiled me of such things as I had: and hardly did I escape, but (being in such extremity) in the end was delivered from them and fortuned to come to the house of a woman that sold wine, called Meroe; old was she, yet not unpleasing; unto whom I opened the causes of my long peregrination and careful home-coming, and of my unlucky robbery; and after that she gently entertained me, and made me more than good cheer, with a supper free of charge; and by and by, being pricked by carnal desire, she brought me to her own bedchamber; where I (poor wretch) from the very first night of our lying together, did purchase to myself this miserable servitude, and I gave her such apparel as the kind thieves had left to cover me withal, and also the little wages that I had gained by carrying bags when still whole and sound, until this good dame and evil fortune brought me to that appearance in which you have just seen me."

'Then said I unto him: "In faith, thou art worthy to sustain the most extreme misery and calamity, and anything there may be even beyond this last, which hast defiled thine own body, forsaken thy wife traitorously and dishonoured thy children, parents and friends for the love of a vile harlot and old strumpet." When Socrates heard me rail against Meroe in such sort, he held up his forefinger to his lips, and, as half astonied, said: "Peace, peace, I pray you," and, looking about lest any person should hear, "I pray you" (quoth he), "Take heed what you say against so venerable a woman as she is, lest by your intemperate tongue you catch some harm." "What?" (quoth I) "This hostess, so mighty and a queen, what manner of woman is she, I pray you tell me?" Then answered he: "Verily, she is a magician, and of divine might, which hath power to bring down the sky, to bear up the earth, to turn the waters into hills and the hills into running waters, to call up the terrestrial spirits into the air, and to pull the gods out of the heavens, to extinguish the planets, and to lighten the very darkness of hell." Then said I unto Socrates: "I pray you leave off this high and tragical kind of talk and away with the scenic curtain and tell the matter in a more plain and simple fashion." Then answered he: "Will you hear one or two or more of the deeds which she hath done? For whereas she enforceth not only the inhabitants of this country here, but also the Indians and Ethiopians and even the Antipodeans to love her in most raging sort, such are but trifles and chips of her occupation; but I pray you give ear, and I will declare of greater matters, which she hath done openly and before the face of all men.

' "This woman had a certain lover whom, by the utterance of one only word, she turned into a beaver because he loved another woman beside her, and the reason why she transformed him into such a beast, is that it is his nature, when he perceives the hunters and hounds to draw after him, to bite off his members and lay them in the way, that the pursuers may be at a stop when they find them, and to the intent that so it might happen unto him (because he fancied another woman) she turned him into that kind of shape. Likewise she changed one of her neighbours, being an old man and one that sold wine, in that he was a rival of her occupation, into a frog, and now the poor wretch swimming in one of his own pipes of wine, and being well nigh drowned in the dregs, doth cry and call with croakings continually for his old guests and acquaintance that pass by. Likewise she turned one of the advocates of the Court (because he pleaded and spake against her) into a horned ram, and now the poor ram doth act advocate. Moreover she caused the wife of a certain lover that she had, because she spake sharply and wittily against her, should never be delivered of her child, but should remain, her womb closed up, everlastingly pregnant, and according to the computation of all men, it is eight years past since the poor woman began first to swell, and now she is increased so big that she seemeth as though she would bring forth some great elephant: and when this was known abroad and published throughout all the town, they took indignation against her, and ordained that the next day she should be most cruelly stoned to death; which purpose of theirs she prevented by the virtue of her enchantments, and as Medea (who obtained of King Creon but one day's respite before her departure) did burn in the flames of the bride's garland all his house, him and his daughter, so she, by her conjurations and invocation of spirits, which she uses over a certain trench, as she herself declared unto me being drunken the next day following, closed all the persons of the town so sure in their houses, by the secret power of her gods, that for the space of two days they could not come forth, nor open their gates nor doors, nor even break down their walls; whereby they were enforced by mutual consent to cry unto her and to bind themselves straitly that they would never after molest or hurt her, and moreover if any did offer her any injury they would be ready to defend her; whereupon she, moved at their promises, released all the town. But she conveyed the principal author of this ordinance, about midnight, with all his house, the walls, the ground and the foundation, into another town distant from thence a hundred miles situate and being on the top of a barren hill, and by reason thereof destitute of water: and because the edifices and houses were so close builded together that it was not possible for the house to stand here, she threw down the same before the gate of the town."

'Then spake I and said: "O my friend Socrates, you have declared unto me many marvellous things and no less cruel, and moreover stricken me also with no small trouble of mind, yea rather with great prick of fear, lest the same old woman, using the like practice, should chance to hear all our communication: wherefore let us now sleep, though it be early, and after that we have done away our weariness with rest let us rise betimes in the morning and ride from hence before day as far as we may."

'In speaking these words, it fortuned that Socrates did fall asleep, and snored very soundly, by reason of his new plenty of meat and wine and his long travail. Then I closed and barred fast the doors of the chamber, and put my bed and made it fast behind the door and so laid me down to rest; but at first I could in no wise sleep for the great fear which was in my heart, until it was about midnight, and then I closed my eyes for a little: but alas, I had just begun to sleep, when behold suddenly the chamber doors brake open; nay, the locks, bolts and posts fell down with greater force than if thieves had been presently come to have spoiled and robbed us. And my bed whereon I lay, being a truckle-bed and somewhat short, and one of the feet broken and rotten, by violence was turned upside down, and I likewise was overwhelmed and covered lying in the same.

'Then perceived I in myself, that certain effects of the mind by nature are turned contrary. For as tears oftentimes are shed for joy, so I being in this fearful perplexity could not forbear laughing, to see how of Aristomenes I was made like unto a tortoise. And while I lay on the ground covered in the happy protection of my pallet, I peeped from under the bed to see what would happen. And behold there entered two old women, the one bearing a burning torch, and the other a sponge and a naked sword. And so in this habit they stood about Socrates being fast asleep. Then she which bare the sword said unto the other: "Behold, sister Panthia, this is my dear Endymion and my sweet Ganymede, which both day and night hath abused my wanton youthfulness; this is he (who little regarding my love) doth not only defame me with reproachful words, but also intendeth to run away. And I shall be forsaken by like craft as Ulysses did use, and shall continually bewail my solitariness as Calypso"; which said she pointed towards me, that lay under the bed, and showed me to Panthia. "This is he," quoth she, "Which is his good counsellor, Aristomenes, and persuadeth him to forsake me, and now (being at the point of death) he lieth prostrate on the ground covered with his bed, and hath seen all our doings, and hopeth to escape scot-free from my hands for all his insults; but I will cause that he shall repent himself too late, nay rather forthwith of his former intemperate language and his present curiosity."

'Which words when I heard, I fell into a cold sweat, and my heart trembled with fear, in so much that the bed over me did likewise rattle and shake and dance with my trembling. Then spake Panthia unto Meroe, and said: "Sister, let us by and by tear him in pieces, or else tie him by the members and so cut them off." Then Meroe (for thus I learned that her name really was that which I had heard in Socrates' tale) answered: "Nay, rather let him live, to bury the corpse of this poor wretch in some hole of the earth," and therewithal she turned the head of Socrates on the other side, and thrust her sword up to the hilt into the left part of his neck, and received the blood that gushed out with a small bladder, that no drop thereof fell beside; this thing I saw with mine own eyes, and then Meroe, to the intent (as I think) she might alter nothing that pertaineth to sacrifice, which she accustomed to make, thrust her hand down through that wound into the entrails of his body, and searching about, at length brought forth the heart of my miserable companion Socrates, who (having his throat cut in such sort) gave out a doleful cry by the wound, or rather a gasping breath, and gave up the ghost. Then Panthia stopped the wide wound of his throat with the sponge and said: "O, sponge sprung and made of the sea, beware that thou pass not over a running river." This being said, they moved and turned up my bed, and then they strode over me and pissed most foully upon me till I was wringing wet.

'When this was ended, they went their ways and the doors closed fast, the hinges sank in their old sockets, the bolts ran into the doorposts, the pins fell into the bars again. But I that lay upon the ground, like one without soul, naked and cold and wringing wet with filth, like to one that were newly born, or rather, one that were more than half dead, yet reviving myself, and appointed as I thought for the gallows, began to say: "Alas, what shall become of me tomorrow when my companion shall be found murdered here in the chamber? To whom shall I seem to tell any similitude of truth, when as I shall tell the truth indeed? They will say: 'If thou, being so great a man, wert unable to resist the violence of the woman, yet shouldst thou have cried at least for help; wilt thou suffer the man to be slain before thy face and say nothing? Or why did not they slay thee likewise? Why did their cruelty spare thee that stood by and saw them commit that horrible fact? Wherefore although thou hast escaped their hands, yet thou shalt not escape ours.' "

'While I pondered these things often with myself the night passed on into day, so I thought best to take my horse secretly before dawn and go fearfully forward on my journey. Thus I took up my packet, unlocked and unbarred the doors, but those good and faithful doors which in the night did open of their own accord could then scarcely be opened with their keys after frequent trials, and when I was out I cried: "Ho, sirrah ostler, where art thou? Open the stable door, for I will ride away before dawn." The ostler lying behind the stable door upon a pallet and half asleep, "What?" quoth he, "Do not you know that the ways be very dangerous with robbers? What mean you to set forth at this time of night? If you perhaps (guilty of some heinous crime) be weary of your life, yet think you not that we are such pumpkin-headed sots that we will die for you." Then said I: "It is well nigh day, and moreover what can thieves take from him that hath nothing? Dost not thou know (fool as thou art) that if thou be naked, if ten trained wrestlers should assail thee, they could not spoil or rob thee?" Whereunto the drowsy ostler half asleep, and turning on the other side, answered: "What know I whether you have murdered your companion whom you brought in yesternight or no, and now seek safety by escaping away?"

'O Lord, at that time I remember that the earth seemed to open, and that I saw at Hell gate the dog Cerberus gaping to devour me, and then I verily believed that Meroe did not spare my throat, moved with pity, but rather cruelly pardoned me to bring me to the gallows. Wherefore, I returned to my chamber and there devised with myself in what violent sort I should finish my life. But when I saw that fortune would minister unto me no other instrument than my bed, I said: "O bed, O bed, most dear unto me at this present, which hast abode and suffered with me so many miseries, judge and arbiter of such things as were done here this night, whom only I may call to witness for my innocence, render (I say) unto me some wholesome weapon to end my life that am most willing to die." And therewithal I pulled out a piece of the rope wherewith the bed was corded, and tied one end thereof about a rafter which stood forth beneath the window, and with the other end I made a sliding knot and stood upon my bed to cast myself from aloft into destruction, and so put my neck into it. But when I pushed away with my foot that which supported me beneath, so that the noose when my weight came upon it might choke the passage of my breath, behold suddenly the rope being old and rotten burst in the middle, and I fell down tumbling upon Socrates that lay nigh me, and with him rolled upon the floor. And even at that very time the ostler came in crying with a loud voice, and said: "Where are you that made such haste at deep night, and now lie wallowing and snoring abed?" Whereupon (I know not whether it was by our fall or by the harsh cry of the ostler) Socrates (as waking out of a sleep) did rise up first and said: "It is not without cause that strangers do speak evil of all such ostlers, for this caitiff in his coming in, and with his crying out, I think under colour to steal away something, hath waked me, that was beside very weary, out of a sound sleep."

'Then I rose up joyful, as I hoped not to be, with a merry countenance, saying: "Behold, good ostler, my friend, my companion and my brother whom thou being drunken in the night didst falsely affirm to be murdered by me." And therewithal I embraced my friend Socrates and kissed him; but he smelling the stink wherewith those hags had embrued me, thrust me away and said: "Away with thee with thy filthy odour," and then he began gently to enquire how that noisome scent happened unto me, but I (with some light jest feigning and colouring the matter for the time) did break off his talk into another path, and take him by the hand and said: "Why tarry we? Why leave we the pleasure of this fair morning? Let us go." And so I took up my packet, and paid the charges of the house, and we departed.

'We had not gone a mile out of the town but it was broad day, and then I diligently looked upon Socrates' throat to see if I could espy the place where Meroe thrust in her sword, and I thought with myself: "What a madman am I, that (being overcome with wine yesternight) have dreamed such terrible things! Behold, I see Socrates is sound, safe and in health. Where is his wound? Where is the sponge? Where is his great and new cut?" And then I spake to him and said: "Verily it is not without occasion that physicians of experience do affirm, that such as fill their gorges abundantly with meat and drink shall dream of dire and horrible sights, for I myself (not restraining mine appetite yesternight from the pots of wine) did seem to see in this bitter night strange and cruel visions, that even yet I think myself sprinkled and wet with human blood"; whereunto Socrates laughing, made answer and said: "Nay, thou art not wet with the blood of men, but thou art embrued with stinking filth: and verily I myself dreamed this night that my throat was cut and that I felt the pain of the wound, and that my heart was pulled out of my belly, and the remembrance thereof makes me now to fear, and my knees do tremble that I totter in my gait, and therefore I would fain eat somewhat to strengthen and revive my spirits." Then said I: "Behold, here is thy breakfast," and therewithal I opened my scrip that hanged upon my shoulder, and gave him bread and cheese, and "Let us sit down," quoth I, "Under that great plane-tree."

'Now I also ate part of the same with him: and while I beheld him eating greedily, I perceived that he wore thin and meagre and pale as boxwood, and that his lively colour faded away, as did mine also, remembering those terrible furies of whom I lately dreamed, in so much that the first morsel of bread that I put in my mouth (which was but very small) did so stick in my jaws that I could neither swallow it down nor yet yield it up; and moreover the number of them that passed by increased my fear, for who is he, that would believe that one of two companions die in the high way without injury done by the other? But when that Socrates had eaten sufficiently he wore very thirsty, for indeed he had well nigh devoured a whole good cheese, and behold there was behind the roots of the plane-tree a pleasant running water which went gently like to a quiet pond, as clear as silver or crystal, and I said unto him: "Come hither, Socrates, to this water and drink thy fill as it were milk." And then he rose, and waiting a little he found a flat space by the river and kneeled down by the side of the bank in his greedy desire to drink; but he had scarce touched the water with his lips when behold, the wound of his throat opened wide, and the sponge suddenly fell into the water and after issued out a little remnant of blood, and his body (being then without life) had fallen into the river, had not I caught him by the leg, and so with great ado pulled him up. And after that I had lamented a good space the death of my wretched companion, I buried him in the sands to dwell for ever there by the river. Which done, trembling and in great fear I rode through many outways and desert places, and as if culpable of murder, I forsook my country, my wife and my children, and came to Aetolia, an exile of my own free will, where I married another wife.'

This tale told Aristomenes, and his fellow which before obstinately would give no credit unto him, began to say: 'Verily there was never so foolish a tale, nor a more absurd lie told than this'; and then he spake unto me, saying: 'Ho, sir, what you are I know not, but your habit and countenance declareth that you should be some honest gentleman, do you believe his tale?' 'Yea, verily,' quoth I, 'Why not? I think nothing impossible; for whatsoever the fates have appointed to men, that I believe shall happen. For many things chance unto me, and unto you, and to divers others, wonderful and almost unheard of; which being declared unto the ignorant be accounted as lies. But verily I give credit unto his tale, and render entire thanks unto him in that (by the pleasant relation of this pretty tale) he hath distracted us so that I have quickly passed and shortened this long and weariful journey, and I think that my horse also was delighted with the same, and I am brought me to the gate of this city without any pain at all, not so much by his back, as by mine own ears.'

Thus ended both our talk and our journey, for they two turned on the left hand to the next village, and I rode up to the first inn that I saw, and I espied an old woman, of whom I enquired whether that city was called Hypata or no, who answered: 'Yes.' Then I demanded whether she knew one Milo, one of the first men of the city, whereat she laughed, and said: 'Verily it is not without cause that Milo is accounted first in the city, for he dwells altogether without the boundary.' To whom I said again: 'I pray thee, good mother, do not mock, but tell me what manner of man he is, and where he dwelleth.' 'Marry,' quoth she, 'Do not you see those bay windows, which on the one side look out upon the city, and the doors on the other side to the next lane: there Milo dwells, very rich both in money and substance, but by reason of his great avarice and covetousness he is evil spoken of, and he is a man that liveth all by usury, and lending his money upon pledges of silver and gold. Moreover he dwelleth in a small house and is ever counting his money, and hath a wife that is a companion of his extreme misery, neither keepeth he any more in his house than one only maid, and he goes apparelled like unto a beggar.'

Which when I heard I laughed with myself and thought: 'In faith, my friend Demeas hath served me well and with forethought, which hath sent me, being a stranger, unto such a man, in whose house I shall not be troubled either with smoke or with the scent of meat,' and therewithal I rode to the door, which was fast barred, and knocked aloud and cried. Then there came forth a maid which said: 'Ho, sirrah, that knocks so fast, in what kind of sort will you borrow money; know you not that we use to take no pledge unless it be either gold or silver?' To whom I answered: 'I pray thee, maid, speak more gently, and tell me whether thy master be within or no.' 'Yes,' quoth she, 'That he is; why do you ask?' 'Marry,' said I, 'I am come from Corinth, and have brought him letters from Demeas his friend.' Then said the maid: 'I pray you tarry here till I tell him so,' and therewithal she closed the doors and went in, and after a while she returned again, and said: 'My master desireth you to come in'; and so I did, where I found him sitting upon a very little bed, just going to supper, and his wife sat at his feet, but there was no meat upon the table; and, pointing at it, 'Behold,' said he, 'Your entertainment.' 'Well,' quoth I, and straightway delivered to him the letters which I brought from Demeas: which when he had quickly read, he said: 'Verily, I thank my friend Demeas very much, in that he hath sent me so worthy a guest as you are': and therewithal he commanded his wife to sit away, and bade me sit in her place, and when I was about refusing by reason of courtesy, he pulled me by the garment and willed me to sit down. 'For we have,' quoth he, 'No other stool here, nor other great store of household stuff for fear of robbing.'

Then I (according to his commandment) sat down: and he fell into communication with me, and said: 'Verily I conjecture (and rightly) by the comely feature of your body, and by the maidenly shamefastness of your face, that you are a gentleman born, as my friend Demeas hath no less declared the same in his letters: wherefore I pray you, take in good part our poor lodgings, and behold, yonder chamber hard by is at your commandment, use it as your own; then you shall both magnify our house by your deigning and shall gain to yourself good report, if, being contented with a humble lodging, you shall resemble and follow the virtuous qualities of your good father's namesake Theseus, who disdained not the slender and poor cottage of old Hecale.' And then he called his maid, which was named Fotis, and said: 'Carry this gentleman's packet into the chamber and lay up safely, and bring quickly from the cupboard oil to anoint him, and a towel to rub him, and other things necessary; and then bring my guest to the nearest baths, for I know he is very weary of so long and difficult travel.' These things when I heard, I partly perceived the manners and parsimony of Milo, and (endeavouring to bring myself further in his favour) I said: 'Sir, there is no need of any of these things, for they are everywhere my companions by the way; and easily I shall enquire my way unto the baths, but my chief care is that my horse be well looked to, for he brought me hither roundly, and therefore, I pray thee, Fotis, take this money and buy some hay and oats for him.'

When this was done and all my things brought into the chamber, I walked towards the baths, but first I went to the provision market to buy some victuals for my supper, whereas I saw great plenty of fish set out to be sold, and so I cheapened part thereof, and that which they first held at an hundred pieces, I bought at length for twenty pence: which when I had done and was departing away, Pythias, one of mine old companions and fellow at Athens, fortuned to pass by, and viewing me a good space, in the end brought me kindly to his remembrance, and gently came and kissed me, saying: 'O my dear friend Lucius, it is a great while past since we two saw each other, and moreover, from the time that we departed from our master Vestius I never heard any news of you; I pray you, Lucius, tell me the cause of your peregrination hither.' Then I answered and said: 'I will make relation thereof unto you tomorrow: but what is this? Verily I think that you have obtained your own desire, whereof I am right glad. For I see these servitors that follow you, and these rods or verges which they bear: and this habit which you wear, like unto a magistrate.' Then answered Pythias: 'I bear the office and rule of the clerk of the market, and therefore if you will aught for your supper, speak and I will purvey it for you.' Then I thanked him heartily and said I had bought fish sufficient already for my dinner, but Pythias, when he espied my basket, took it and shook it, so that the fish might come to view, and demanded of me what I paid for all my sprats. 'In faith,' quoth I, 'I could scarce enforce the fishmonger to sell them for twenty pence'; which when he heard, he seized my hand and brought me back again into the market, and enquired of me of whom I had bought such wretched stuff. I showed him the old man which sat in a corner, whom straightway (by reason of his office) he did greatly blame, and said: 'Is it thus that you serve and handle strangers? And especially our friends? Wherefore sell you this fish so dear which is not worth a halfpenny? Now perceive I well that you are an occasion to make this place, which is the flower of all Thessaly, to be forsaken of all men and reduce it into an uninhabitable rock, by reason of your excessive prices of victuals; but assure yourself that you shall not escape without punishment, and you shall know what mine office is, and how I ought to punish such as do offend.' Then he took my basket and cast the fish on the ground, and commanded one of his servants to tread them all under his feet; so doing was Pythias well pleased with the severity he showed in his office, and bade me farewell, and said that he was content with the shame and reproach done unto the old caitiff. So I went away, all amazed and astonished, towards the baths, considering with myself, and devising of the strong hand of that so imprudent companion of mine, Pythias, whereby I had lost both my money and my meat: and there, when I had washed and refreshed my body, I returned again to Milo's house, and so got into my chamber.

Then came Fotis immediately unto me, and said that her master desired me to come to supper, but I (not ignorant of Milo's abstinence) prayed courteously that I might be pardoned, since I thought best to ease my weary bones rather with sleep and quietness than with meat. When Fotis had told this unto Milo, he came himself and took me by the hand to draw me gently with him, and while I did hold back and modestly excuse me, 'I will not,' quoth he, 'Depart from this place until such time as you shall go with me,' and to confirm the same he bound his words with an oath, whereby with insistence he enforced me all against my will to follow him and he brought me into his chamber, where he sat me down upon the bed, and demanded of me how his friend Demeas did, his wife, his children, and all his family; and I made him answer to every question; and specially he enquired the causes of my peregrination and travel; which when I had declared, he yet busily enquired of the state of my country, and the chief citizens, and principally of our Lieutenant and Viceroy. And when he perceived that I was not only wearied by my hard travel but also with talk, and that I fell asleep in the midst of my tale, and further that I spake nothing directly or advisably, but babbled only in imperfect words, he suffered me to depart to my chamber. So escaped I at length from the prattling and hungry supper of this rank old man, and being heavy with sleep and not with meat (as having supped only with talk) I returned unto my chamber and there betook me to my quiet and long-desired rest.

BOOK TWO

As soon as night was past and the new day began to spring, I fortuned
to awake and rose out of my bed as half amazed, and indeed very
desirous to know and see some marvellous and strange things,
remembering with myself that I was in the midst part of all Thessaly,
where, by the common report of all the world, is the birthplace of
sorceries and enchantments, and I oftentimes repeated with myself
the tale of my companion Aristomenes whereof the scene was set in
this city; all agog moreover (being moved both by desire and my own
especial longing) I viewed the whole situation thereof with care.
Neither was there anything which I saw there that I did believe to be
the same which it was indeed, but everything seemed unto me to be
transformed into other shapes by the wicked power of enchantment,
in so much that I thought the stones against which I might stumble
were indurate and turned from men into that figure, and that the
birds which I heard chirping, and the trees without the walls of the
city, and the running waters were changed from men into such
feathers and leaves and fountains. And further I thought that the
statues and images would by and by move, and that the walls would
talk, and the kine and other brute beasts would speak and tell strange
news, and that immediately I should hear some oracle from the
heaven and from the ray of the sun.

Thus being astonished and dismayed, nay dumbfounded with the
longing that did torment me, though I found no beginning nor
indeed any trace to satisfy my curious desire, I went nevertheless from
door to door, and at length, like some luxurious person strolling at
my ease, I fortuned unawares to come into the market-place, where I
espied a certain woman accompanied with a great many servants,
walking apace, towards whom I drew nigh and viewed her precious
stones set with gold and her garments woven with the same in such
sort that she seemed to be some noble matron: and there was an old
man which followed her: who (as soon as he had espied me) said:
'Verily this is Lucius,' and then he came and embraced me, and by

and by he went unto his mistress, and whispered in her ear, and came to me again, saying: 'How is it, Lucius, that you will not salute your dear cousin and friend?' To whom I answered: 'Sir, I dare not be so bold as to take acquaintance of an unknown woman.' Howbeit as half ashamed with blushes and hanging head I drew back, she turned her gaze upon me and said: 'Behold how he resembleth the same noble dignity as his modest mother Salvia doth; behold his countenance and body agreeing thereto in each point, behold his comely stature, his graceful slenderness, his delicate colour, his hair yellow and not too foppishly dressed, his grey and quick eyes shining like unto the eagle's, his blooming countenance in all points, and his grave and comely gait.' And moreover she said: 'O Lucius, I have nourished thee with mine own proper hands, and why not? For I am not only of kindred unto thy mother by blood, but also her foster-sister; for we are both descended of the line of Plutarch, sucked the same paps, and were brought up together as sisters in one house; and further there is no other difference between us two, but that she is married more honourably than I: I am the same Byrrhaena whom you have perhaps often heard named as one of those that reared you. Wherefore I pray you to come with all confidence to my house — nay, use it as your own.' By whose words my blushes had time to disperse, and I said: 'God forbid, cousin, that I should forsake mine host Milo without any just and reasonable cause, but verily I will do as much as I may without hurt to the duties of a guest, and as often as I have occasion to pass by your house I will come and see how you do.'

While we went talking thus together, in a very few steps we came to her house; and behold the court of the same was very beautiful set with pillars quadrangularwise, on the top whereof were placed carven statues and images of the goddess of Victory, so lively and with such excellency portrayed and with wings spread forth, their dewy feet just poised upon motionless globes, that you would verily have thought that they had flown, and were hovering with their wings hither and thither. There also the image of Diana, wrought in white marble, stood in the midst of all, holding all in balance, which was a marvellous sight to see, for she seemed as though the wind did blow up her garments, striding briskly forward, so that she was now to encounter with them that came into the house, a goddess very venerable and majestic to see: on each side of her were dogs made also of stone, that seemed to menace with their fiery eyes, their pricked ears, their wide nostrils and their grinning teeth, in such sort that if any dogs in the neighbourhood had bayed and barked, you would have thought the sound came from their stony throats. And moreover (which was a greater marvel to behold) the excellent carver and deviser of this work had fashioned the dogs to stand up fiercely with their former feet ready to run, and their hinder feet set firmly on the ground. Behind the back of the goddess was carved a stone rising in manner of a cavern, environed with moss, herbs, leaves, sprigs, green branches, and boughs of vines growing in and about the same, and within the image of the statue glistened and shone marvellously upon the stone; under the brim of the rock hung apples and grapes polished finely, wherein art (envying nature) showed its great cunning: for they were so lively set out that you would have thought that now autumn, the season of wine, had breathed upon them the colour of ripeness, and that they might have been pulled and eaten; and if, bending down, thou didst behold the running water, which seemed to spring and leap under the feet of the goddess, thou mightest mark the grapes which hung down and seemed even to move and stir like the very grapes of the vine. Moreover amongst the branches of the stone appeared the image of Acteon looking eagerly upon the goddess: and both in the stream and in the stone he might be seen already beginning to be turned into a hart as he waited to spy Diana bathe.

And while I was greatly delighted with exploring the view of these things, Byrrhaena spake to me and said: 'Cousin, all things here be at your commandment.' And therewithal she willed secretly the residue to depart from our secret conference, who being gone she said: 'My most dear cousin Lucius, I swear by this goddess Diana that I do greatly fear for your safety, and am as careful for you long before, as if you were mine own natural child; beware I say, beware of the evil arts and wicked allurements of that Pamphile that is the wife of Milo, whom you call your host, for she is accounted the most chief and principal magician and enchantress of every necromantic spell: who, by breathing out certain words and charms over boughs and stones and other frivolous things, can throw down all the light of the starry heavens into the deep bottom of hell, and reduce them again to the old chaos. For as soon as she espieth any comely young man, she is forthwith stricken with his love, and presently setteth her eye and whole affection on him: she soweth her seed of flattery, she invadeth his spirit, and entangleth him with continual snares of immeasurable love. And then if any afford not to her filthy desire, so that they seem loathsome in her eye, by and by in a moment she either turneth them into stones, sheep, or some other beast as herself pleaseth, and some she presently slays and murders; of whom I would you should earnestly beware. For she burneth continually, and you, by reason of your tender age and comely beauty, are capable of her fire and love.'

Thus with great care Byrrhaena charged me, but I nevertheless, that was curious and coveted after such sorcery and witchcraft, as soon as I heard its name, little esteemed to beware of Pamphile, but willingly determined to bestow abundance of money in learning of that teacher, and even to leap of my own accord into that very pit whereof Byrrhaena had warned me, and so I waxed mad and hasty, and wresting myself out of her company, as out of links or chains, I bade her farewell, and departed with all speed towards the house of mine host Milo. Then as I hastened by the way like one bereft of wit, I reasoned thus with myself: 'O Lucius, now take heed, be vigilant, have a good care, for now thou hast time and place to satisfy thy longing, and mayest gain the desire thou hast so long nourished and fill thy heart with marvels. Now shake off thy childishness and come close to this matter like a man, but specially temper thyself from the love of thine hostess, and abstain from violation of the bed of worthy Milo; but strongly attempt to win the maiden Fotis, for she is beautiful, wanton and pleasant in talk. Nay yester-eve when thou wentest to sleep, she brought thee gently into thy chamber, and tenderly laid thee down in thy bed, and lovingly covered thee, and kissed thy head sweetly, and showed in her countenance how unwillingly she departed, and cast her eyes oftentimes back and stood still; then good speed to thee; then hast thou a good occasion ministered unto thee, even if it betide thee ill, to prove and try the mind of Fotis.'

Thus while I reasoned with myself, I came to Milo's door persevering still in my purpose, but I found neither Milo nor his wife at home, but only my dear and sweet love Fotis mincing pigs' meat as if for stuffing, and slicing flesh, and making pottage for her master and mistress, and I thought I smelled even from thence the savour of some haggis very sweet and dainty. She had about her middle a white and clean apron, and she was girded high about her body beneath her breasts with a girdle of red shining silk, and she stirred the pot and turned the meat with her fair and white hands, in such sort and with such stirrings and turning the same that her loins and hips did likewise gently move and shake, which was in my mind a comely sight to see. These things when I saw I was half amazed, and stood musing with myself, and my courage came then upon me which before was scant. And I spoke unto Fotis at last, and said: 'O Fotis, how trimly, how merrily, with shaking your hips you can stir the pot, and how sweet do you make the pottage. O happy and thrice happy is he to whom you give leave and license to dip his finger therein." Then she, being likewise witty and merrily disposed, gave answer: 'Depart, I say, wretch, from me; depart from my fire, for if the flame thereof do never so little blaze forth it will burn thee inwardly, and none can extinguish the heat thereof but I alone, who know well how with daintiest seasoning to stir both board and bed.'

When she had said these words she cast her eyes upon me and laughed, but I did not depart from thence until such time as I had viewed her in every point: but why should I speak of other things? When as it hath always been my chief care both abroad to mark and view the head and hair of every dame and afterwards delight myself therewith privately at home, and this is my firm and fixed judgement, for that is the principal part of all the body, and is first open to our eyes; and whatsoever flourishing and gorgeous apparel doth for the other parts of the body, this doth the natural and comely beauty set forth on the head. Moreover there be divers, that (to the intent to show their grace and loveliness) will cast off their partlets and habiliments, and do more delight to show the fairness and ruddiness of their skin in beauty unadorned than to deck themselves up in raiment of gold. But, though it be a crime unto me to say it, and I pray there may be no example of so foul a thing, know ye that if you spoil and cut off the hair of any woman or deprive her of the natural colour of her face, though she were never so excellent in beauty, though she were thrown down from heaven, sprung of the seas, nourished of the floods, though she were Venus herself, accompanied with the Graces, waited upon by all the court of Cupids, girded with her beautiful scarf of love, sweet like cinnamon and bedewed with balsam; yet if she appeared bald she could in no wise please, no, not her own Vulcan. O how well doth a fair colour and a brilliant sheen upon the glittering hair! Behold it encountereth with the beams of the sun like swift lightning, or doth softly reflect them back again, or changeth clean contrary into another grace. Sometimes the beauty of the hair, shining like gold, resembles the colour of honey; sometimes, when it is raven black, the blue plume and azure feathers about the necks of doves, especially when it is anointed with the nard of Arabia, or trimly tuffed out with the teeth of a fine comb; and if it be tied up in the nape of the neck, it seemeth to the lover that beholdeth the same as a glass that yieldeth forth a more pleasant and gracious comeliness. The same is it if it should be gathered thick on the crown of the head, or if it should hang down scattering behind on the shoulders of the woman. Finally, there is such a dignity in the hair, that whatsoever she be, though she never be so bravely attired with gold, silks, precious stones, and other rich and gorgeous ornaments, yet if her hair be not curiously set forth, she cannot seem fair.

But in my Fotis not her studied care thereof but rather its disorderliness did increase her beauty: her rich tresses hung gently about her shoulders, and were dispersed abroad upon every part of her neck hanging from the nape, and fell fairly down enwound in a kerchief, until at last they were trussed up upon her crown with a knot: then I, unable to sustain the torture of the great desire that I was in, ran upon her and kissed very sweetly the place where she had thus laid her hair upon her crown, whereat she turned her face and cast her sidelong and rolling eyes upon me, saying: 'O scholar, thou hast tasted now both honey and gall; take heed that the sweetness of thy pleasure do not turn into the bitterness of repentance.' 'Tush!' quoth I: 'My sweetheart, I am contented for such another kiss to be broiled here upon this fire'; wherewithal I embraced her more closely and began to kiss her. Then she embraced and kissed me with like passion of love, and moreover her breath smelled like cinnamon, and the liquor of her tongue was like sweet nectar. Wherewith when my mind was greatly delighted, I said: 'Behold, Fotis, I am yours and shall presently die, nay, I am already dead, unless you take pity upon me,' which when I had said, she eftsoons kissed me and bade me be of good courage. 'And I will,' quoth she, 'Satisfy your whole desire, and it shall be no longer delayed than until night, when as (assure yourself) I will come to your chamber; wherefore go your ways and prepare yourself, for I intend valiantly and courageously to encounter with you this night.' Thus when we had lovingly talked and reasoned together, we departed for that time.

When noon was just now come Byrrhaena sent unto me a present
of a fat pig, five hens, and a flagon of old wine and rare. Then I called
Fotis and said: 'Behold how Bacchus, the aider and abettor of Venus,
doth offer himself of his own accord; let us therefore drink up this
wine, that we may do utterly away with the cowardice of shame and
get us the courage of pleasure, for the voyage of Venus wanteth no
other provision than this, that the lamp may be all the night
replenished with oil, and the cups filled with wine.'

The residue of the day I passed away at the baths, and then to
supper, for I was bid by the worthy Milo, and so I sat down at his
little table, so neatly furnished, out of Pamphile's sight as much as I
could, being mindful of the commandment of Byrrhaena, and only
sometimes I would cast mine eyes upon her, as if I should look upon
the lakes of hell; but then I (eftsoons turning my face behind me, and
beholding my Fotis ministering at the table) was again refreshed and
made merry. And behold, when it was now evening and Pamphile
did see the lamp standing on the table, she said: 'Verily we shall have
much rain tomorrow,' which when her husband did hear, he
demanded of her, by what reason she knew it. 'Marry,' quoth she,
'The light on the table doth show the same': then Milo laughed and
said: 'Verily we nourish and bring up a Sibyl prophesier in this lamp,
which doth divine from its socket of celestial things, and of the sun
itself, as from a watch-tower.'

Then I mused in my mind and said unto Milo: 'Of truth now is my
first experience and proof of divination, neither is it any marvel, for
although this light is but a small light and made by the hands of man,
yet hath it a remembrance of that great and heavenly light as of its
parent, and by its divine spirit of prophecy doth both know and show
unto us, what he will do in the skies above: for I knew among us at
Corinth a certain man of Assyria, who by his answers set the whole
city in a turmoil, and for the gain of money would tell every man his
fortune: to some he would tell the days they should marry; to others
he would tell when they should build, so that their edifices should
continue; to others when they should best go about their affairs; to
others when they should travel by land; to others when they should
go by sea; and to me (enquiring of my journey hither) he declared
many things strange and variable. For sometimes he said that I should
win glory enough, sometimes that mine should be a great history,
sometimes an incredible tale and the subject of books.'

Whereat Milo laughed again, and enquired of me of what stature this man of Assyria was, and what he was named. 'In faith,' quoth I, 'He is a tall man and somewhat black, and he is called Diophanes.' Then said Milo: 'The same is he and no other, who likewise hath declared many things unto many of us, whereby he got and obtained no small profit, indeed much substance and treasure, but fell at length, poor wretch, into the hands of unpropitious fate, or I might say fate unfaithful. For being on a day amongst a great assembly of people, to tell the bystanders their fortune, a certain merchant called Cerdo came unto him, and desired him to tell when it should be best for him to take his voyage, the which when he had done, Cerdo had already opened his purse and already poured forth his money and counted out a hundred pence to pay him for the pains of his soothsaying; whereupon came a certain young nobleman from behind and took Diophanes by the garment, and turned him about and embraced and kissed him close, and Diophanes kissed him again and desired him to sit down by him. And astonished with this sudden chance, he forgot the present business that he was doing, and said: "O dear friend, you are heartily welcome; I pray you when arrived you, whom we have looked for so long, into these parts?" Then answered he: "Just this last evening; but, brother, I pray you tell me of your sudden coming from the Isle of Euboea, and how you sped by the way, both of sea and land?" Whereunto Diophanes, this notable Assyrian, not yet come unto his mind but half amazed, gave answer and said: "I would to God that all our enemies and evil-willers might fall into the like dangerous peregrination, as troublesome as Ulysses' was, for the ship which we were in (after that it was by the waves of the sea and by the great tempest tossed hither and thither, in great peril, and after that both the rudders brake alike in pieces) was but just brought to the further shore, but sunk utterly into the water, and so we did swim and hardly escaped to land with loss of all that we had: and after that, whatsoever was given unto us in recompense of our losses, either by the pity of strangers or by the benevolence of our friends, was taken away from us by a band of thieves, whose violence when mine only brother Arignotus did essay to resist, he was cruelly murdered by them before my face." While he was still sadly declaring these things, the merchant Cerdo took up his money again, which he had told out to pay for the telling of his fortune, and ran away: and then Diophanes coming to himself perceived what he had done, how his imprudence had ruined him, and we all that stood by laughed greatly. But surely, I pray that unto you, O Lucius, did Diophanes tell the truth, if to you alone, and may you be happy, and give a prosperous journey.'

Thus Milo reasoned with me, but I groaned within myself and was not a little sorry that I had by my own doing turned him into such a vein of talk so unseasonably, that I was like to lose a good part of the night, and the sweet pleasure thereof, but at length I boldly swallowed my shame and said unto Milo: 'Let Diophanes farewell with his evil fortune, and disgorge again to sea and land that spoil that he wins from all nations, for I verily do yet feel the weariness of my travel of yesterday; wherefore I pray you pardon me, and give me license, being very tired, to depart early to bed,' wherewithal I rose up and went to my chamber, where I found all manner of meats finely prepared, and the servants' bed (so that they should not hear, methinks, our tattling of the night) was removed far off without the chamber door. By my bed a table was set, all covered with no small store of such meats as were left at supper, generous cups were filled half full with liquor, leaving room only for enough water to temper and delay the wine, the flagon stood ready prepared, its neck opened with a wide and smooth cut, that one might the easier draw from it, and there did nothing lack which was necessary for the preparation of Venus.

Now when I was just entered into the bed, behold my Fotis (who had brought her mistress to sleep) drew nigh, with bunches of rose garlands and rose blooms in her apron, and she kissed me closely and tied a garland about my head, and cast the residue about me. Which when she had done, she took up a cup of wine, and tempered it with hot water, and proffered it me to drink, and before I had drunk up all, she gently pulled it from my mouth, and sipping it slowly and looking upon me the while, she drank that which was left, and in this manner we emptied the pot twice or thrice together. Thus when I had well replenished myself with wine, and was now ready not only in mind but also in body, I showed to Fotis my great impatience and said: 'O my sweetheart, take pity upon me and help me: for as you see, I am prepared unto the battle now approaching which yourself did appoint without the herald's aid, for after that I felt the first arrow of cruel Cupid within my breast I bent my bow very strong, and now fear (because it is bended so hard) lest the string should break: but that thou mayest the better please me, unbrace thy hair and come and embrace me lovingly'; wherewithal she made no long delay, but set aside all the meat and wine, and then unapparelled herself and unattired her hair, presenting her amiable body unto me in manner of fair Venus, when she goeth under the waves of the sea, and for a short while covering her smooth mount of Venus with her rosy hand rather from saucy knowingness than from modesty. 'Now,' quoth she, 'Is come the hour of jousting, now is come the time of war, wherefore show thyself like unto a man, for I will not retire, I will not fly the field; see then thou be valiant, see thou be courageous, since there is no time appointed when our skirmish shall cease.' In saying these words she climbed up onto the bed and, sitting herself astride of me, ever and anon she writhed upwards and curving her pliant back with flexible motions, she sated me with the joys of love experienced from beneath, utterly worn down with our spirits exhausted and our limbs enfeebled, we both collapsed together, breathing out our souls amid our mutual embraces. We passed all night amid these struggles and other such, and never slept till it was day; but we would ever refresh our weariness and provoke our pleasure by drinking of wine. In which sort we pleasantly passed many nights following.

It fortuned on a day that Byrrhaena desired me to sup with her, and she would in no wise take any excuse. Whereupon I must go unto Fotis to ask counsel of her as of some divine, who (although she was unwilling that I should depart one foot from her company) yet at length she gave me license to be absent for a while from amorous debate, saying: 'Look you, beware that you tarry not long at supper there, for there is a rabble of well-born youths that disturbeth the public peace, and you may see many murdered about in the streets, neither can the armies of the governor, for that they are afar off, rid the city of this great plague. And they will the sooner set upon you, by reason of your high station and for that they will disdain you being a foreigner.' Then I answered and said: 'Have no care for me, Fotis, for I esteem the pleasure which I have with thee above the dainty meat that I eat abroad, and I will take away that fear that you have by returning again quickly. Nevertheless, I mind not to go without company, for I have here my sword by my side, whereby I hope to defend myself.'

And so in this sort I went to supper, and behold I found at

Byrrhaena's house a great company of strangers, the very flower of the citizens, for that she was one of the chief and principal women of the city. The tables (made of citron-wood and ivory) were richly adorned, the couches spread with cloth of gold, the cups were great and garnished preciously in sundry fashion, but were of like estimation and price: here stood a glass gorgeously wrought, there stood another of crystal finely chased, there stood a cup of glittering silver, and here stood another of shining gold, and here was another of amber artificially carved, and precious stones made to drink out of; finally, there were all things that might never be found. A crowd of servitors brought orderly the plentiful meats in rich apparel, the pages curled and arrayed in silk robes did fill great gems made in form of cups with ancient wine.

Then one brought in candles and torches: and when we were sat down and placed in order we began to talk, to laugh and be merry. And Byrrhaena spoke to me, and said: 'I pray you, cousin, how like you our country? Verily I think there is no other city which hath the like temples, baths and other commodities as we have here: further we have abundance of household stuff, we have freedom for him that will rest, and when a busy merchant cometh, he may find here as many as at Rome; but for a stranger that will have quiet there is peace as at a country-house: and in fine, all that dwell within this province (when they purpose to solace and repose themselves) do come to this city.'

Whereunto I answered: 'Verily you tell truth, for I have found no place in all the world where I may be freer than here; but I greatly fear the blind and inevitable hits of witchcraft, for they say that not even the graves of the dead are safe, but the bones and slices of such as are slain be digged up from tombs and pyres to afflict and torment such as live: and the old witches as soon as they hear of the death of any person do forthwith go and uncover the hearse and spoil the corpse before ever it be buried.'

Then another sitting at the table spoke and said: 'In faith you say true, neither yet do they spare or favour the living. For I know one not far hence that was cruelly handled by them and hath suffered much with all manner of cutting of his face'; whereat all the company laughed heartily, and looked upon one that sat apart at the board's end, who being amazed at all their gazing and angry withal, murmured somewhat and would have risen from the table had not

Byrrhaena spoken to him and said: 'I pray thee, friend Thelyphron, sit still, and according to thy accustomed courtesy declare unto us thy story, to the end that my son Lucius may be delighted with the pleasantness of thy tale.' To whom he answered: 'Ah dame, you are always the same in the office of your bounty and thoughtfulness, but the insolence of some is not to be supported.' This he said very angrily, but Byrrhaena was earnest upon him and conjured him by her own life that he should, how unwilling soever, tell his tale, whereby he was enforced to declare the same: and so (lapping up the end of the table-cloth into an heap) he leaned with his elbow thereon, and sat up upon the couch and held out his right hand in the manner of an orator, shutting down the two smaller fingers and stretching out the other three, and pointing up with his thumb a little, and said:

'When I was a young man I went from the city called Miletus to see the games and triumphs called Olympian, and being desirous also to come into this famous province, after that I had travelled over all Thessaly, I fortuned in an evil hour to come to the city Larissa, where, while I went up and down to view the streets, to take some relief for my poor estate (for I had spent near all my money) I espied a tall old man standing upon a stone in the midst of the market-place, crying with a loud voice, and saying that if any man would watch a dead corpse that night he should be rewarded and a price be fixed for his pains. Which when I heard I said to one that passed by: "What is here to do? Do dead men use to run away in this country?" Then answered he: "Hold your peace; for you are but a babe and a stranger here, and not without cause you are ignorant how you are in Thessaly, where the women witches do bite off by morsels the flesh of the faces of dead men, and thereby work their sorceries and enchantments." "Then," quoth I, "In good fellowship tell me the order of this custody of the dead and how it is?" "Marry," quoth he, "First you must watch all the night, with your eyes staring and bent continually upon the corpse, without winking, never looking off nor even moving aside: for these witches do change their skin and turn themselves at will into sundry kinds of beasts, whereby they deceive the eyes even of the sun and of very Justice; sometimes they are transformed into birds, sometimes into dogs and mice, and sometimes into flies; moreover they will charm the keepers of the corpse asleep, neither can it be declared what means and shifts these wicked women do use to bring their purpose to pass: and the reward for such dangerous watching is no more than four or six pieces of gold. But hearken further, which I had well nigh forgotten, if the keeper of the dead do not render on the morning following the corpse whole and sound as he received the same, he shall be punished in this sort. That is; if the corpse be diminished or spoiled in any part, the same shall be diminished and spoiled in the face of the keeper to patch it up withal."

'Which when I heard I took a good heart and went unto the crier and bade him cease, for I would take the matter in hand, and so I demanded what I should have. "Marry," quoth he, "A thousand pence; but beware I say, young man, that you do well defend the dead corpse from the wicked witches, for he was the son of one of the chiefest of the city." "Tush," said I, "You speak you cannot tell what; behold I am a man made all of iron, and have never desire to sleep, and am more quick of sight than Lynceus or Argus, and must be all eyes."

'I had scarce spoken these words, when he took me by the hand, and brought me to a certain house, the gate whereof was closed fast, so that I went through a small wicket, and then he brought me into a chamber somewhat dark, the light being shut out, and showed me a matron clothed in mourning vesture and weeping in lamentable wise: and he stood by and spake unto her and said: "Behold here is one that is employed to watch the corpse of your husband faithfully this night." Which when she heard, she pushed aside her hair that hung before her blubbered face that was yet very fair, and turned her unto me, saying: "Mark you, young man, take good heed and see you be vigilant to your office." "Have no care," quoth I, "So that you will give me something above that which is due to be given," wherewith she was contented; and then rose and brought me into another chamber, wherein the corpse lay covered with white sheets, and she called seven witnesses, before whom she removed the cloth, and wept long over him, then showed the dead body and every part and parcel thereof, and with weeping eyes desired them all to testify the matter, which done she said these words that she had composed of set purpose, while one wrote and noted the same in tables: "Behold his nose is whole, his eyes safe, his ears without scar, his lips untouched, and his chin sound: do you, good citizens, bear witness hereto": and then was all inscribed with the hands of the witnesses to confirm the same.

'This done, I said unto the matron: "Madam, I pray you bid that I

may have all things here necessary." "What is that?" quoth she.
"Marry," said I, "A great lamp replenished with oil, pots of wine, and
warm water to temper the same, a cup, and some other dainty dish
that was left at supper." Then she shook her head, and said: "Away,
fool as thou art, thinkest thou to play the glutton here, and to look for
dainty meats, where so long time hath not been seen any smoke at
all? Comest thou here to revel, rather than weep and lament suitably
to the place?" And therewithal she turned back and commanded her
maiden Myrrhine to deliver me a lamp with oil, and to close in the
watcher and depart from the room.

'Now when I was alone to keep the corpse company, I rubbed
mine eyes to arm them for watching, and to the intent that I would
not sleep I solaced my mind with singing, and so I passed the time till
it was dark, and then night deeper and deeper still, and then
midnight, when behold, as I grew already more afraid, there crept in
a weasel into the chamber, and she came against me and fixed a sharp
look upon me and put me in very great fear, in so much that I
marvelled greatly of the audacity of so little a beast. To whom I said:
"Get thee hence, thou filthy brute, and hie thee to the mice thy
fellows, lest thou feel my fingers. Why wilt thou not go?" Then
incontinently she ran away, and when she was quite gone from the
chamber, I fell on the ground so fast in the deepest depth of sleep that
Apollo himself could not well discern whether of us two was the
dead corpse, for I lay prostrate as one without life, and needed a
keeper likewise, and had as well not been there.

'At length the cocks began to crow declaring night past and that it
was now day, wherewithal I waked and, being greatly afraid, ran unto
the dead body with the lamp in my hand, and I uncovered his face
and viewed him closely round about; all the parts were there: and
immediately came in the wretched matron all blubbered with her
witnesses, and threw herself upon the corpse, and eftsoons kissing
him, examined his body in the lamplight, and found no part
diminished. Then she turned and commanded one Philodespotus,
her steward, to pay the good guardian his wages forthwith, which
when he had done, he said: "We thank you, gentle young man, for
your pains, and verily for your diligence herein we will account you
as one of the family."

'Whereupon I, being joyous of my unhoped gain, and rattling my
money in my hand, as I gazed upon its shining colour, did answer:

"Nay, madam, I pray you, esteem me as one of your servitors; and as often as you need my services at any time, I am at your commandment."

'I had not fully declared these words, when as behold, all the servants of the house did curse the dreadful ominousness of my words, and were assembled to drive me away with all manner of weapons; one buffeted me about the face with his fists, another thrust his elbows into my shoulders, some struck me in the sides with their hands, some kicked me, some pulled me by the hair, some tore my garments, and so I was handled amongst them and driven from the house even as the proud young man Adonis who was torn by a boar, or Orpheus the Muses' poet.

'When I was come into the next street to recover my spirit, I mused with myself too late mine unwise and unadvised words which I had spoken, whereby I considered that I had deserved much more punishment, and that I was worthily beaten for my folly: and by and by the corpse came forth, after the last words of the farewell and lamentation, which (because it was the body of one of the chiefs of the city) was carried in funeral pomp round about the market-place, according to the rite of the country there. And forthwith stepped out an old man weeping and lamenting and tearing his venerable and aged hair, and ran unto the bier and embraced it, and with deep sighs and sobs cried out in this sort: "O masters, I pray you, by the duty which you owe to the public weal, take pity and mercy upon this dead corpse, who is miserably murdered, and do vengeance on this wicked and cursed woman his wife, which hath committed this fact, for it is she and no other that hath poisoned her husband, my sister's son, to the intent to maintain her adultery and to get his heritage."

'In this sort the old man complained before the face of all the people. Then they, astonished at these sayings and because the thing seemed to be true, began to be very angry and cried out: "Burn her, burn her," and they sought for stones to throw at her, and willed the boys in the street to do the same; but she, weeping in lamentable wise with feigned tears, did swear by all the gods that she was not culpable of this crime.

'Then quoth the old man: "Let us refer the judgement of truth to the divine providence of God. Behold here is one Zatchlas, an Egyptian, who is the most principal prophesier in all this country, and who was hired of me long since to bring back the soul of this man from hell for a short season, and to revive his body from beyond the threshold of death for the trial hereof"; and therewithal he brought forth a certain young man clothed in linen raiment, having on his feet a pair of sandals of palm-leaves and his crown shaven; and he kissed his hands often and touched even his knees, saying: "O Priest, have mercy, have mercy, I pray thee by the celestial planets, by the powers infernal, by the virtue of the natural elements, by the silences of the night, by the temples nigh unto the town of Coptos, by the increase of the flood of Nile, by the secret mysteries of Memphis, and by the rattles* of Pharos: have mercy, I say, and call again to the light of the sun for a short moment this dead body, and make that his eyes which be closed and shut for ever, may be opened awhile and see; howbeit we mean not to strive against the law of death, neither intend we to deprive the earth of its right, but (to the end that vengeance may be done) we crave but a small time and space of life."

'At this the prophet was moved, and took a certain herb, and laid it three times upon the mouth of the dead, and he took another, and laid it upon his breast in like sort: thus when he had done he turned himself unto the East, and made silently certain orisons unto the proud and rising sun, which caused all the people to marvel greatly at the sight of this solemn acting, and to look for the strange miracle that should happen.

'Then I pressed in amongst them nigh behind the bier, and got upon a stone to look curiously upon this mystery, and behold incontinently his breast did swell, the dead body began to receive spirit, his principal veins did move, his life came again, and he held up his head, and spoke in this sort: "Why do you call me back again to the duties of this transitory life, that have already tasted of the water of Lethe, and likewise floated upon the waters of Styx? Leave off, I pray, leave off, and let me lie in quiet rest." When these words were uttered by the dead corpse, the prophet, moved with anger, said: "I charge thee to tell, before the face of all the people here, the secret occasion of thy death. What? Dost thou think that I cannot by my conjurations call up the Furies and by my puissance torment thy weary limbs?"

'Then the corpse moved up his head again, and with a deep groan thus made reverence unto the people, and said: "Verily, I was poisoned by the evil arts of my newly wedded wife, and so yielded

* The sistrum or rattle of Isis.

my bed, still warm, unto an adulterer." Whereat his excellent wife, taking present audacity and reproving his sayings, with a cursed mind did deny it. The people were in a turmoil and divided in sundry ways; some thought best the vile woman should be buried alive with her husband, but some said there ought no credit to be given unto the dead body that spake falsely: which opinion was clean taken away by the words which the corpse spoke again with deeper groaning, and said: "Behold, I will give you an evident token, which never yet any other man knew, whereby you shall perceive that I declare the truth," and by and by he pointed towards me that stood on the stone, and said: "When this, the good guardian of my body, watched me diligently in the night, and the wicked witches and enchantresses came into the chamber to spoil me of my limbs, and to bring such their purpose to pass, did transform themselves into the shape of beasts; and when they could in no wise deceive or beguile his vigilant eyes, they cast him at last into so dead and sound a sleep that by their witchcraft he seemed without spirit or life. After this they called me by my name, and did never cease till the cold members of my body began by little and little to revive to obey their magic arts: then he, being lively indeed, howbeit buried in sleep, because he and I were named by one name, rose up when they called, and walked as one without sense like some lifeless ghost: and they, though the door was fast closed, came in by a certain hole and cut off first his nose and then his ears, and so that butchery was done to him, which was appointed to be done to me. And that such their subtlety might not be perceived, they made him very exactly like a pair of ears of wax, and fitted it exactly upon him, and a nose like his they made also, wherefore you may see that the poor wretch for his diligence hath received no reward of money, but loss of his members."

'Which when he said I was greatly astonished, and (minding to feel my face) put my hand to my nose, and my nose fell off, and put my hand to my ears, and my ears fell off. Whereat all the people pointed and nodded at me, and laughed me to scorn: but I (being striken in a cold sweat) crept between their legs for shame and escaped away. So I, disfigured and ridiculous, could never return home again, but covered the loss of mine ears with my long hair and glued this clout to my face to hide the shame of my nose.'

As soon as Thelyphron had told his tale they which sat at the table, replenished with wine, laughed heartily; and while they cried for a toast after their fashion to Laughter, Byrrhaena spoke to me and said: 'From the first foundation of this city, we alone of all men have had a custom to celebrate with joyful and pleasant rites the festival day of the god Laughter, and tomorrow is the feast, when I pray you to be present to set out the same more honourably, and I would with all my heart that you could find or devise somewhat merry of yourself, that you might the more honour so great a god.' To whom I answered: 'Verily, cousin, I will do as you command me, and right glad would I be if I might invent any laughing or merry matter to please or satisfy Laughter withal.' Then at the warning of my servant, who told me the night was late, being also well drunken with wine, I rose from the table, took leave of Byrrhaena, and departed with tottering steps on my homeward way.

But when we came into the first street, the torch whereunto we trusted went out with a sudden gust of wind, so that with great pain we could scarce get out of this sudden darkness to our lodging, weary with our toes stumbling against the stones. And when we were well nigh come to the door, behold I saw three men of great stature heaving and lifting at Milo's gates to get in. And when they saw me, they were nothing afraid, but assayed with more force to break down the doors, whereby they gave me occasion, and not without cause, to think that they were strong thieves. Whereupon I straightway drew my sword which I carried for that purpose under my cloak, and ran in amongst them, and wounded them deeply as each thrust against me, in such sort that they fell down for their many and great wounds before my feet and gave up the ghost. Thus when I had slain them all, I knocked, sweating and breathing, at the door, till Fotis, awaked by the tumult, let me in. And then full weary with the slaughter of these three thieves, like Hercules when he fought King Geryon, I went to my chamber and laid me down to sleep.

BOOK THREE

So soon as morning was come, and Aurora had lifted her rosy arm to drive her bright coursers through the shining heaven, and night tore me from peaceful sleep and gave me up to the day, my heart burned sore with remembrance of the murder which I had committed on the night before: and I rose and sat down on the bed with my legs across, and clasping my hands over my knees with fingers intertwined I wept bitterly. For I imagined with myself that I was brought before the judge in the judgement-place, and that he awarded sentence against me, and that the hangman was ready to lead me to the gallows. And further I imagined and said: 'Alas, what judge is he that is so gentle or benign that he will think I am unguilty of the slaughter and murder of these three men, and will absolve me, stained with the innocent blood of so many of the city? Thus forsooth the Assyrian Diophanes did firmly assure unto me, that my peregrination and voyage hither should be prosperous.'

But while I did thus again and again unfold my sorrows and greatly bewail my fortune, behold I heard a great noise and cry at the door; in a moment the gates were flung open, and in came the magistrates and officers, and all their retinue, that filled all the place, and commanded two sergeants to lay hands on me and lead me to prison, whereunto I was willingly obedient; and as we came to the mouth of our lane all the city gathered together in a thick throng and followed me, and although I looked always on the ground, nay, even to the very pit of death for misery, yet sometimes I cast my head aside, and marvelled greatly that amongst so many thousand people there was not one but laughed exceedingly. Finally, when they had brought me through all the streets of the city, and to every nook and corner, in manner of those as go in procession and do sacrifice to mitigate the ire of the gods, they placed me in the judgement-hall before the seat of the judges: and after that the magistrates had taken their seat on a high stage, and the crier had commanded all men to keep silence, the people instantly cried out with one voice and desired the judges to give sentence in the great theatre by reason of the great multitude that was there, whereby they were in danger of stifling. And behold they ran and very quickly filled the whole pit of the theatre, and the press of people increased still; some climbed to the top of the house, some got upon the beams, some hung from the images, and some thrust in their heads through the windows and ceilings, little regarding the dangers they were in, so they might see me. Then the officers brought me forth openly into the middle of the place like some victim, that every man might behold me, and made me to stand in the midst of the stage. And after that the crier had made an 'Oyez' and willed all such as would bring any evidence against me should come forth, there stepped out an old man with an hour-glass of water in his hand, wherein, through a small hole like to a funnel, the water dropped softly, that he might have liberty to speak during the time of the continuance of the water; and he began his oration to the people in this sort:

'O most reverend and just judges, the thing which I purpose to declare unto you is no small matter, but toucheth the estate and tranquillity of this whole city, and the punishment thereof may be a right good example to others. Wherefore I pray you, most venerable fathers, to whom and to every of whom it doth appertain to provide for the dignity and safety of the common weal, that you would in no wise suffer this wicked homicide embrued with the blood of so many murders to escape unpunished. And think you not that I am moved by private envy or hatred, but by reason of mine office, in that until this day no man alive can accuse me to be remiss in the same. Now I will declare all the whole matter, orderly, as it was done this last night. For when at about the third watch of this night past I diligently searched every part of the city, spying everything close from one door to another, behold I fortuned to espy this cruel young man, sword drawn out for murder, and already three by his fierce onslaught dead at his feet, their bodies still breathing, in a welter of blood. Now this when he had done (moved in his conscience at so great a crime) he ran away and aided by reason of darkness slipped into a house and there lay hidden all night; but, by the providence of the gods, which suffereth no heinous offences to remain unpunished, he was taken up this morning before he escaped any further by secret ways, and so I have brought him hither to your honourable presence to receive his desert accordingly. So have you here a culpable homicide, one caught in the very act, and an accused stranger; wherefore pronounce the judgement against this man being an alien, even as you would most severely and sharply revenge such an offence found in a known citizen.'

In this sort the cruel accuser finished and ended his terrible tale: then the crier commanded me to speak if I had anything to say for myself, but I could in no wise utter any word at all for weeping: yet verily I esteemed not so much his rigorous accusation, as I did consider mine own miserable conscience. Howbeit (being inspired by divine audacity) at length I began to say:

'Verily I know that it is a hard thing for him that is accused to have slain three persons, to persuade you, being so many, that he is innocent, although he should declare the whole truth, and confess the matter how it was in deed; but if your Honours will vouchsafe to give me audience, I will show you that if I be condemned to die, I have not deserved it by mine own desert, but that I was moved by the fortune of reasonable anger to do that deed. For returning somewhat late from supper yesternight (being well tippled with wine, which I will not deny) and approaching nigh unto my lodging, which was in the house of good Milo, a citizen of this city, I fortuned to espy three great thieves attempting to break down his walls and gates, and to open the locks to enter in, by tearing away all the doors from the posts and by dragging out the bolts, which were most firmly fixed; and they consulted amongst themselves how they would cruelly handle such as they found in the house And one of them being of more courage and of greater stature than the rest, spoke unto his fellows, urging them on, and said: "Come, boys, take men's hearts unto you, and let us enter into every part of the house, and attack them that slumber therein. No delay, no cowardice in your hearts; let murder with drawn sword go throughout the dwelling. Such as we find asleep let us slay, and such likewise as resist let us kill, and so by that means we shall escape without danger if we leave none alive therein.' Verily, ye judges, I confess that I drew out my sword, which I bore for this manner of danger, against those three abandoned robbers, willing to terrify and drive them away; for I thought that it was the office and duty of one that beareth good will to this common weal so to do, especially since they put me in great fear, both for myself and for mine host. But when those cruel and terrible men would in no case run away, nor fear my naked sword, but boldly resisted against me, I ran upon them and fought valiantly. One of them which was the captain and leader of the rest invaded me strongly and drew me by the hair with both his hands, and would have beaten me with a great stone, but while he groped therefor, I proved the hardier man, and threw him down at my feet and killed him. I took likewise the second that clasped about my legs and bit me, and slew him also, thrusting him through the shoulder. And the third that came running carelessly upon me, after that I had struck him full in the stomach, fell down dead. Thus when I had restored peace and delivered myself, the house, mine host, and all his family from this present danger, I thought that I should not only escape unpunished, but also have some great reward of the city for my pains. Moreover I that have always been clear and unspotted of crime and well looked upon in mine own country, and that have esteemed mine innocency above all the treasure of the world, can find no reasonable cause why, having justly punished these evil robbers, I should now be accused and condemned to die; since there is none that can affirm that there has been at any time either grudge or hatred between us, or that we were aught but men mere strangers and of no acquaintance: and last of all, no man can prove that I committed that deed for any lucre or gain.'

When I had ended my words in this sort, behold I wept again piteously, and holding up my hands, I prayed all the people by their common mercy and for the love of their poor infants and children to show me some pity and favour. And when I believed their hearts somewhat relented and moved by my lamentable tears, I called upon the eyes of the sun and of Justice to witness that I was not guilty of the crime, and so to the divine providence I committed my present estate; but lifting up somewhat mine eyes again, I perceived that all the people laughed with exceeding laughter, and especially my good friend and host Milo. Then thought I with myself: 'Alas! where is faith, where is conscience? Behold for the safeguard of mine host and his family I am a slayer of men, and brought to the bar as a murderer. Yet is he not contented with coming not to comfort and help me, but likewise laugheth with all his heart at my destruction.'

When this was a-doing, out came a woman weeping into the middle of the theatre arrayed in mourning vesture, and bearing a child in her arms. And after her came an old woman in ragged robes crying and howling likewise: and these brought with them olive-boughs, and going about the bier whereon lay the three slain bodies all covered up, with loud lamentation cried out miserably in this manner: 'O right judges, we pray you by the public pity and the humanity which is due to all, to have mercy upon these persons so foully slain, and succour our widowhood and loss of our dear husband and solace us with vengeance; and especially help this poor infant, who is now an orphan and deprived of all good fortune, and execute your justice by order and law upon the blood of this thief who is the occasion of all our sorrows.'

When they had spoken these words, the most ancient of the judges did rise and say to the people: 'Touching this murder which deserveth great punishment, this malefactor himself cannot deny it: but one duty further is left us, to enquire and try out whether he had no coadjutors to help him in this great crime. For it is not likely that one man alone could kill three such great and valiant persons: wherefore the truth must be tried out by the rack, for the slave that was with him fled secretly away, and so we must needs put him to the question, that we may learn what other companions he had, and root out the nest of these mischievous murderers.' And there was no long delay, for, according to the custom of Greece, the fire, the wheel, and many other torments were brought in: then straightway my sorrow increased or rather doubled, in that I could not at least end my life with whole and unperished members. But by and by the old woman, who had troubled all the court with her howling, implored the judges, saying: 'Before ye send to the gallows this thief that hath destroyed my wretched children, let him uncover the bodies which he hath slain, that every man may see their comely shape and youthful beauty and be the more enraged thereat, and that he may receive condign and worthy punishment, according to the quality of the offence.'

Therewithal they were delighted at her words, and the judge commanded me forthwith to discover the bodies of the slain that lay upon the bier, with my own hand; but when I refused a good space, by reason I would not anew make my deed apparent to the eyes of all men, the sergeants charged me by commandment of the judges, and thrust me forward to do the same, and forced my hand, to its own undoing, from my side over the bier. I then (being enforced by necessity) though it were against my will, drew away the pall and uncovered their bodies: but, O good Lord, what a strange sight did I see! What a monster! What sudden change of all my sorrows! For I, who had seemed as though I were already one of the house of Proserpina and of the family of death, could not sufficiently express the form of this new sight, so far was I amazed and astonished thereat; for why? The bodies of the three slain men were no bodies, but three blown bladders, mangled in divers places, and they seemed to be wounded in those parts where I remembered I had wounded the thieves the night before.

Then did that laughter, which they had before artfully concealed, break out exceedingly among the people. Some rejoiced marvellously with the remembrance thereof, some held their stomachs that ached with joy, but every man delighted at this passing sport, gazing on me, and so departed out of the theatre. But I, from the time that I uncovered the bodies, stood still as one turned to stone and cold as ice, no otherwise than as the other statues and pillars there, neither came I up from this hell of mine, until such time as Milo, mine host, came and took me by the hand and with civil violence led me away weeping and sobbing, whether I would or no; and so that I might not be seen, he brought me through many blind ways and lanes to his house, where he went about to comfort me, that was sad and yet fearful, with gentle entreaty of talk; but he could in no wise mitigate my impatience of the injury which I conceived within my mind.

And behold, by and by the very magistrates and judges, with their ensigns, entered into the house and endeavoured to pacify me in this sort, saying: 'O Lucius, we are advertised of your dignity, and know the dignity of your ancient lineage, for the nobility of your kin do possess the greatest part of all this province. And think not that you have suffered the thing wherefore you weep to any reproach of yours or ignominy; put away then all sorrow out of your heart and banish this anguish of mind: for this day, which we celebrate once a year in honour of the god Laughter, is always renowned with some solemn novel prank, and the god doth everywhere graciously accompany with the inventor and doer thereof, and he will not suffer that you should be sorrowful, but he will diligently make glad your countenance with serene beauty. And verily all the city, for the grace that is in you, hath rewarded you with great honours, and hath written you down their patron: and, further, that your statue or image shall be set up in copper for a perpetual remembrance.' To whom I answered: 'As for such benefits as I have received already of this famous city of

Thessaly, I yield and render most entire thanks, but as touching the setting up of any statues or images, I would wish that they should be reserved for such as are more worthy and greater than I.' When I had spoken these words somewhat modestly with a more cheerful countenance, and showed myself more merry than I was before, the judges and magistrates departed, and I reverently took my leave of them and bade them farewell.

And behold, by and by there came one running to me in haste, and said: 'Sir, your cousin Byrrhaena desireth you to take the pains, according to your promise yesternight, to come to supper; for it is ready.' But I, greatly fearing, and shrinking even afar at the very thought of her house, said unto the messenger: 'My friend, I pray you to tell my cousin, your mistress, that I would willingly be at her commandment, but for breaking my troth and credit. For mine host Milo enforced me to assure him, and compelled me by the feast of this present day, that I should pledge me to his dinner and company, and he goeth not forth nor suffereth me to depart from him; wherefore I pray you to excuse me and to defer my promise until another time.' And while I was speaking these words, Milo took me by the hand and led me towards the next bath; but by the way I went crouching under him to hide myself from the sight of men, because I had ministered such an occasion of laughter. And when I had washed and wiped myself and returned home again, I never remembered any such thing, so greatly was I ashamed at the nodding and pointing of every person.

Then I went to supper with Milo, where God wot we fared but poorly: wherefore (feigning that my head did ache by reason of my sobbing and weeping all the day) I desired license to depart to my chamber, and so I went to bed, and there I began to call to mind all the sorrows and griefs that I was in the day before, until such time as my love Fotis (having brought her mistress to sleep) came into the chamber not as she was wont to do, for she seemed nothing pleasant neither in countenance nor talk, but with a sour face and frowning look, and began to speak slowly and fearfully in this sort: 'Verily I confess that I have been the occasion of all thy trouble this day,' and therewithal she pulled out a whip from under her apron, and delivered it to me, saying: 'Revenge thyself of me, mischievous harlot that I am, or rather slay me. Yet think not that I did willingly procure this anguish and sorrow unto you; I call the gods to witness. For I had rather suffer mine own body to be punished than that you should receive or sustain any harm by my means, but that which I was bidden to do was wrought for some other purpose, but behold the unlucky chance fortuned on you by mine evil occasion.' Then I, very envious and desirous to know the secret cause of the matter, answered: 'In faith,' quoth I, 'This most pestilent and evil-favoured whip (which thou hast brought to scourge thyself withal) shall first be broken in a thousand pieces, than it should touch or hurt thy delicate and dainty skin; but I pray you tell me truly what deed of yours has been turned by the perversity of fortune to my trouble and sorrow. For I dare swear by the love that I bear unto you that I will not be persuaded (though you yourself endeavour the same) that ever you went about to trouble or harm me: and moreover no chance, though it be uncertain or even unlucky, can make a crime of harmless and innocent intentions.' When I had spoken these words, I perceived that Fotis's eyes were wet and trembling and dull with desire, and now half closed, so that I embraced and kissed her sweetly, and greedily drank therefrom.

Now when she was somewhat restored unto joy she desired me that she might shut the chamber door, lest by the intemperance of her tongue in uttering any unfitting words there might grow further inconvenience. Wherewithal she barred and propped the door and came to me again, and embracing me lovingly about the neck with both her arms, spoke with a whispering soft voice and said: 'I do greatly fear to discover the privities of this house, and to utter the secret mysteries of my dame, but I have such a confidence in you and in your wisdom, by reason that you are come of so noble a line and endued with so profound sapience, and further instructed in so many holy and divine things that you will faithfully keep silence, and that whatsoever I shall reveal or declare unto you, you would close them within the bottom of your heart, and never discover the same, but rather repay the simple tale that I shall tell you by keeping it utterly hidden and dark; for I ensure you the love that I bear you enforceth me, that alone of mortals know aught thereof, to utter it. Now shall you know all the estate of our house, now shall you know the hidden secrets of my mistress, unto which the powers of hell do obey, and by which the celestial planets are troubled, the gods made weak, and the elements subdued.

'Neither is the violence of her art in more strength and force than when she espieth some comely young man that pleaseth her fancy, as oftentimes happeneth. For now she loveth to distraction one young Boeotian, a fair and beautiful person, on whom she employeth all her sorcery and enchantment; and I heard her threaten with mine own ears yesternight, that because the sun had not then presently gone down and the night come to minister convenient time to work her magical enticement, she would veil the same sun with a thick shadow of cloud and bring perpetual darkness over all the world. And you shall know that when she saw yesternight this Boeotian sitting at the barber's, when she came from the baths, she secretly commanded me to gather some of the hair of his head which lay dispersed upon the ground, and to bring it home; which when I thought to have done, gathering it up secretly with care, the barber espied me, and by reason it was bruited throughout all the city that we were witches and enchantresses, he seized upon me and cried out, and chid me, saying: "Will you never leave off stealing of handsome young men's hairs? In faith I assure you, unless you cease your wicked sorceries, I will complain to the justices." Wherewithal he came angrily towards me and took away the hair which I had gathered out of mine apron, which grieved me very much. For I knew my mistress's manners, that she would not be contented, but beat me cruelly. Wherefore I intended to run away, but the remembrance of you put always that thought out of my mind, and so I came homeward very sorrowful; but because I would not seem to come in my mistress's sight with empty hands, I saw a man shearing of blown goat-skins. Now these were well tied up and blown out, and were hanging up, and the hair he had shorn off was yellow, and much resembled the hair of the Boeotian: and I took a good deal thereof, and dissembling the truth I brought it to my mistress.

'And so when night came, before your return from supper, Pamphile my mistress, being now out of her wits, went up to a high gallery of her house, blown upon by all the winds of heaven, opening to the east and all other parts of the world; well prepared for these her practices, she gathered together all her accustomed substance for fumigations, she brought forth plates of metal carved with strange characters, she prepared the bones of birds of ill-omen, she made ready the members of dead men brought from their tombs. Here she set out their nostrils and fingers, there the nails with lumps of flesh of such as were hanged, the blood which she had reserved of such as were slain, and skulls snatched away from the jaws and teeth of wild beasts. Then she said certain charms over entrails still warm and breathing, and dipped them in divers waters, as in well water, cow milk, mountain honey and mead; which when she had done she tied and lapped up the hair together, and with many perfumes and smells threw it into a hot fire to burn. Then by the strong force of this sorcery, and the invisible violence of the gods so compelled, those bodies, whose hair was burning in the fire, received human breath, and felt, heard, and walked, and, smelling the scent of their own hair, came and rapped at our doors instead of the Boeotian. Then came you being well tippled, and deceived by the obscurity of the night, and drew out your sword courageously, like furious Ajax, and killed, not as he did whole herds of living beasts, but three blown skins, a deed more brave than his, to the intent that I, after the slaughter of so many enemies without effusion of blood, might embrace and kiss not an homicide, but an utricide.'

Thus pleasantly Fotis, but I again mocked and taunted her, saying: 'Verily now may I for this first achieved enterprise be numbered with Hercules, who by his valiant prowess performed the twelve notable labours, as Geryon with three bodies, and as Cerberus with three heads: for I have slain three blown goatskins. But to the end I may pardon thee with all my heart of that which thou hast committed, bringing upon me so much grief and pain, perform the thing which I shall most earnestly desire of thee, that is, bring me that I may see and behold when thy mistress goes about any sorcery or enchantment, and when she prays unto her gods, but most of all when she changes her form, for I am very desirous of knowing more closely that art of magic, and as it seems unto me, thou thyself hast some experience in the same. For this I know and plainly feel, that (whereas I have always irked and loathed the embracings and love even of noble matrons) I am so stricken and subdued with thy shining eyes, ruddy cheeks, glittering hair, close kisses, and sweet-smelling breasts, that thou holdest me bound and tied to thee like a slave with my own goodwill, and I neither have mind to go home, nor to depart hence, but esteem the pleasure I shall have with thee this night above all the joys of the world.' 'Then,' quoth she, 'O my Lucius, how willing would I be to fulfil your desire, but besides that she is of a grudging and surly disposition, she gets herself into solitary places and out of the presence of every person when she mindeth to make her enchantments; howbeit I regard more to gratify your request than I do esteem the danger of my life: and I will look for opportunity and time for that which you desire, but always upon this condition, that, as I bade you before, you secretly keep close such things as are done.' Thus as we reasoned together the courage of Venus assailed as well our desires as our members; and so we cast aside all our clothes and, utterly naked, gave ourselves to lustful revelry, and Fotis giving me all that she might and more, at last drowsy and unlusty sleep came upon our eyes and we were constrained to lie still until it was now high day.

Now when we had thus delightfully passed a few nights on this wise, on a day Fotis came running to me in great trembling and said that her mistress, for that she could not any the more gain towards that she loved, intended, the night following, to transform herself into a bird, and to fly to him she desired; wherefore she willed me privily to prepare myself to see the same. And about the first watch of the night she led me, walking a-tiptoe and very softly, into that high chamber, and bade me look through the chink of a door. Where first I saw how Pamphile put off all her garments, and took out of a certain coffer sundry kind of boxes, of the which she opened one and tempered the ointment therein with her fingers, and then rubbed her body therewith from the sole of the foot to the crown of the head: and when she had spoken much privily with the lamp, she shaked all the parts of her body, and as they gently moved behold I perceived a plume of feathers did burgeon out upon them, strong wings did grow, her nose was more crooked and hard, her nails turned into claws, and so Pamphile became an owl: then she cried and screeched like a bird of that kind, and willing to prove her force, moved herself from the ground by little and little, till at last she leaped up and flew quite away.

Thus by her sorcery she transformed her body into what shape she would, which when I saw I was greatly astonished, and although I was enchanted by no kind of charm, yet I thought I seemed not to have the likeness of Lucius, for so was I vanished from my senses, amazed in madness, that I dreamed waking, and felt mine eyes to know whether I were asleep or no. But when I was come again to myself, I took Fotis by the hand, and moved it to mine eyes, and said: 'I pray thee, while occasion doth serve, that I may have the fruition of the fruits of thy love towards me, and grant me some of this ointment. O Fotis, my honey, I pray thee by thy sweet breasts, and I will ever hereafter be bound unto you by a mighty gift and obedient to your commandment, if you will but make that I may be turned into a bird, and stand, like Cupid with his wings, beside you my Venus.' Then said Fotis: 'Will you go about to deceive me now, my love, like a fox, and enforce me to work mine own sorrow?* Do I hardly now save you, that are without defence, from these she-wolves of Thessaly, and then if you be a bird where shall I seek you? And when shall I see you?' Then answered I: 'God forbid that I should commit such a crime, for though I could fly into the air as an eagle, or though I were the sure messenger or joyful armour-bearer of Jupiter, yet would I have recourse to nest with thee for all that glory of wings: and I swear by the knot of thy amiable hair, that wherewith you have fast bound my spirit, I love not any other person rather than Fotis. Moreover, this cometh to my mind, that if by virtue of the ointment I shall become a bird, I will take heed that I come nigh no man's house: for how prettily and wittily would these matrons handle their lovers if they were owls: for when they fly into any place by night and are taken, they are nailed upon posts, and so they are worthily rewarded with torment because it is thought that they bring evil fortune to the house by their ill-omened flight. But I pray you (which I had almost forgotten) tell me by what means, when I am an owl, I shall return to my pristine shape and become Lucius again?' 'Fear not for that,' quoth she,' For my mistress hath taught me the way to bring all to pass, and to turn again the figures of such as are transformed into the shapes of men. Neither think you she did it for any goodwill or favour to me, but to the end I might help her and minister this remedy to her when she returneth home. Consider, I pray you, with yourself, with what frivolous trifles and herbs so marvellous a thing is wrought, for I give her nothing else, save a little dill and laurel-leaves in well-water, the which she drinketh, and washeth herself withal.'

Which when she had often spoken she went all trembling into the chamber, and took a box out of the coffer, which I first kissed and embraced, and prayed that I might have good success in my purpose to fly. And then I put off all my garments and greedily thrust my hand into the box and took out a good deal of ointment, and after that I

---

* *Lit.* 'to apply the axe to my own legs'.

had well rubbed every part and member of my body, I hovered with mine arms, and moved myself, looking still when I should be changed into a bird as Pamphile was; and behold neither feathers did burgeon out nor appearance of wings, but verily my hair did turn into ruggedness and my tender skin wore tough and hard; my fingers and toes leaving the number of five grew together into hooves, and from the end of my back grew a great tail, and now my face became monstrous and my mouth long and my nostrils wide, my lips hanging down, and mine ears exceedingly increased with bristles; neither could I see any comfort of my transformation, save that the nature of my members was increasing likewise to the great discomfiture of Fotis, and so without all help (viewing every part of my poor body) I perceived that I was no bird, but a plain ass. Then I thought to blame Fotis, but being deprived as well of language as human gesture, I did all that I could, and looked upon her with hanging lips and watery eyes, as though to reproach her; but she (as soon as she espied me in such sort) smote her face angrily with her hands and cried out: 'Alas, poor wretch that I am, I am utterly cast away. The fear that I was in and my haste hath beguiled me, but especially the mistaking of the box hath deceived me. But it matters not so much, since sooner a medicine may be gotten for this than for any other thing: for if thou couldst get roses and eat them, thou shouldst be delivered from the shape of an ass, and become my Lucius again. And would to God I had gathered some garlands this evening past according to my custom; then shouldst thou not have continued an ass one night's space: but in the morning I will seek thee this remedy.'

Thus Fotis lamented in pitiful sort, but I that was now a perfect ass, and for Lucius a brute beast, did yet retain the sense and understanding of a man. And I did devise a good space with myself, whether it were best for me to kill this mischievous and wicked harlot by tearing her with my mouth and kicking her with my heels. But a better thought reduced me from so rash a purpose, for I feared lest by the death of Fotis I should be deprived of all remedy and help. Then drooping and shaking my head, and dissimulating my ire for the nonce, and bending to my adversity, I went into the stable to my own good horse that once carried me, where I found another ass of Milo's sometime mine host, and I did verily think that my own horse (if there were any natural conscience or faithfulness in brute beasts) would know me and take pity upon me, and proffer me a good lodging for that night. But fie upon Jupiter that is the god of hospitality and the secret divinity of Faith! For see, my good horse and the ass as it were consented together to work my harm lest I should eat up their provender, and scarce did they see me come nigh the manger, but they put down their ears and kicked me with their heels from their meat, which I myself had given that grateful servant of mine, the horse, the night before.

Then I, being thus handled by them and driven away, got me into a corner of the stable, where (while I remembered the uncourtesy of my colleagues, and how on the morrow I should return to Lucius by the help of a rose, and then revenge myself on my own horse) I fortuned to espy, on the midmost pillar sustaining the rafters of the stable, the image of the goddess Epona,* in the midst thereof in a small shrine which was prettily garnished and decked round about with fair fresh roses; then in hope of a present remedy I leaped up with my fore feet as high as I could, and stretching out my neck and lengthening my lips, I coveted exceedingly to snatch some roses. But in an evil hour did I go about that enterprise, for behold, the boy to whom I gave always charge of my horse suddenly spied me and ran in great anger towards me and said: 'How long shall we suffer this vile ass that doth not only eat up his fellows' meat, but also would spoil the images of the gods? Why do I not make lame and weak this wretch?' Therewithal looking about for some cudgel, he espied where lay a faggot of wood, and choosing out a crabbed truncheon of the biggest he could find, did never cease beating of me, poor wretch, until such time as by great noise and rumbling, he heard the doors of the house burst open, and the neighbours crying 'Thieves' in lamentable sort, so that, being stricken in fear, he fled away.

And by and by the doors were broken down and a troop of thieves entered in, and kept every part and corner of the house with weapons. And as men resorted to aid and help them which were within the doors, the thieves resisted and kept them back, for each one was armed with his sword and a torch in his hand, the glimpses whereof did yield out such light as if it had been day. Then they broke out with their axes a great chest shut and sealed with double locks, wherein was laid in the middle of the house all the treasures of Milo, and ransacked the same, which when they had done, they

---

* The patron goddess of horses and stables.

packed it up and gave everyone a portion to carry; but when they had more bags to bear away than men to carry them, they were at their wits' end for the abundance of all this exceeding wealth, and so they came into the stable and took us two poor asses and my horse and loaded us with the greatest trusses that we were able to bear. And when we were out of the house, they followed and threatened us with great staves, and willed one of their fellows to carry behind and bring them tidings what was done concerning the robbery, and so they beat us forward over great hills out of the high way.

But I, what with my heavy burden and the steep side of the mountain, and my long journey, did nothing differ from a dead ass; wherefore I determined with myself, though late yet in good earnest, to seek some remedy of the civil power, and by invocation of the awful name of the Emperor to be delivered from so many miseries. And on a time when it was high day, as I passed through a village of much people, where was a great fair, I came amongst a multitude, and I thought to call upon the renowned name of the Emperor in that same Greek tongue, and I cried out cleverly and aloud, 'O,' but 'Caesar' I could in no wise pronounce: but the thieves, little regarding my unmusical crying, did lay on and beat my wretched skin in such sort, that after it was neither apt nor meet for leather nor sieves. Howbeit, at last Jupiter ministered unto me an unhoped remedy. For when we had passed by many farms and great houses, I fortuned to espy a pleasant garden, wherein, besides many other flowers of delectable hue, were new and fresh roses that dripped with the morning dew, and gaping on these (being very joyful and brisk to catch some as I passed by) I drew nearer and nearer. Now while my lips watered upon them, I thought of a better advice more profitable for me: lest if from being an ass I should become Lucius again, I might fall into the hands of the thieves, and either by suspicion that I were some witch, or for fear that I would utter their theft, I should be slain of a surety; wherefore I abstained for that time, for it was needful, from eating of the roses, and (enduring my present adversity) I ate hay as other asses did.

BOOK FOUR

When noon was come, and now the broiling heat of the sun had most power, we turned into a village to certain old men of the thieves' acquaintance and friends, for verily their meeting and embracing together did give me (poor ass) cause to deem the same: and they took the truss from my back, and gave them part of the treasure that was in it, and they seemed to whisper and tell them that it was stolen goods; and after that we were unladen of our burdens they let us loose into a meadow to pasture, but I would not feed there with my own horse and Milo's ass, for that I was not wont to eat hay, but I must seek my dinner in some other place. Wherefore I leaped into a garden which was behind the stable, and being well nigh perished with hunger, although I could find nothing there but raw and green salads, yet I filled my hungry guts therewithal abundantly, and praying unto all the gods, I looked about in every place if I could espy any roses in the gardens by, and my solitary being alone did put me in good hope, that if I could find any remedy, being far from the public road and hidden by the bushes, I should presently out of the low gait of a beast be changed out of everyone's sight into a man walking upright.

Now while I tossed on the flood of these cogitations, I looked about, and behold I saw afar off a shadowed valley adjoining to a wood, where, amongst divers other herbs and pleasant verdures, I thought I saw many flourishing roses of bright damask colour. So that I said within my mind, which was not wholly bestial: 'Verily the place is the grove of Venus and the Graces, where secretly glittereth the royal hue of so lively and delectable a flower.' Then I, desiring the help of the god of good fortune, ran lustily towards the wood, in so much that I felt myself no more an ass but a swift-coursing horse, but my agility and quickness could not prevent the cruelty of my fortune; for when I came to the place, I perceived that they were no roses neither tender nor pleasant, neither moistened with the heavenly drops of dew nor celestial liquor, which grow out of the rich thicket and thorns. Neither did I perceive that there was any valley at all, but only the bank of the river environed with great thick trees, which had long branches like unto laurel, and bear a flower without any manner of scent but somewhat red of hue, and the common people call them by the name of laurel-roses, which are very poisonous to all manner of beasts. Then was I so entangled with unhappy fortune, that I little esteemed mine own life, and went willingly to eat of those roses, though I knew them to be present poison. But as I drew near very slowly, I saw a young man that seemed to be the gardener come upon me, the same that I had devoured up all his herbs in the garden, and he, knowing now full well his great loss, came swearing with a great staff in his hand, and laid upon me in such sort that I was well nigh dead, but I speedily devised some remedy for myself, for I lifted up my legs and kicked him with my hinder heels, so that I left him lying at the hill foot well nigh slain, and so I ran away: incontinently came out a certain woman, doubtless his wife, who, seeing from above her husband lying half dead, cried and howled in pitiful sort, hasting towards her husband, to the intent that by her loud cries she might purchase to me present destruction; for all the persons of the town, moved and raised by her noise, came forth and cried for dogs, and hied them on madly to tear me down. Out came a great company of bandogs and mastiffs, more fit to pull down bears and lions than me, whom when I beheld I thought verily that I should presently die, so that I took what counsel I might from the occasion; and thought no more of flight, but turned myself about and ran as fast as ever I might to the stable whither we had lodged. Then the men of the town called in their dogs, which they scarce could hold, and took me, and bound me to the staple of a post with a great thong, and scourged me till I was well nigh dead: and they would undoubtedly have slain me, had it not come to pass that my belly, narrowed with the pain of their beating and reeking with the green herbs that lay therein, caught such a looseness that I all besprinkled the faces of some with my liquid dung which exploded in a jet, and with the filthy stench thereof enforced the others to leave my sides now well nigh broken.

Not long after, which was now towards eventide, the thieves loaded us again, and especially me, with the heaviest burden, and brought us forth out of the stable, and when we had gone a good part of our journey, what with the long way, my great burden, the beating of staves, and my worn hooves, lame and tottering, I was so weary that I could scarcely go; then as I walked by a little river running with fair water, I said to myself: 'Behold, now I have found a good occasion. For I will fall down when I come yonder, bending my legs beneath me, and surely I will not rise again for any scourging or beating, and not only will I defy the cudgel, but even be pierced by the sword, if they shall use it upon me.' And the cause why I determined so to do was this: I thought that I was so utterly feeble and weak that I deserved my discharge for ill health, and certainly that the robbers (partly for that they would not stay in their journey, partly in haste to flee) would take off the burden from my back, and put it upon my two fellows, and so for my further punishment leave me as a prey to the wolves and ravenous beasts. But evil fortune prevented so good a consideration; for the other ass, being of the same purpose that I was of, and forestalling me, by feigned and coloured weariness fell down first with all his burden upon the ground as though he were dead, and he would not rise neither with beating nor pricking, nor stand upon his feet, though they pulled him all about by the tail, by his legs, and by his ears; which when the thieves beheld, as without all hope, they said one to another: 'What, should we stand here so long about a dead or rather a stony ass? Let us be gone'; and so they took his burden and divided some to me and some to my horse. And then they drew their swords and cut through all his hamstrings, and dragged him a little from the way, and threw his body while he yet breathed from the point of a hill down into a great valley. Then I, considering with myself of the evil fortune of my poor companion, purposed now to forget all subtlety and deceit and to play the good ass to get my masters' favour, for I perceived by their talk that we were well nigh come home to our journey's end where they lived and had their dwelling. And after that we had passed over a little hill, we came to our appointed place, where when we were unladen of our burdens and all things carried in, I tumbled and wallowed in the dust to refresh myself instead of water.

The thing and the time compel me to make description of the places and especially of the den where the thieves did inhabit: I will prove my wit what I can do, and then consider you whether I was an ass in judgement and sense, or no. First there was an exceeding great hill compassed about with big trees, very high, with many turning bottoms, surrounded by sharp rocks, whereby it was inaccessible;

there were many winding and hollow valleys environed with thickets and thorns, and naturally fortressed round about. From the top of the hill ran a spring both leaping and bubbling which poured down the steep slope its silvery waves, and then scattering abroad into many little brooks watered all the valleys below, that it seemed like unto a sea enclosed, or a standing flood. Before the den, where was no more hill, stood a high tower, and at the foot thereof, and on either side, were sheep-cots fenced and wattled with clay; before the gate of the house were walls enclosing a narrow path, in such sort that I well warrant you would judge it to be a very den for thieves, and there was nothing else near save a little cot covered roughly with thatch, wherein the thieves did nightly accustom to watch by order, as after I perceived.

And when they were all crept crouching into the house, and we fast tied with strong halters at the door, they began to chide with an old woman there, crooked with age, who had the government and rule of all those young men, and said: 'How is it, old witch, old trot, that art the shame of life and rejected of very death, that thou sittest idly all day at home, and (having no regard to our perilous labours) hast provided nothing for our suppers thus late, but sittest doing nought but swilling wine into that greedy belly of thine from morning to night?' Then the old woman trembled and began to say in a terrified and harsh voice: 'Behold, my puissant and faithful masters, you shall have meat and pottage enough by and by, cooked with a sweet savour. Here is first store of bread, wine plenty, filled in clean rinsed pots, likewise hot water prepared to bathe you hastily after your wont.' Which when she had said, they but off all their garments and refreshed themselves by a great fire, and after that they were washed with the hot water and anointed with oil, they sat down at the table garnished with all kinds of dainty meat.

Now they were no sooner set down, but in came another company of young men, more in number than was before, whom you would judge at once likewise to be thieves; for they also brought in their prey of gold and silver money, and plate, and robes both silken and gold-embroidered, and when they had likewise washed, they sat amongst the rest, and casting lots they served one another by order. The thieves drank and ate exceedingly, laying out the meat in heaps, the bread in mounds, and the wine-cups like a marching army, crying, laughing, and making such noise, that I thought I was amongst the tyrannous and wild drunken Labiths and Centaurs. At length one of them, more stout than the rest, spoke in this sort: 'We verily have manfully conquered the house of Milo of Hypata, and besides all the riches and treasure which by force we have brought away, we are all come home safe, none being lost, and are increased the more, if it be worthy of mention, by the eight feet of this horse and this ass. But you, that have roved about among the towns of Boeotia, have lost your valiant captain Lamachus, whose loss I more regarded than all this treasure which you have brought. But it is his own bravery that hath destroyed him, and therefore the memory of him shall be renowned for ever amongst the most noble kings and valiant captains; but you accustom when you go abroad, like doughty robbers indeed, to creep through every corner and hole for every trifle, doing a paltry business in baths and the huts of aged women.'

Then one of them that came last answered: 'Why, are you only ignorant, that the greater the house is, the sooner it may be robbed and spoiled? For though the family of servants be great and dispersed in divers lodgings, yet every man had rather defend his life than save at his own hazard the riches of his master; but when the people be few and poor and live alone, then will they hide and protect very fiercely, even at the danger of their lives, their substance, how little or great soever it be. And to the intent you will believe me, I will show you our story as an example. We were scarce come nigh unto seven-gated Thebes, and began at once to enquire of the fortunes of the greatest men thereof, which is the fountain of our art and science, and we learned at length where a rich chuff called Chryseros did dwell, who, for fear of offices and burdens in the public weal, with great pains dissimulated his estate and lived sole and solitary in a small cot (howbeit well fortified) and huddled daily in ragged and torn apparel over his bags of gold. Wherefore we devised with ourselves to go first to his house and spoil him of all his riches, which we thought we should easily do if we had but to fight against him alone. And at once when night came we quickly drew towards his door, which we thought best neither to move it, nor lift it out of the hinges, and we would not break it open lest by the noise we should raise up (to our harm) the neighbours by. Then our strong and valiant captain Lamachus, trusting his own strength and force, thrust in his hand through a hole of the door, which was made for the key, and thought to pull back the bolt; but the covetous caitiff Chryseros, vilest of all that go on two feet, being awake and seeing all, but making no noise, came softly to the door and caught his hand, and with a great nail nailed it fast to a post of the gate, which when he had done, and had left him thus crucified, he ran up to a high chamber of his hovel, and in a very loud voice called every one of his neighbours by name, desiring them to look to their common safety with all possible speed, for his house was afire. Then everyone, for fear of the danger that was nigh him, came running out to aid him; wherewith we (fearing our present peril) knew not what was best to be done, whether we should leave our companion there, or yield ourselves to die with him; but by his consent we devised a better way, for we cut through the joint of this our leader where the arm joins to the shoulder, and so let it hang there, and then bound up his wound with clouts lest we should be traced by the drops of blood, and so we took all that was left of Lamachus and led him away. Now when we hurried along, trembling for our affection to him, and were so nigh pursued that we were in present danger, and Lamachus could not keep our company by reason of faintness (and on the other side it was not for his profit to linger behind) he spoke unto us as a man of singular courage and virtue, desiring us by much entreaty and prayer, and by the puissance of the god Mars and the faith of our confederacy, to deliver our brave comrade from torment and miserable captivity: and further he asked how was it possible that so courageous a captain could live without his hand, wherewith alone he could rob and slay so many people, but he would rather think himself sufficiently happy if he might be slain by the hand of a friend. But when he saw that we all refused to commit any such wicked deed he drew out his sword with his other hand, and after that he had often kissed it, he thrust it with a strong blow clean through his body. Then we honoured the corpse of so puissant a man, and wrapped it in linen clothes and threw it into the sea to hide it: so lieth our master Lamachus buried and hid in the grave of water.

Now he ended his life worthily of his courage, as I have declared; but Alcimus, though he were a man of great enterprise, yet could he not void himself from evil fortune: for on a day when he had entered into an old woman's hut that slept, to rob her, he went up into the higher chamber, where he should first have strangled her, but he had more regard to throw down everything out of the window to us that stood under: and when he had cleverly despoiled all, he would leave nothing behind, but went to the old woman's bed where she lay asleep and threw her from it, and would have taken off the coverlet to have thrown down likewise, but the old hag awaked and fell at his knees, and desired him in this manner: "O sir, I pray you, cast not away such torn and ragged clouts into my neighbours' houses, whither this window looks; for they are rich enough and need no such things." Then Alcimus (thinking her words to be true) was brought in belief that such things as he had thrown out already, and such things as he should throw out after, were not fallen down to his fellows, but into other men's houses; wherefore he went to the window to see, and especially to behold the places round about, as she had told him, thrusting his body out of the window; but while he strove to do this, strongly indeed but somewhat rashly, the old trot marked him well, and came behind him softly, and although she had but small strength, yet with a sudden force she took him by the heels and thrust him out headlong while his body was balancing and unsure; and beside that the height was very great, he fell upon a marvellous great stone that lay near and burst his ribs, whereby he vomited and spewed flakes of blood, and when he had told us all, he suffered not long torment, but presently died. Then we gave unto him the same burial and sent him a worthy comrade to Lamachus, as we had done before.

'When we had thus lost two of our companions, we liked not Thebes, but marched towards the next city called Plataea, where we found great fame concerning a man named Demochares that purposed to set forth a great game, where should be a trial of all kinds of weapons: he was come of a good house, marvellous rich, liberal, and well deserved that which he had, and had prepared many shows and pleasures for the common people: in so much that there is no man can either by wit or eloquence show in fit words all the manifold shapes of his preparations, for first he had provided gladiators of a famous band, then all manner of hunters most fleet of foot, then guilty men without hope of reprieve who were judged for their punishment to be food for wild beasts. He had ordained a machine made of beams fixed together, great towers and platforms like a house to move hither and thither, very well painted, to be places to contain all the quarry: he had ready a great number of wild beasts and all sorts of them, especially he had brought from abroad those noble creatures that were soon to be the death of so many condemned persons. But amongst so great preparations of noble price, he bestowed the most part of his patrimony in buying of a vast multitude of great bears, which either by chasing he had caught himself, or which he dearly bought or which were given him by divers of his friends, who strove one with another in making him such gifts: and all these he kept and nourished to his very great cost. Howbeit for all his care of the public pleasure, he could not be free from the malicious eyes of envy: for some of them were well nigh dead, with too long tying up; some meagre with the broiling heat of the sun; some languished with long lying, but all (having sundry diseases) were so afflicted that they died one after another, and there were well nigh none left, in such sort that you might see their wrecks piteously lying in the streets and all but dead: and then the common people, having no other meat to feed on, and forced by their rude poverty to find any new meat and cheap feasts, would come forth and fill their bellies with the flesh of the bears.

'Then by and by Babulus and I devised a pretty sport to suit this case; we drew to our lodging one of the bears that was greater of bulk than all the rest, as though we would prepare to eat thereof, where we flayed off his skin and kept his claws whole, but we meddled not with the head, but cut it off by the neck, and so let it hang to the skin. Then we razed off the flesh from the back, and cast dust thereon, and set it in the sun to dry: and while it was drying by the heat of the heavenly fire, we made merry with the flesh, and then we devised with ourselves with an oath that one of us, being more valiant than the rest, not so much in body as in courage (so that he would straightway consent thereto) should put on the skin, and feigning that he were a bear, should be led to Demochares' house in the night, by which means we thought to be received and easily let in. Many of our brave brotherhood were desirous to play the bear in this subtle sleight, but especially one Thrasyleon of a courageous mind was chosen by all our band to take the risk of this enterprise. Then we put him, very calm in mind and face, into the bear's skin, which was soft and fitted him finely in every point; we buckled fast the edges thereof with fine stitching, and covered the same, though small, with the thick hair growing about it that it might not be seen: we thrust his head into the opening of the bear's throat where his neck had been cut out, and after this we made little holes through his nostrils and eyes for Thrasyleon to see out and take wind at, in such sort that he seemed a very lively and natural beast: when this was done, we brought him into a cage which we hired with a little money for the purpose, and he crept nimbly in after like a bear with a good courage.

'Thus we began our subtlety, and then we imagined thus: we feigned letters as though they came from one Nicanor which dwelt in the country of Thrace, which was of great acquaintance with this Demochares, wherein we wrote that he had sent him, being his friend, the first-fruits of his coursing and hunting. When night was come, we took cover of the darkness, and brought Thrasyleon's cage and our forged letters, and presented them to Demochares. When Demochares wonderingly beheld this mighty bear, and saw the timely liberality of Nicanor his friend, he was glad, and commanded his servant to deliver unto us that brought him this joy ten gold crowns, as he had great store in his coffers: then (as the novelty of a thing doth accustom to stir men's minds to behold the same) many persons came on every side to see this bear, but Thrasyleon (lest they should by curious viewing and prying perceive the truth) ran often upon them to put them in fear, so that they durst not come nigh. Then the people said with one voice: "Verily Demochares is right happy, in that, after the death of so many beasts, he hath gotten, in spite of fortune, so goodly a bear to supply him afresh.' He commanded that with great care his servants should put him into the park close by, but I immediately spoke unto him and said: "Sir, I pray you, take heed how you put a beast tired with the heat of the sun and with long travel amongst others which (as I hear say) have divers maladies and diseases; let him rather lie in some open place of your house, where the breeze blows through, yea nigh to some water, where he may take air and ease himself, for do not you know that such kind of beasts do greatly delight to couch under shadow of trees and dewy caves, nigh unto pleasant wells and waters?" Hereby Demochares, admonished and remembering how many he had before that perished, was contented that we should put the bear's cage where we would. Moreover we said unto him: "We ourselves are determined to lie all night nigh unto the bear, to look unto him, which is tired with the heat and his long journey, and to give him meat and drink at his due hour." Then he answered: "Verily, masters, you need not to put yourselves to such pains: for I have men, yea, almost all my family of servants, that serve for nothing but for this purpose of tending bears."

'Then we took leave of him and departed, and when we were come without the gates of the town we perceived before us a great sepulchre standing out of the highway, in a privy and secret place. And thither we went and opened there certain coffins, half rotted with age, wherein we found the corruption of man, and the ashes and dust of his long-buried body, which should serve to hold the prey we were very soon to get: and then, according to the custom of our band, having a respect to the dark and moonless time of the night when we thought that every man was sunk in his first and strongest sleep, we went with our weapons and besieged the doors of Demochares round about, in earnest that we were soon to plunder the same. Then Thrasyleon was ready at hand, seizing upon that time of night which is for robbers most fit, and crept out of the cage and went to kill all such of his guards as he found asleep; but when he came to the porter he slew him also and took the key and opened the gates and let us all in: and he showed us now in the midst of the house a large counter, wherein looking sharply he saw put the night before a great abundance of treasure: which when by violence of us all we had broken open, I bade every one of my fellows take as much gold and silver as they could quickly bear away, and carry it to the sepulchre, and there quickly hide it in the house of those dead who were to us most faithful allies, and then come soon back to take another burden; but I, for our common weal, would stand alone at the gate watching diligently when they would return, and the bear running about the house would make such of the family afraid as fortuned to wake and come out: for who is he that is so puissant and courageous, that at the sight of so great a monster would not quail and flee away and keep his chamber well barred, especially in the night?

'Now when we had brought this matter to so good a point, there chanced a pitiful case; for as I looked for my companions that should come from the sepulchre, behold there was a boy of the house that fortuned to he awaked by the noise, as fate would have it, and look out of a window and espy the bear running freely about the house, and he went back on his steps a-tiptoe and very secretly, and told all the servants, and at once the house was filled with the whole train of them. Incontinently they came forth with torches, lanterns, candles and tapers, and other lights, that they might see all the yard over; they came not unarmed, but with clubs, spears, and naked swords, to guard the entrances, and they set on greyhounds and mastiffs, even those with great ears and shaggy hair, to subdue the poor beast. Then I, during this broil, thought to run away, but because I would see Thrasyleon fighting wonderfully with the dogs, I lay behind the gate to behold him. And although I might perceive that he was at the very term or limit of life, yet remembered he his own faithfulness and ours, and valiantly resisted the gaping and ravenous mouths of the hound of Hell: for he took well to play the part which he so willingly had taken in hand himself, and with much ado, so long as the breath was in him, now flying and now pursuing, with many twistings and turnings of his body, tumbled at length out of the house; but when he was come to liberty abroad, yet could he not save himself by flight, for all the dogs of the street (which were fierce and many) joined themselves to the greyhounds and mastiffs that had just come out of the house, to chase him like a great host: alas, what a pitiful sight it was when our poor Thrasyleon was thus environed and compassed with so many furious dogs that tore and rent him miserably! Then I, impatient of so great his misery, ran in amongst the press of the people, and aiding my comrade secretly with my words (for no more could I do) exhorted all the leaders of this chase in this manner: "O great extreme mischance, what a precious and excellent beast do we lose!" but my words did nothing prevail to help the poor wretch. For there came running out a tall man with a spear in his hand, that thrust him clean through, and afterwards many that stood by, released of their fear, drew out their swords, and so they killed him. But verily our brave captain Thrasyleon, the great honour of our band, when his life, that was worthy never to die, was utterly overcome, but not his fortitude, would not bewray the league between us, either by crying, howling, or any other means, but (being torn with dogs, and wounded with weapons) did still send forth a bellowing cry more like that of a beast than of a man: and taking his present fortune in good part, with courage and glory enough did finish his life with such a terror unto the assembly, that no person was so hardy (until it was morn, nay, until it was high day) as to touch him, though he were a beast stark dead: but at last there came a butcher more valiant than the rest, who (opening the paunch of the beast) slit off the skin from the hardy and venturous thief. In this manner there was lost to us also our captain Thrasyleon, but there was not lost to him his fame and honour. When all this was done, we packed up our treasure which the faithful dead in the sepulchre had kept for us, and we got us out of the bounds of Plataea, thinking always with ourselves that there was no fidelity to be found amongst the living; and no wonder, for that it hath passed over to the ghosts and the dead in hatred of our deceitfulness. And so, being wearied with the weight of our burdens, and very tired with our rough travel, having thus lost three of our soldiers, we are come home with this present prey that you see.'

Thus when they had spoken and poured libation of pure wine from cups of gold in memory of their slain companions, they sung hymns to the god Mars to pacify him withal, and laid them down to sleep. Then the old woman gave us fresh barley in plenty without measure, in so much that my horse, the only lord of all that abundance, might well think he was at some priestly banquet that day. But I, that was accustomed to eat flour finely milled and long cooked with broth, thought that but a sour kind of meat; wherefore espying a corner where lay the loaves of bread left by all the band, I got me thither, and used upon them my jaws which ached with long famine and seemed to be full of cobwebs. Now when the night was come the thieves awaked and rose up: and when they had buckled on their weapons and disguised their faces with vizors, like unto spectres, they departed, and yet for all the great sleep that came upon me, I could in no wise leave eating, and whereas, when I was a man, I could be contented with one or two loaves at the most, now my guts were so greedy that three panniers full would scarcely serve me; and while I laboured at this business, the morning came, and being moved by even an ass's shamefastness, I left my food at last (though well I liked it) and at a stream hard by I quenched my thirst. And suddenly after, the thieves returned home careful and heavy, bringing no burdens with them, no not so much as one poor cloke, but with all their swords and strength, yea even with the might of their whole band, only a maiden that seemed by her habit to be some gentlewoman born, and the daughter of some noble of that country, who was so fair and beautiful, that though I were an ass, yet I swear that I had a great affection to her. The virgin lamented and tore her hair, and spoiled her garments for the great sorrow she was in, but the thieves brought her within the cave, and essayed to comfort her in this sort: 'Weep not, fair gentlewoman, we pray you, for be you assured that we will do no outrage or violence to your person, but take patience awhile for our profit; for necessity and poor estate hath compelled us to this enterprise: we warrant you that your parents (although they be covetous) from their great store will be contented to give us money enough to redeem and ransom you, that are their own blood, from our hands.'

With such flattering words they endeavoured to appease the gentlewoman: howbeit she would in no case be comforted, but put her head between her knees and cried piteously. Then they called the old woman and commanded her to sit by the maiden, and pacify her dolour as much as she might. And they departed away to rob, as they accustomed to do, but the virgin would not assuage her griefs nor mitigate her sorrow by any entreaty of the old woman, but howled and sobbed, shaking her bosom with her sighs, in such sort that she made me (poor ass) likewise to weep, and thus she said: 'Alas! can I, poor wretch, that am come of so good a house, being now forsaken of all my dear parents, my many friends and great house and family, made a rapine and prey, closed servilely in this stony prison, deprived of all the pleasures wherein I have been brought up, thrown in danger, ready to be rent in pieces amongst so many sturdy thieves and dreadful robbers, can I (I say) cease from weeping or live any longer?' Thus she cried and lamented, and after she had wearied herself with sorrow and beating of her breast, she closed the windows of her hollow eyes to sleep: but scarce had she slept, but she rose again, like a furious and mad woman, and did afflict herself more violently than before, and beat her breast and comely face with her cruel hands. Then the old woman enquired the cause of her new and sudden lamentation, to whom (sighing in pitiful sort) she answered: 'Alas! now I am utterly undone, now I am out of all hope. O, give me a knife to kill me or a halter to hang me, or a precipice that I may throw me down therefrom': whereat the old woman was more angry, and severely commanded her to tell her the cause of her sorrow, and why after her sleep she should renew her dolour and miserable weeping. 'What, think you,' quoth she, 'To deceive our young men of the price of your ransom? No, no; therefore cease your crying, for the thieves do little esteem your tears, and if you will still weep, I will surely burn you alive.'

Hereat the maiden was greatly afraid, and kissed her hand and said: 'O mother, take pity upon me and my wretched fortune, for the sake of human kindness, for I think there be mercy ripe and frank in your venerable hoar head, and hear the sum of my calamity. There was a comely young man of the first rank in the city, who for his bounty and grace was beloved entirely as a son of all the town, my cousin-germain, and but three years older than I; from our early years we two were nourished and brought up in one house, and lay under one roof, aye, in one chamber and bed, and at length by promise of marriage and by consent of our parents we were by law contracted together; the marriage day was come, my spouse was accompanied with his parents, kinsfolk, and friends, and made sacrifice in the temples and public places; the whole house was garnished with laurel, and torches were set in every place as they chanted in honour of Hymenaeus, and when my unhappy mother was pampering me in her lap and decking me like a bride, kissing me sweetly and praying earnestly for the hope of future children, behold there came in suddenly a great multitude of thieves, armed like men of war, with naked swords in their hands, who went not about to do any slaughter, neither to take anything away, but brake into the chamber where I was, and violently took me, now half dead with fear, out of my mother's arms, when none of the family would fight nor resist ever so little. In this sort was our marriage broken and disturbed, like the marriage of Hippodamia and Protesilaus: but behold, good mother, now my unhappy fortune is renewed and increased: for I dreamed in my sleep that I was pulled out of our house, out of our chamber, and out of my bed, and that I roamed about in solitary and unknown places, calling upon the name of my unfortunate husband, and that he, when he was robbed of my embrace, even still smelling of perfumes and crowned with garlands, did trace me by my steps as I fled on feet not mine own, desiring the aid of the people to assist him, in that his fair wife was violently stolen away: and as he went crying up and down, one of the thieves, moved with indignation by reason of his pursuit, took up a great stone that lay at his feet and threw it at my husband, poor youth, and killed him: by the terror of which sight I awaked in fear from so dreadful a sleep.' Then the old woman, rendering out like sighs, began to speak in this sort: 'My lady, take a good heart unto you, and be not afraid at feigned or strange visions or dreams, for as the visions of the day are accounted false and untrue, so the visions of the night do often chance contrary: and indeed to dream of weeping, beating, and killing is a token of good luck and prosperous change, whereas contrary, to dream of laughing, filling the belly with good cheer, or dalliance of love, is sign of sadness of heart, sickness of body, or other displeasure. But I will tell thee a pleasant old wives' tale to put away all thy sorrow and to revive thy spirits'; and so she began in this manner:

'There was sometime a certain king, inhabiting in a certain state, who had to wife a noble dame, by whom he had three daughters exceeding fair: of whom the two elder were of most comely shape and beauty, yet they did not excel all the praise and commendation of mortal speech; but the singular passing beauty and maidenly majesty of the youngest daughter was so far excellent, that no earthly tongue could by any means sufficiently express or set out the same: by reason whereof the citizens and strangers there, being inwardly pricked by zealous affection to behold her famous person, came daily by thousands to see her, and as astonied with admiration of her incomparable beauty did no less worship and reverence her, bringing their right hands to their lips,* with the forefinger laid against the thumb, as tokens, and with other divine adorations, as if she were Lady Venus indeed: and shortly after the fame was spread into the next cities and bordering regions that the goddess whom the deep seas had borne and brought forth, and the froth of the foaming waves had nourished (to the intent to show her high magnificency and power in earth to such as before did honour and worship her) was now conversant amongst mortal men, or else that the earth and not the seas, by a new concourse and influence of the celestial planets, had budded and yielded forth a new Venus, endued with the flower of virginity. So daily more and more increased this opinion, and now was her flying fame dispersed into the next islands and well nigh into every part and province of the whole world. Whereupon innumerable strangers resorted from far countries, adventuring themselves by long journeys on land and by great travels on water, to behold this wonder of the age. By occasion whereof such a contempt grew towards the goddess Venus, that no person travelled unto the town Paphos nor unto Cnidos, no nor to the isle Cythera to worship her. Her liturgies were left out, her temples defaced, her couches†

---

* As in the modern actress's gesture of 'blowing a kiss'. Pliny (*Natural History*, xxviii, 2) tells us that 'in adoring the gods and doing reverence to their images, we use to kiss our right hand and turn about with our whole body'.

† *Pulvinaria*: cushions used in certain public feasts and processions of the gods.

contemned, her ceremonies neglected, and her bare altars unswept and foul with the ashes of old burnt sacrifice. For why, every person honoured and worshipped this maiden instead of Venus, calling upon the divinity of that great goddess in a human form, and in the morning at her first coming abroad, offered unto her oblations, provided banquets, called her by the name of Venus which was not Venus indeed, and in her honour, as she walked in the streets, presented flowers and garlands in most reverent fashion.

'This sudden change and alteration of celestial honour unto the worship of a mortal maiden did greatly inflame and kindle the mind of very Venus, who (unable to temper herself from indignation, shaking her head in raging sort) reasoned with herself in this manner: "Behold I, the original of nature, the first beginning of all the elements, behold I, the Lady Venus of all the world, am now joined with a mortal maiden as a partaker of my honour; my name, registered in the city of heaven, is profaned and made vile by terrene absurdities. If I shall suffer any mortal creature to present my majesty in earth, and must be content with sharing the godhead and receiving worship through other, or that any girl that one day is to die shall bear about a false surmised shape of my person, then in vain did Paris that shepherd (in whose just judgement and confidence the great Jupiter had affiance) prefer me above the other great goddesses for the excellency of my beauty: but she, whatsoever she be, shall not for nought have usurped mine honour, but she shall shortly repent her of her unlawful loveliness."

'Then by and by she called her winged son Cupid, rash enough and hardy, who by his evil manners, contemning all public justice and law, armed with fire and arrows, running up and down in the nights from house to house, and corrupting the lawful marriages of every person, doth nothing (and yet he is not punished) but that which is evil: and although he were of his own proper nature sufficient prone to work mischief, yet she egged him forward with words and brought him to the city, and showed him Psyche (for so the maiden was called) and having told him of her rival beauty, the cause of her anger, not without great rage, "I pray thee," quoth she, "My dear child, by the motherly bond of love, by the sweet wounds of thy piercing darts, by the pleasant heat of thy fire, revenge fully the injury which is done to thy mother upon the false and disobedient beauty of a mortal maiden; and this beyond all I pray thee without delay, that she may fall in desperate love with the most miserable creature living, the most poor, the most crooked, and the most vile, that there may be none found in all the world of like wretchedness.' When she had spoken these words, she embraced long and kissed often her son, and took her voyage towards the shore hard by, where the tides flow to and fro: and when she was come there, and had trodden with her rosy feet upon the top of the trembling waters, then the deep sea became exceeding calm upon its whole surface, and at her will, as though she had before given her bidding, straightway appeared her servitors from the deep: for incontinent came the daughters of Nereus singing with tunes melodiously; Portunus with his bristled and rough beard of azure; Salacia with her bosom full of fish; Palaemon the little driver of the dolphin; and the bands of Triton trumpeters leaping hither and thither, the one blowing on his shell with heavenly noise, another turning aside with a silken veil the burning heat of the fierce sun, another holding her mirror before his lady's eyes, others, yoked two together, swimming beneath her car. Such was the company which followed Venus marching towards the middest Ocean.

'In the mean season Psyche with all her beauty received no fruit of her honour. She was wondered at of all, she was praised of all, but she perceived that no king nor prince nor any of the inferior sort did repair to woo her. Everyone marvelled at her divine beauty, but only as it were at some image well painted and set out. Her other two sisters, whose lesser beauty was nothing so greatly exalted by the people, were royally married to two kings, but the virgin Psyche sitting at home alone lamented her solitary life, and being disquieted both in mind and body (although she pleased all the world) yet hated she in herself her own beauty.

Whereupon the miserable father of this unfortunate daughter, suspecting that the gods and powers of heaven did envy her estate, went into the town called Miletus to receive the most ancient oracle of Apollo, where he made his prayers and offered sacrifice, and desired a husband for his neglected daughter; but Apollo, though he were a Grecian of the country of Ionia, yet for the sake of him that telleth this Milesian tale, gave answer in Latin verse, the sense whereof was this:

Let Psyche's corpse be clad in mourning weed
    And set on rock of yonder hill aloft:
Her husband is no wight of human seed,
    But serpent dire and fierce as may be thought,
Who flies with wings above in starry skies
    And doth subdue each thing with fiery flight.
The gods themselves and powers that seem so wise
    With mighty Jove be subject to his might;
The rivers black and deadly floods of pain
And darkness eke as thrall to him remain.

The king, beforetimes happy, when he heard the prophecy of Apollo, returned home sad and sorrowful, and declared to his wife the miserable and unhappy fate of his daughter: then they began to lament and weep, and passed over many days in great sorrow. But now was the sad fulfilment of the oracle at hand, now the time approached of Psyche's funeral marriage; preparation was made, the torches burned weakly with black and sooty flame, the pleasant sound of the nuptial flute was turned into the sad Lydian strains, the melody of Hymenaeus was ended with deadly howling, the maiden that should be married did wipe her eyes with her veil; all the people of the city wept likewise the gloomy fate of a fallen house; and with great lamentation was ordained a public mourning for that day.

'But necessity compelled that poor Psyche should be brought to her appointed doom, according to the divine commandment; and when the solemnity of the wretched wedding was ended with great sorrow, all the people followed the living corpse, and they went to bring this sorrowful spouse, not to her marriage, but to her final end and burial. And while the father and mother of Psyche did go forward, weeping and crying and delaying to do this enterprise, Psyche spake unto them in this sort: "Why torment you your unhappy age with continual dolour? Why trouble you your breath, which is more rather mine than yours, with these many cryings? Why soil ye with useless tears your faces which I ought to adore and worship? Why tear you my eyes when ye tear yours? Why pull you your hoar hairs? Why knock you your breasts that are holy to me? Now you see the reward of my excellent beauty: now, now, you perceive (but too late) the deadly plague of envy. When the people did honour me with divine honours and all together call me new

Venus, then you should have grieved, then you should have wept, then you should have sorrowed, as though I had been then dead: for now I see and perceive that I am come to this misery by the only name of Venus. Bring me, and (as fortune hath appointed) place me on the top of the rock; I greatly desire to end my happy marriage, I greatly covet to see my noble husband. Why do I delay? Why should I refuse him that is appointed to destroy all the world?" Thus ended she her words, and thrust herself with strong gait amongst the people that followed: then they brought her to the appointed rock of the high hill, and set her thereon and so departed. The torches and lights were put out with the tears of the people, and every man gone home with bowed heads: the miserable parents, well nigh consumed with sorrow, closed themselves in their palace and gave themselves to everlasting darkness. Thus poor Psyche being left alone weeping and trembling on the highest top of the rock, there came a gentle air of softly breathing Zephyrus and carried her from the hill, with a meek wind, which retained her garments up, and by little and little brought her down into a deep valley, where she was laid in a soft grassy bed of most sweet and fragrant flowers.

BOOK FIVE

'Thus fair Psyche being sweetly couched amongst the soft and tender herbs, as in a bed of dewy grass and fragrant flowers, and having qualified the troubles and thoughts of her restless mind, was now well reposed: and when she had refreshed herself sufficiently with sleep, she rose with a more quiet and pacified mind, and fortuned to espy a pleasant wood environed with great and mighty trees, and likewise a running river as clear as crystal; in the middest and very heart of the woods, well nigh at the fall of the river, was a princely edifice, wrought and builded, not by the art or hand of man, but by the mighty power of a god: and you would judge at the first entry therein, that it were some pleasant and worthy mansion for the powers of heaven. For the embowings above were curiously carven out of citron and ivory, propped and undermined with pillars of gold; the walls covered and seeled with silver, divers sorts of beasts were graven and carved, that seemed to encounter with such as entered in: all things were so curiously and finely wrought, that it seemed either to be the work of some demigod, or God himself, that put all these beasts into silver. The pavement was ill of precious stone, divided and cut one from another, whereon was carved divers kinds of pictures, in such sort that blessed and thrice blessed were they which might go upon such a pavement of gems and ornaments: every part and angle of the house was so well adorned by the precious stones and inestimable treasure there, and the walls were so solidly built up with great blocks of gold, that glittered and shone in such sort that the chambers, porches, and doors gave out the light of day as it had been the sun. Neither otherwise did the other treasure of the house disagree unto so great a majesty, that verily it seemed in every point a heavenly palace fabricated and builded for Jupiter himself wherein to dwell among men.

'Then Psyche, moved with delectation, approached nigh, and taking a bold heart entered into the house led on by the beauty of that sight, and beheld everything there with great affection: she saw storehouses brought exceeding fine, and replenished with abundance of riches, and finally, there could nothing be devised which lacked there, but amongst such great store of treasure, this was more marvellous, that there was no closure, bolt, or lock, and no guardian to keep the same. And when with great pleasure she viewed all these things, she heard a voice without any body, that said: "Why do you marvel, lady, at so great riches? Behold all that you see is at your commandment: wherefore go you into the chamber and repose yourself upon the bed, and desire what bath you will have, and we, whose voices you hear, be your servants, and ready to minister unto you according to your desire: in the mean season, when you have refreshed your body, royal meats and dainty dishes shall be prepared for you."

'Then Psyche perceived the felicity of divine providence, and according to the advertisement of the incorporeal voices she first reposed herself upon the bed, and then refreshed her body in the bath. This done, she saw the table garnished with meats, and a round chair to sit down, and gladly reposed herself beside the array for dining, which she thought was set very conveniently for her refreshment. Then straightway all sorts of wines like nectar were brought in, and plentiful dishes of divers meats, not by anybody but as it were by some divine spirit or breath, for she could see no person before her, but only hear words falling on every side, and she had only voices to serve her. After that all the rich services were brought to the table, one came in and sang invisibly, another played on the harp, and that, too, could not be seen; the harmony of a large concourse did so greatly thrill in her ears, that though there were no manner of person, yet seemed she in the midst of a great quire.

'All these pleasures finished, when night approached Psyche went to bed; and when she was laid, and the night far advanced, still a sweet sound came about her ears; then she greatly feared for her virginity, because she was alone; she trembled and quaked the more for that she knew not what evil might come to pass. Then came her unknown husband to her bed, and after that he had made her his very wife, he rose in the morning before day and departed. Soon after came those invisible voices, consoling the bride for that virginity she had lost, and thus she passed a great while: and so (as it naturally happened) that which was first a novelty, by continual custom did at last bring her great pleasure, but specially the sound of the voices was a comfort unto her being alone and knowing nothing of her estate. During this time her father and mother did nothing but weep and lament in their old age, and the fame of it was all blown abroad, and her two sisters, hearing of her most miserable fortune, came with great dolour and sorrow to see and speak with their parents.

'Now on that very night Psyche's husband spake unto her (for she might not know him with her eyes, but only with her hands and ears) and said: "O my sweet spouse and dear wife, fortune doth menace unto thee imminent peril and danger, whereof I wish thee greatly to beware: for know thou that thy sisters, thinking thou art dead, be greatly troubled and will soon come to the mountain by thy footsteps; whose lamentations, if thou fortune to hear, beware that thou do in no wise either make answer or look up toward them. For if thou do, thou shalt purchase to me a great sorrow, and to thyself utter destruction. Psyche (hearing her husband) promised that she would do all things as he commanded, but after that he was departed, and the night passed away, she lamented and cried all day following, thinking that now she was past all hope of comfort in that she was both closed within the walls of a fine prison, deprived of human conversation, and commanded not to aid or assist her sorrowful sisters, no, nor once to see them. Thus she passed all the day in weeping, and went to bed at night without any reflection of meat or bathing, but incontinently after came her husband earlier than he was wont, who (when he had embraced her sweetly) as she still wept, began to say: "Is it thus that you perform your promise, my sweet wife? What do I find here, that am your husband? What have I to hope? Pass you all the day and the night in weeping, and will you not cease even in your husband's arms? Go to, do what you will, purchase your own destruction, and when you find it so, then remember my words and repent, but too late."

'Then she desired her husband more and more, assuring him that she should die, unless he would grant her desire that she might see her sisters, whereby she might speak with them and comfort them; whereat at length he was contented, and moreover he willed that she should give them as much gold and jewels as she would, but he gave her a further charge, warning her often, and saying that she should beware that she should covet not (being moved by the pernicious counsel of her sisters) to see the shape of his person, lest by her wicked curiosity she should be deprived of so great and worthy estate and nevermore feel his embrace. Psyche being glad herewith rendered unto him most entire thanks and said: "My honey, my husband, I had rather die an hundred times than be separate from your sweet company; for whosoever you be, I love and retain you within my heart, as if you were mine own spirit, and I make you not less than if you were Cupid himself: but I pray you grant this likewise, that you would command your servant Zephyrus to bring my sisters down into the valley, as he brought me, and place them here": wherewithal she kissed him sweetly, and desired him with tender words to grant her request, and clasped him closely to her bosom, calling him her spouse, her sweetheart, her joy, her own very soul, whereby she enforced him by the power of her love (though unwilling) to her mind, and he promised to do her will, and when morning came he departed away from her arms.

'After long search made, the sisters of Psyche came unto the hill where she had been set on the rock, and cried with a loud voice and beat their breasts in such sort that the rocks and stones with echoes answered again their frequent howlings: and when they called their sister by her name, so that their lamentable cries came down the mountain unto her ears, she came forth, very anxious and now almost out of her mind, and said: "Behold, here is she for whom you weep; I pray you torment yourself no more, and dry those tears with which you have so long wetted your cheeks, for now may you embrace her for whom you mourned."

'By and by she commanded Zephyrus by the appointment of her husband to bring them down; neither did he delay, for with gentle blasts he retained them up, and laid them softly in the valley: I am not able to express the often embracing, kissing, and greeting which was between them three; and those tears which had been then laid apart sprang forth again for joy. "Come in," quoth Psyche, "Into our house with gladness and refresh your afflicted minds with me your sister." After this she showed them the storehouses of treasure, she caused them to hear the great company of voices which served her, the fair bath was made ready, and she entertained them richly with dainty meats of her celestial table, and when they had eaten and filled themselves with divine delicacies they conceived great envy within their hearts: and one of them being very curious in every point, did not cease to demand what her husband was, and who was the lord of so precious a house; but Psyche, remembering the promise which she

made to her husband, did not let it go forth from the secret places of
her heart, but with timely colour feigned that he was a young man of
comely stature with soft down, rather than a beard, just beginning to
shadow his cheeks, and had great delight in hunting in the hills and
dales hard by: and lest by her long talk she should be found to trip or
fail in her words and betray her secret counsel, she filled their laps
with gold and ornaments of jewels, and commanded Zephyrus to
carry them away.

'When this was done these worthy sisters took rays homeward to
their own houses, and the poison of envy that they bare against
Psyche grew hot within them, so that they murmured with much
talk between them; and one began: "Behold a cruel and contrary
fortune! Doth it please thee that we (born all of one parent) have
divers destinies, but especially we, that are the elder two, be married
to strange husbands, made as handmaidens, and as it were banished
from our country and friends; whereas our younger sister, last born,
which is ever the weakest, hath so great abundance of treasure and
gotten a god to her husband, but hath no skill how to use so great
plenty of riches. Saw you not, sister, what was in the house? What
great store of jewels, what glittering robes, what gems, yea, what gold
we trod on? So that if she have a goodly husband according as she
affirmeth there is none that liveth this day more happy in all the
world than she. And so it may come to pass that at length, if the great
affection and love which he beareth unto her do continually increase,
he may make her a goddess, for (by Hercules) such was her port, so
she behaved herself. Now already she holds up her countenance, now
she breathes the goddess, that as a woman hath voices to serve her,
and lays her commands upon the winds. But I, poor wretch, have
first married a husband older than my father, more bald than a coot,*
more weak than a child, and one that locketh up all the house with
bolts and chains."

Then said the other sister: "And in faith I am married to a husband
that hath the gout, bent crooked, not courageous in paying the debt
of love; I am fain to rub and mollify his crabbed and stony fingers,
and I soil my white and dainty hands with stinking plasters and rank-
smelling salves and with the corruption of filthy clouts, so that he uses
me not like a wife, but more like a surgeon's servant. And you, my

* The Latin uses another comparison: 'balder than a pumpkin'.

sister, seem to bear this with a patient, nay (that I may speak freely)
with a servile mind, but I cannot abide to see our younger sister so
unworthy in such great felicity. Saw you not, I pray, how proudly
and arrogantly she handled us even now, and how in vaunting herself
she uttered her presumptuous mind, how she cast grudgingly a little
gold into our laps, and (being weary of our company) commanded
that we should be borne and blown and whistled away? Verily, I live
not nor am I a woman, but I will cast her utterly down from her rich
estate: and if you, my sister, as you should, be so far made bitter
herewith as I, let us consult boldly together, and not show this that
we have to any person, no, nor yet to our parents, nor tell that we
know that she liveth. For it sufficeth that we have seen her, whom it
repenteth to have seen: neither let us declare her good fortune to our
father, nor to all the world, for they be not wealthy, whose riches are
unknown: so shall she know that she hath not abject slaves, but very
elder sisters. But now let us go home to our husbands and poor
houses, that be yet honest enough, and when we are better instructed
with most careful plotting, let us return the stronger to suppress her
pride." So this evil counsel seemed good to these two evil women,
and they hid that great treasure which Psyche gave them, and tare
their hair and befouled their faces renewing their false and forged
tears. Thus did they terrify their father and mother, and doubled their
sorrows and griefs; and then full of ire and farced with envy they took
their voyage homeward devising the hurt, nay the slaughter and
destruction of their harmless sister.

'In the mean season the husband of Psyche, whom she knew not,
did warn her again in the night with these words: "Seest thou not,"
quoth he, "What peril and danger evil fortune doth threaten unto
thee from afar? Whereof if thou take not good heed in time, it will
shortly come upon thee: for the unfaithful harlots do greatly
endeavour to set their snares to catch thee, and their purpose is to
make and persuade thee to behold my face, which if thou once
fortune to see (as I have often told thee) thou shalt see no more:
wherefore if these naughty hags, armed with wicked minds, do
chance to come again (as I think not otherwise but that they will)
take heed that thou talk not with them, but simply suffer them to
speak what they will; howbeit, if thou canst not restrain thyself for
thy natural simplicity and for the tender years of thy mind, beware
that thou have no communication of thy husband, nor answer a

word if they fortune to question of me. So will we increase our stock, and thou hast a young and tender child couched in this young and tender belly of thine, who shall be made, if thou conceal my secret, an immortal god, but otherwise a mortal creature." Then Psyche was very glad that she should bring forth a divine babe, and proud of the pledge that was to be born, and very joyful in that she should be honoured as a mother: she reckoned and numbered carefully the days and months that passed, and being never with child before, did marvel greatly that her belly should swell so big from so small a beginning.

'But those pestilent and wicked furies, breathing out their serpentine poison, were hastening with wicked speed to bring their enterprise to pass. Then Psyche was warned again by her husband, while he briefly tarried with her, in this sort: "Behold the last day and the extreme case. The enemies of thy own sex and blood have armed themselves against us, pitched their camps, set their host in array, sounded for advance, and are now marching towards us, for thy two sisters have drawn their swords and are ready to slay thee. Oh with what force and slaughter are we assailed this day, sweet Psyche: I pray thee to take pity on thyself, and on me, keep a seal on thy lips, and deliver thy husband, and thyself, and this infant within thy belly from so great and imminent a danger, and see not neither hear these cursed women, which are not worthy to be called thy sisters, for their great and murderous hatred, and breach of sisterly amity, for they will come (like Sirens) to the mountain, and yield out therein their piteous and lamentable cries."

'When Psyche had heard these words, she sighed sorrowfully and said: "O dear husband, this long time you have had experience and trial of my faith and my silence, and doubt you not but that I will persevere in the same steadfastness of mind: wherefore command you our servant Zephyrus that he may do as he hath done before, to the intent that instead of your form that you have forbidden me to see, yet I may comfort myself with the sight of my sisters. I pray you by this lovely and fragrant hair of yours that hangs down, by these round cheeks, delicate and tender like mine own, by your pleasant warm breast, by that shape and face that I shall learn at length by the child in my belly, hear the solemn prayer of my anxious beseeching, grant the fruit of my desire that I may embrace my sisters, refresh your dear spouse Psyche with joy, who is bound and linked unto you for ever. I little esteem to see your visage and figure, little do I regard the night and darkness, for I hold you in my arms, my only light." Her husband (being as it were enchanted with these words, and compelled by violence of her often embracing, wiping away her tears with his hair) did yield unto his wife, and promised that which she desired, and before morning was come departed as he accustomed to do.

'Now her sisters, their plot well compacted, arrived on land, and without even visiting of their father and mother never rested till they came to the rock, and there leaped down rashly from the hill themselves, waiting not for the breeze that was to bear them; forgat not then Zephyrus the divine commandment, and brought them down in the bosom of the wind (though it were against his will) and laid them in the valley without any harm. By and by they went into the palace to their sister without leave, and when they had eftsoons embraced their prey, falsely assuming the show of sisters, and hiding the store of their malice beneath a smiling face, with flattering words they said: "O dear sister Psyche, know you that you are now no more so slim and slender, but already almost a mother? O what great joy bear you unto us in your belly! What a comfort will it be unto all the house! How happy shall we be that shall see this golden infant increase and grow! – who, if he be like his parents in beauty, as it is necessary he should, there is no doubt but a new Cupid shall be born."

'By this kind of pretended love they went about to win Psyche by little and little; but because they were weary with travel, they sat them down in chairs, and after that they had washed their bodies in warm and pleasant baths, they went into a parlour, where all those wonderful meats and goodly haggis were ready prepared. Psyche commanded the harp to play, and it was done; the flute to sound, and so it was; to make a quire, and song brake forth: but no person was seen, by whose sweet harmony and modulation the sisters of Psyche were greatly delighted. Howbeit the wickedness of these cursed women was nothing suppressed by the sweet and honeyed noise of these instruments, but they settled themselves to work their treason and snare against Psyche, demanding with guile who was her husband, and of what parentage or race he was: then she (having forgotten, by too much simplicity, that which she had before spoken of her husband) invented a new answer, and said that her husband was of a near province, a merchant in great affairs, and a man of a middle age, having his head interspersed with a few grey hairs; which when she had shortly said (because she would have no further talk) she filled their lap full of the richest gifts, and bade them again be borne away of the wind.

'In their return homeward, carried aloft by the gentle breath of Zephyrus, they murmured with themselves, saying: "How say you, sister, to so great and apparent a lie of doting Psyche? For first she said that her husband was a young man with the down of his chin but just beginning to spring, and now she saith that he hath a head half grey with age: what is he that in so short space can suddenly become so old? You shall find it no otherwise, my sister, but that either this cursed quean hath invented a great lie or else that she never saw the shape of her husband: and whichever be true, we must, as soon as may be, drive her forth from that rich estate of hers. And if it be so that she never saw him, then verily she is married to some god, and hath a young god for us in her belly; but if it be a divine babe of the which she shall soon be called the mother (as God forbid it should) then may I go and hang myself: wherefore let us go now to our parents, and with such forged lies as this let us colour the matter."

'After they were thus inflamed and had proudly visited their parents, having passed the night in fitful watchings, they returned again to the mountain, and by the aid of the wind Zephyrus were carried down into the valley; and after they had strained their eyelids to enforce themselves to weep, they called unto Psyche in this sort: "Thou (ignorant of so great evil) thinkest thyself sure and happy, and sittest at home nothing regarding thy peril, whereas we go about thy affairs, and are exceeding sorry for the harm that shall happen unto thee: for we are credibly informed, neither can we but utter it unto thee, that are the companions of thy grief and mishap, that there is a great serpent of many coils, full of deadly poison, with a ravenous and gaping throat, that lieth with thee secretly every night. Remember the oracle of Apollo, who pronounced that thou shouldest be married to a dire and fierce beast; and many of the inhabitants hereby, and such as hunt about in the country, affirm that they have seen him towards evening returning from pasture and swimming over the river: whereby they do undoubtedly say that he will not pamper thee long with delicate meats, but when the time of delivery shall approach, he will devour both thee and thy child as a more tender morsel. Wherefore advise thyself, whether thou wilt agree unto us that are careful for thy safety, and so avoid the peril of death, and be contented to live with thy sisters, or whether thou wilt remain with the most cruel serpent, and in the end be swallowed into the gulf of his body. And if it be so that thy solitary life, thy conversation with voices, and this servile and dangerous pleasure, that is the secret and filthy love of the poisonous serpent, do more delight thee; say not but that we have played the parts of natural sisters in warning thee."

'Then the poor simple Psyche was moved with the fear of so dreadful words, and (being amazed in her mind) did clean forget the admonitions of her husband and her own promises made unto him. And (throwing herself headlong into extreme misery) with a wan and sallow countenance, scantly uttering and stammering forth her words, at length began to say in this sort: "O my most dear sisters, I heartily thank you for your great kindness towards me, and I am now verily persuaded that they which have told you hereof, have told you of nothing but truth, for I never saw the shape of my husband, neither know I from whence he came; only I hear his voice in the night, in so much that I have an unknown husband, and one that loveth not the light of the day; which causeth me to suspect that he is some beast as you affirm. Moreover I do greatly fear to see him, for he doth menace and threaten great evil unto me, if I should go about to spy, and behold his shape; wherefore, my loving sisters, if you have any wholesome remedy for your sister in danger, give it now presently: for if ye be now careless so to do, ye will make of none effect the kindness of your watchfulness that was before."

'Then those wicked women, opening the gates of their sister's heart, did put away now all privy guile, and egged her forward in her fearful thoughts, drawing openly the sword of deceit, and persuading her to do as they would have her; and one of them began and said: "Because that we, obliged by our kinship with you, little esteem any peril or danger to save your life, we intend to show you the best way and means to safety as we may possibly do, and we have long thought thereon. Take a sharp razor, whetted upon the palm of your hand to its finest edge, and put it under the pillow of your bed, and see that you have ready a privy burning lamp with oil, hid under some part of the hanging of the chamber; and (finely dissimulating all the matter) when, according to his custom, he cometh to bed and stretcheth him fully out and sleepeth soundly, breathing deep, arise you secretly, and with your bare feet treading a-tiptoe, go and take your lamp, with the razor lifted high in your right hand, from the ward of its hiding-place that you may borrow from its light the occasion of a bold deed, and with valiant force cut off the head of the poisonous serpent at the knot of his neck: wherein we will aid and assist you, and when by the death of him you shall be made safe, we will bring quickly away all these riches and marry you, that are a woman, to some comely man, and no beast." After they had thus inflamed the heart of their sister, who was already alight (fearing lest some danger might happen unto them by reason of their privity in so wicked a deed) they left her and were carried by the wind Zephyrus to the top of the mountain, and so they ran away, and took shipping.

'When Psyche was left alone (saving that she seemed not to be alone, being stirred by so many furies) she was in a tossing mind, like the waves of the sea, and although her will was obstinate and fixed to put in execution the counsel of her sisters, yet when she was now ready to do the deed, she was in doubtful and divers opinions touching her calamity. Sometimes she would, sometimes she would not, sometimes she is bold, sometimes she feareth, sometimes she mistrusteth, sometimes she is moved, and at last in one person she hateth the beast and loveth her husband; but at length the evening came, when she made preparation for her wicked intent. Then was it night, and soon after her husband came, and when he had kissed and embraced her he fell asleep: then Psyche (somewhat feeble in body and mind, yet strengthened by cruelty of fate) received boldness and brought forth the lamp, and took the razor, so that by her audacity she changed herself to masculine kind. But when she took the lamp and the secret parts of the bed were made light, she saw the most meek and sweetest beast of all beasts, even fair Cupid, couched fairly, at whose sight the very lamp increased its light for joy, and the razor turned its edge. But when Psyche saw so glorious a body, she greatly feared, and amazed in mind, with a pale countenance, all trembling, fell on her knees, and thought to hide the razor, yea verily in her own heart; which she had undoubtedly done, had it not, through fear of so wicked an enterprise, fallen out of her rash and hasty hands. And now she was faint and had lost her strength, but when she saw and beheld the beauty of his divine visage, she was well recreated in her mind; she saw his hairs of gold, that were drenched with ambrosia and yielded out a sweet savour thereof; his neck more white than milk; his ruddy cheeks upon which his hair hanged comely behind and before, the brightness whereof did darken the light of the lamp; the tender plume feathers of that flying god dispersed upon his shoulders with shining gleam, and though his wings were at rest, the tender down of their edges trembling hither and thither, and the other parts of his body so smooth and soft that it could not repent Venus to bear such a child. At the bed's feet lay his bow, quiver and arrows that be the gentle weapons of so great a god: which when Psyche did curiously behold, and marvelling at the weapons of her husband took one of the arrows out of the quiver, and trying the sharpness thereof with her finger, she pricked herself withal: wherewith she was so grievously wounded that some little drops of blood followed, and thereby of her own accord she fell in love with Love. Then more and more broiling in the love of Cupid, she embraced him and kissed him a thousand times, fearing the measure of his sleep.

'But alas, while she was in this great joy, and her spirit languished and wavered, whether it were for foul envy, or for desire to touch this amiable body likewise, there fell out a drop of burning oil from the lamp upon the right shoulder of the god. O rash and bold lamp, the vile ministry of love, how darest thou be so bold as to burn the god of all fire, when surely some lover invented thee, to the intent that he might with more joy pass the nights in pleasure? The god being burned in this sort, and perceiving that promise and faith was broken, he fled away without utterance of any word from the kisses and hands of his most unhappy wife. But Psyche fortuned to catch him as he was rising by the right thigh with both hands, and held him fast as he flew about in the air, hanging to him (poor wretch) through his cloudy journey, until such time that, constrained by weariness, she let go and fell down upon the ground: but Cupid left her not altogether, but followed her down and lighted upon the top of a cypress-tree, and angrily spake unto her in this manner: "O simple Psyche, consider with thyself, how I (little regarding the commandment of my mother, who willed me that thou shouldest be married to a man of base and miserable condition) did come myself from heaven to love thee. This have I very wantonly done, I know (and I have wounded mine own body with my proper weapon) to have thee to my spouse, and did I seem a beast unto thee, that thou shouldest go about to cut off my head with a razor, yea this head with its eyes that love thee so well? Did not I always give thee in charge against this danger? Did not I gently will thee to beware? But those cursed aiders and counsellors of thine shall be worthily rewarded for their pains. As for thee, thou shalt be sufficiently punished by my absence." And when he had spoken these words he took his flight into the air.

'Then Psyche fell flat on the ground, and as long she might see her husband, she cast her eyes after him into the air, weeping and lamenting piteously: but when he was flown clean away out of her sight, she threw herself into the next running river, for the great anguish and dolour that she was in, for the lack of her husband; howbeit the gentle water would not suffer her to be drowned, but took pity upon her, in the honour of Cupid which accustomed to broil and burn the very river, and so fearing for himself would not harm her, but threw her upon the bank amongst the herbs. Then Pan the rustical god was sitting on the river-side, embracing and teaching the goddess Echo of the mountains to tune her songs and pipes, by whom were feeding upon the grass of the margin the young and tender goats; and after that this goat-footed god perceived poor Psyche in so sorrowful case, not ignorant (I know not by what means) of her miserable estate, he called her gently beside him and endeavoured to pacify her in this sort: "O fair maid, I am a rustic and rude herdsman, howbeit (by reason of my old age) expert in many things; for as far as I can learn by conjecture, which (according as wise men do term) is called divination, I perceive by your uncertain and trembling gait, your pale hue, your sobbing sighs, aye and your watery eyes, that you are greatly in love. Wherefore hearken to me, and go not about to slay yourself, nor weep not at all, but rather adore and worship the great god Cupid, and win him unto you, that is a delicate and wanton youth, by your gentle promise of service."

'When the god of shepherds had spoken these words, she gave no answer, but made reverence unto him as to a god, and so departed: and after that she had gone more than a little way with weary feet, she fortuned unawares to take a certain path, and towards evening to come to a city where the husband of one of her sisters did reign; which when Psyche did understand, she caused that her sister had knowledge of her coming. And so they met together, and after great embracing and salutation the sister of Psyche demanded the cause of her travel thither. "Marry," quoth she, "Do not you remember the counsel that you gave me, whereby you would that I should kill with a razor the beast, who under colour of my husband did lie with me every night, before he should utterly devour miserable me? You shall understand that as soon as, by thy further advice, I brought forth the lamp to see and behold his shape, I perceived a wonderful and even a divine sight; for it was the son of Venus, even Cupid himself, that lay softly asleep. Then I, being stricken with the sight of so great pleasure, and distraught by exceeding great joy, could not thoroughly assuage my delight, but, alas (by evil chance) the boiling oil of the lamp fortuned to fall on his shoulder, which caused him to awake; and he, aroused by the pain thereof, seeing me armed with fire and weapon, began to say: 'How darest thou be so bold as to do so great a mischief? Depart from me, and take such things as thou diddest bring:* for I will have thy sister' (and named you) 'to my wife, and she shall be joined in true wedlock with me'; and by and by he commanded Zephyrus to carry me away from the bounds of his house."

'Psyche had scantly finished her tale, but her sister (pierced with the prick of carnal desire and wicked envy) ran home, and feigning to her husband with a cunningly made lie that she had heard somewhat of the death of her parents, took shipping and came to the mountain. And although there blew a contrary wind, yet being brought in a vain hope, she cried: "O Cupid, take me a more worthy wife, and thou, Zephyrus, bear down thy mistress," and so she cast herself down from the mountain. But she fell not into the valley neither alive nor dead, for all the members and parts of her body were torn amongst the rocks, whereby she was made a prey to the birds and wild beasts, as she worthily deserved, and so she perished. Neither was the vengeance of the other delayed: for Psyche, travelling with wandering feet, fortuned to come to another city, where her other sister did dwell; to whom when she had declared all such things as she told to her first sister, she also was caught in the snare, and being very jealous of her marriage, ran likewise unto the rock, and was slain in like sort.

'In the meantime, Psyche travelled about in the country to seek her husband Cupid, but he was gotten into his mother's chamber, and there bewailed the sorrowful wound which he caught by the oil of the burning lamp. Then the white bird the gull, which swimmeth

---

* The Roman formula of divorce; and Cupid was to re-marry the sister by *confarreatio*, the solemn and ceremonial tie confined to patricians and priests.

with his wings over the waves of the water, flew down to the Ocean sea, where she found Venus washing and bathing herself: to whom she declared her son was burned and suffering from a grievous wound and in danger of death, and moreover that it was a common report in the mouth of every person to speak evil of all the family of Venus; "Thy son," quoth she, "Doth nothing but haunt harlots in the mountain, and thou thyself dost use to riot on the sea, whereby they say there is now nothing any more gracious, nothing pleasant, nothing gentle, but all is become uncivil, monstrous, and horrible; moreover, there are no more loving marriages, nor friendships of amity, nor loving of children, but all is disorderly, and there is a very bitter hatred of weddings as base things." This the wordy and curious gull did clatter in the ears of Venus, reprehending her son. But Venus began to be very angry, and said: "What, hath my son gotten any love? I pray thee, gentle bird, that dost alone serve me so faithfully, tell me what she is and what is her name, that hath troubled my simple and beardless* son in such sort, whether she be any of the tribe of the Nymphs, of the number of the Seasons, of the company of the Muses, or of the ministry of my Graces?" To whom the bird answered that could never be silent: "Madam, I know not what she is; but this I know, that he loveth her greatly, and that she is called Psyche." Then Venus with indignation cried out: "What, is it she? The usurper of my beauty, the vicar of my name? And this is more and worse; will the brat think that I am a bawd, by whose showing he fell acquainted with the maid?"

'Thus she complained, and immediately departed and went to her golden chamber, where she found her son wounded, as it was told unto her; whom when she beheld she stood at the door and cried out very loudly in this sort: "Is this an honest thing? Is this honourable to thy parents and to thine own good name? Is this reason that thou hast first violated and broken the commandment of thy mother and sovereign mistress? And whereas thou shouldest have vexed my enemy with a loathsome and base love, thou hast done contrary: for (being but of tender and unripe years) thou hast with too licentious appetite embraced her, that my most mortal foe shall be made a daughter unto me. Thou presumest and thinkest (thou trifling boy, thou varlet, and without all love) that thou art alone my true child,

---

* *Lit.* 'not yet clothed as a man'.

and that I am not able by reason of mine age to have another son; but this I could do, and thou shouldest well understand that I would bear a more worthier than thou: but to work thee a greater despite, I do determine to adopt one of my servants, and to give him these wings, this fire, this bow and these arrows, and all other furniture which I gave to thee, though not for this purpose; for of all this nothing came to thee from thy father to thy furnishment. But first thou hast been evil brought up and instructed in thy youth: thou hast thy hands ready and sharp: thou hast often most rudely struck and beaten thy ancients, and especially thy own mother, myself I say, thou hast robbed me daily, thou very parricide, and hast pierced me with thy darts, thou contemnest me as a widow, neither dost thou regard thy valiant and invincible stepfather, but to anger me more thou settest him after wenches that I may be jealous: but I will cause that thou shalt shortly repent thee of this sport, and that this marriage shall be bitter to thee and dearly bought. To what a public scorn am I now driven? What shall I do? Whither shall I go? How shall I repress this beast? Shall I ask aid of mine enemy Sobriety, whom I have often offended because of thy wantonness? But I hate to seek for counsel from so poor and rustical a woman. No, no, howbeit I will not cease from my vengeance, whencesoever it cometh; to her must I have recourse for help, and to none other (I mean to Sobriety) who may correct sharply this trifler, take away his quiver, deprive him of his arrows, unbend his bow, quench his fire, and subdue his body with punishment still more bitter, and when that she hath razed and cut off this his hair, which I have dressed with mine own hands and made to glitter like gold, and when she hath clipped his wings which I myself have dyed with the immortal fountain of my breast, then shall I think to have sufficiently revenged myself for the injury which he hath done."

'When she had spoken these words she departed in a great rage out of her chamber full of the bitterness of very Venus; and immediately as she was going away, came Juno and Ceres, and seeing her angry countenance, they demanded the cause of her anger, and why with so gloomy a frown she had dimmed the glory of her shining eyes. Then Venus made answer: "Verily you are come in good time to carry into effect the purpose of my furious heart; but I pray you with all diligence to seek out one whose name is Psyche, who is a vagabond, and runneth about the countries, and I think you are not ignorant of the bruit of my son Cupid, and of his demeanour, which I am ashamed to declare." Then they understanding and knowing the whole matter, endeavoured to mitigate the ire of Venus in this sort: "What is the cause, madam, or how hath your son so offended that you should so greatly accuse his love, and blame him by reason that he is amorous? And why should you seek the death of her whom he doth fancy? What is his fault, we pray, if he have accorded to the mind of a fair maiden? What, do not you know that he is a man and a young man? Or have you forgotten of what years he is? Doth he seem always to you to be a child because he beareth well his age? You are his mother and a kind and understanding woman; will you continually search out his dalliance? Will you blame his luxury? Will you bridle his love? And will you reprehend your own art and delights in your lovely son? What god or man is he, that can endure that you should sow or disperse your seed of love in every place, and at the same time make a restraint of that same love within your own doors, and entirely close and shut up that factory where the natural faults of women are made?" In this sort these goddesses endeavoured to excuse Cupid with all their power (although he were absent) for fear of his dart and shafts of love. But Venus would in no wise assuage her heat, but (thinking that they did but trifle and taunt at her injuries) she departed from them, and took her voyage again towards the sea in all haste.

BOOK SIX

'In the mean season Psyche hurled herself hither and thither, seeking day and night for her husband with unquiet mind, eager the more because she thought that if he would not be appeased with the sweet flattery of his wife, yet he would take mercy upon her at her servile and continual prayers. And (espying a church on the top of a high hill) she said: "How can I tell whether my husband and master be there or no?" Wherefore she went swiftly thitherward, and with great pain and travail, yet moved by hope and desire, after that she had stoutly climbed to the top of the mountain, she went up to the sacred couch, where behold, she espied sheaves of corn lying on a heap, blades twisted into garlands, and reeds of barley; moreover she saw hooks, scythes, sickles, and other instruments to reap, but everything lay out of order, and as it were cast down carelessly in the summer heat by the hands of labourers; which when Psyche saw, she gathered up and put everything duly in order, thinking that she would not despise or contemn the temples of any of the gods, but rather get the favour and benevolence of them all.

'By and by Lady Ceres came in and beholding her busy and curious in her chapel, cried out afar off and said: "O Psyche, needful of mercy, Venus searcheth anxiously for thy steps in every place, mad at heart to revenge herself and to punish thee grievously with all the power of her godhead, but hast thou more mind to be here and to look after my affairs, and carest for nothing less than thy safety?" Then Psyche fell on her knees before her, watering her feet with her tears, wiping the ground with her hair, and with great weeping and many supplications desired pardon, saying: "O great and holy goddess, I pray thee by thy plenteous and liberal right hand, by thy joyful ceremonies of harvest, by the secrets of thy baskets, by the flying chariots of the dragons thy servants, by the tillage of the ground of Sicily which thou hast invented, by the chariot of the ravishing god,* by the earth that held

* Pluto, who carried off Proserpina to Hell from the plains of Henna, in Sicily.

thy daughter fast, by the dark descent to the unillumined marriage of
Proserpina, by thy diligent inquisition of her and thy bright return, and
by the other secrets which are concealed within the temple of Eleusis
in the land of Athens, take pity on me thy servant Psyche, and help my
miserable soul, and let me hide myself a few days amongst these
sheaves of corn until the ire of so great a goddess be past, or until that I
be refreshed of my great labour and travail." Then answered Ceres:
"Verily, Psyche, I am greatly moved by thy prayers and tears and desire
with all my heart to aid thee, but if I should suffer thee to be hidden
here, I should incur the displeasure of my good cousin, with whom I
have made a treaty of peace and an ancient promise of amity:
wherefore I advise thee to depart from this my temple, and take it in
good part in that I do not keep and guard thee as a prisoner here."

'Then Psyche driven away, contrary to her hope, was doubly
afflicted with sorrow, and so she returned back again: and behold, she
perceived afar off in a valley a temple standing within a glimmering
forest, fair and curiously wrought; and minding to overpass no place
whither better hope did direct her, although it might be uncertain,
and to the intent she would desire the pardon of every god, she
approached nigh to the sacred doors. There she saw precious riches
and vestments engraven with letters of gold, hanging upon branches
of trees and the posts of the temple, testifying the name of the goddess
Juno to whom they were dedicated and the reason of their offering.
Then she kneeled down upon her knees, and embracing the altar
(which was yet warm) with her hands, and wiping her tears away,
began to pray in this sort: "O dear spouse and sister of the great god
Jupiter, which art adored among the great temples of Samos alone
made famous by thy birth, and infant crying, and nurture; or
worshipped at high and happy Carthage, as a maid, being carried
through heaven by a lion; or whether the rivers of the flood Inachus
do celebrate thee, ruling over the notable walls of Argos, and know
that thou art the wife of the great thunderer and the goddess of
goddesses: all the east part of the world hath thee in veneration as
Zygia, all the west world calleth thee Lucina: I pray thee to be mine
advocate and Saviour* in my tribulations; deliver me from the great

* Psyche appeals to Juno in her threefold aspect: Zygia, as goddess of
marriage; Lucina, as goddess of childbirth; and Sospita, as protectress and
deliverer.

peril which pursueth me, and save me that am wearied with so long labours and sorrow, for I know that it is thou that succourest and helpest such women as are with child and in danger." Then Juno, hearing the prayers of Psyche, appeared unto her in all the royal dignity of her godhead, saying: "Certes, Psyche, I would gladly help thee; but I am ashamed to do anything contrary to the will of my daughter-in-law Venus, whom always I have loved as mine own child; and moreover I shall incur the danger of the law entitled *De servo corrupto*, whereby I am forbidden to retain any servant fugitive against the will of his master."

'Then Psyche, terrified at this new shipwreck of fortune, as without all hope of her safety and the recovery of her husband, reasoned with herself in this sort: "Now what comfort or remedy is left to my afflictions, when as my prayers will nothing avail with the goddesses, though they be willing enough to help me? What shall I do? Whither shall I go, that am set about and surrounded with such snares? In what cave or darkness shall I hide myself to avoid the piercing eyes of Venus? Why do I not take a good heart, renouncing my vain hopes, and offer myself with humility (though it be late) unto her whose anger I have wrought and so try to soften her great fury? What do I know whether he whom I seek for so long be not in the house of his mother?" Thus unto a doubtful service, nay unto certain destruction, Psyche prepared herself how she might make her orison and prayer unto Venus.

'But Venus, after that she was weary with searching over all the earth for Psyche, returned towards heaven and commanded that one should prepare the chariot which her husband Vulcanus had most curiously shaped and given unto her as a marriage gift before that she had first entered the bridal chamber; and it was so finely wrought that it had been made the more precious even of the very gold which the file had taken away. Four white doves, out of all those that stood sentinel to the chamber of their lady, stepped very briskly in front and bowed their rainbow-coloured necks to the yoke of precious gems, and when Venus was entered in, bore up the chariot with great diligence. After her chariot there followed a number of sparrows chirping about, making sign of joy, and all other kind of birds sang very sweetly with honeyed notes, foreshowing the coming of the great goddess: the clouds gave place, the heavens opened and the upper air received her joyfully, the birds that followed, being the tuneful choir of Venus, nothing feared the eagles, hawks, and other ravenous fowl in the air. Incontinently she went unto the royal palace of the god Jupiter, and with proud and bold petition demanded the service of Mercury the herald in certain of her affairs, whereunto Jupiter consented, nodding with his azure brow; then with much joy she descended from heaven with Mercury, and gave him an earnest charge to put in execution her words, saying: "O my brother, born in Arcadia, thou knowest well that I (who am thy sister) did never enterprise to do anything without thy presence: thou knowest also how long I have sought for a girl that is a-hiding and cannot find her: wherefore there resteth nothing else save that thou do publicly pronounce the reward to such as take her. See thou put in execution my commandment, account the signs by which she may be known, and declare that whatsoever he be that retaineth her wittingly against my will, he shall not defend himself by any mean or excusation." And when she had spoken this, she delivered unto him a paper wherein was contained the name of Psyche and the residue of his publication; which done, she departed away to her lodging.

'By and by Mercurius, obeying her commands, proclaimed throughout all the world that whatsoever he were that could bring back or tell any tidings of a king's fugitive daughter, the servant of Venus, named Psyche, let him bring word to Mercury, behind the Murtian temple, and for reward of his pains he should receive seven sweet kisses of Venus and one more sweetly honeyed from the touch of her loving tongue. After that Mercury had pronounced these things, every man was inflamed with desire of so great a guerdon to search her out, and this was the cause that put away all doubt from Psyche, who was all but come in sight of the house of Venus: but one of her servants called Custom came out, who, espying Psyche, cried with a loud voice: "O wicked harlot as thou art, now at length thou shalt know that thou hast a mistress above thee; what, beside all thy other bold carriage, dost thou make thyself ignorant, as if thou diddest not understand what travail we have taken in searching for thee? I am glad that thou art come into my hands, thou art now in the claws of Hell, and shalt abide the pain and punishment of thy great contumacy"; and therewithal she seized her by the hair, and brought her before the presence of Venus.

'When Venus espied her brought into her presence, she began to laugh loudly, as angry persons accustom to do, and she shaked her head and scratched her right ear,* saying: "Have you now deigned at length to visit your mother? Or perchance to visit your husband, that is in danger of death by your means? Be you assured I will handle you like a daughter; where be my maidens Sorrow and Sadness?" To whom, when they came, she delivered Psyche to be cruelly tormented. They fulfilled the commandment of their mistress, and after they had piteously scourged her with whips and had otherwise tormented her, they presented her again before Venus. Then she began to laugh again, saying: "Behold, she thinketh that by reason of her great belly, which she hath gotten by playing the whore, to move me to pity, and to make me a happy grandmother to her noble child. Am not I happy, that in the flourishing time of all mine age shall be called a grandmother, and the son of a vile harlot shall be accounted the grandson of Venus. Howbeit I am a fool to term him by the name of a son, since as the marriage was made between unequal persons, in no town, without witnesses, and not by the consent of their parents, therefore the marriage is illegitimate, and the child (that shall be born) a bastard, if indeed we fortune to suffer thee to live till thou be delivered."

'When Venus had spoken these words, she leaped upon poor Psyche, and (tearing everywhere her apparel) took her violently by the hair, and dashed her head upon the ground. Then she took a great quantity of wheat, barley, millet, poppy-seed, pease, lentils, and beans, and mingled them all together on a heap, saying: "Thou art so evil-favoured, girl, that thou seemest unable to get the grace of thy lovers by no other means, but only by diligent and painful service: wherefore I will prove what thou canst do; see that thou separate all these grains one from another, disposing them orderly in their quality, and let it be done to my content before night." When she had appointed this heap of seeds unto Psyche, she departed to a great banquet for a marriage that was prepared that day. But Psyche went not about to dissever the grain (as being a thing impossible to be brought to pass, by reason it lay so confusedly scattered) but being astonied at the cruel commandment of Venus, sat still and said nothing. Then the little pismire the ant, that dwelleth in the fields, knowing and taking pity of the great difficulty and labour of the consort of so great a god, and cursing the cruelness of so evil a

* Pliny, *Natural History*, XI, 45: 'Behind the right ear likewise is the proper place of *Nemesis*.'

mother, ran about nimbly hither and thither, and called to her all the
ants of the country, saying: "I pray you, my friends, ye quick
daughters of the ground the mother of all things, take mercy on this
poor maid espoused to Cupid, who is in great danger of her person; I
pray you help her with all diligence." Incontinently they came, the
hosts of six-footed creatures one after another in waves, separating
and dividing the grain, and after that they had put each kind of corn
in order, they ran away again in all haste from her sight.

'When night came, Venus returned home from the banquet well
tippled with wine, smelling of balm, and all her body crowned with
garlands of roses, who when she espied with what great diligence the
work was done, began to say: "This is not the labour of thy hands,
vile quean, but rather of his that is amorous of thee to thy hurt and
his." Then she gave her a morsel of brown bread, and went to sleep.
In the mean season Cupid was closed fast in the most surest chamber
of the house, partly because he should not hurt himself the more with
wanton dalliance, and partly because he should not speak with his
love. So was the night bitterly passed by these two lovers divided one
from another beneath the same roof. But when Aurora was driving in
through the morning sky, Venus called Psyche, and said: "Seest thou
yonder forest that extendeth out in length with the river-banks, the
bushes whereof look close down upon the stream hard by? There be
great sheep shining like gold, and kept by no manner of person; I
command thee that thou go thither and bring me home some of the
wool of their fleeces."

'Psyche arose willingly, not to do her commandment, but to throw
herself headlong into the water to end her sorrow. But then a green
reed, nurse of sweet music, inspired by divine inspiration with a
gracious tune and melody, began to say: "O Psyche, harried by these
great labours, I pray thee not to trouble or pollute my holy water by
thy wretched death, and yet beware that thou go not towards the
terrible wild sheep of this coast until such time as the heat of the sun
be past; for when the sun is in his force, then seem they most dreadful
and furious with their sharp horns, their stony foreheads, and their
poisonous bites wherewith they arm themselves to the destruction of
mankind: but until the midday is past and the heat assuaged, and until
the flock doth begin to rest in the gentle breeze of the river, thou
mayest hide thyself here by me under this great plane-tree, which
drinks of the river as I do also, and as soon as their great fury is past

and their passion is stilled, thou mayest go among the thickets and
bushes under the wood-side and gather the locks of their golden
fleeces which thou shalt find hanging upon the briars." Thus spake
the gentle and benign reed, showing a mean to most wretched
Psyche to save her life, which she bare well in memory, and with all
diligence went and gathered up such locks as she found and put them
in her apron and carried them home to Venus: howbeit the danger of
this second labour did not please her, nor give her sufficient witness
of the good service of Psyche, but twisting her brows with a sour
resemblance of laughter, she said: "Of a certainty I know that another
is the author of this thy deed, but I will prove if thou be truly of so
stout a courage and singular prudence as thou seemest. Seest thou the
high rock that overhangs the top of yonder great hill, from whence
there runneth down water of black and deadly colour which is
gathered together in the valley hard by and thence nourisheth the
marshes of Styx and the hoarse torrent of Cocytus? I charge thee to
go thither and bring me a vessel of that freezing water from the
middest flow of the top of that spring": wherewithal she gave her a
bottle of carven crystal, menacing and threatening her more
rigorously than before.

'Then poor Psyche went in all haste to the top of the mountain,
rather to end her wretched life than to fetch any water, and when she
was come up to the ridge of the hill, she perceived that it was very
deadly and impossible to bring it to pass, for she saw a great rock, very
high and not to be approached by reason that it was exceeding
rugged and slippery, gushing out most horrible fountains of waters,
which, bursting forth from a cavernous mouth that sloped down-
wards, ran below and fell through a close and covered watercourse
which it had digged out, by many stops and passages, into the valley
beneath. On each side she saw great dragons creeping upon the
hollow rocks and stretching out their long and bloody necks, with
eyes that never slept devoted to watchfulness, their pupils always
awake to the unfailing light, which were appointed to keep the river
there: the very waters protected themselves with voices, for they
seemed to themselves likewise saying: "Away, away, what wilt thou
do? Fly, fly, or else thou wilt be slain." Then Psyche (seeing the
impossibility of this affair) stood still as though she were transformed
into stone, and although she was present in body, yet was she absent
in spirit and sense, overcome by reason of the great and inevitable

peril which she saw, in so much that she could not even comfort herself with weeping. Yet the sorrow of this innocent escaped not the watchful eyes of good Providence, and the royal bird of great Jupiter, the eagle, swept down on wings stretched out, remembering his old service which he had done, when by the leading of Cupid he brought up the Phrygian boy to the heavens, to be made the butler of Jupiter, and minding to show the like service in the person of the wife of Cupid, and came from the high house of the skies, and flying past the girl's face said unto Psyche: "O simple woman, without all experience of such things, dost thou think to get or dip up any drop of this dreadful water? No, no, assure thyself thou art never able to come nigh it, for the gods themselves, and even very Jupiter, do greatly fear so much as to name those waters of Styx; what, have you not heard that as it is a custom among men to swear by the puissance of the gods, so the gods do swear by the majesty of the river Styx? But give me thy bottle": and suddenly he took it and held it, and hastened on the poise of his beating wings betwixt the ravening teeth and terrible darting tongues of the dragons by right and by left, and filled it with the water of the river which yet came willingly that he might depart unharmed: for he feigned that he sought it by the command of Venus, so was his coming made somewhat more easy. Then Psyche, being very joyful thereof, took the full bottle and quickly presented it to Venus. Nor would the furious goddess even yet be appeased, but menacing more and more, and smiling most cruelly, said: "What? Thou seemest unto me a very witch and a most deep enchantress, thou hast so nimbly obeyed my commands. Howbeit thou shalt do one thing more, my poppet; take this box and go to Hell and the deadly house of Orcus, and desire Proserpina to send me a little of her beauty, as much as will serve me the space of one day, and say that such as I had is consumed away in tending my son that is sick: but return again quickly, for I must dress myself therewithal, and go to the theatre of the gods."

'Then the poor Psyche clearly perceived the end of all her fortune, seeing that all pretence was thrown off, and manifestly she was being driven to present destruction; and not without cause, as she was compelled to go upon her own feet to the gulf and furies of Hell. Wherefore without any further delay, she went up to a high tower to throw herself down headlong (thinking that it was the next and readiest way to Hell): but the tower (as inspired) spake suddenly unto her, saying: "O poor wretch, why goest thou about to slay thyself? Why dost thou rashly yield unto thy last peril and danger? Know thou that if thy spirit be once separate from thy body thou shalt surely go to Hell, but never to return again; wherefore hearken to me. Lacedaemon, a city of Greece, is not far hence: go thou thither and enquire for Taenarus, which is hidden in waste places, whereas thou shalt find a hole, the breathing-place of Hell, and through the open gate is seen a pathless way: hereby if thou enter across that threshold, thou shalt come by a straight passage even to the palace of Pluto. But take heed that thou go not with empty hands through that place of darkness: but carry two sops sodden in the flour of barley and honey in the hands, and two halfpence in thy mouth; and when thou hast passed a good part of that deadly way thou shalt see a lame ass carrying of wood, and a lame fellow driving him, who will desire thee to give him up certain sticks that fall down from his burden, but pass thou on silently and do nothing. By and by thou shalt come unto the dead river, whereas Charon is ferryman, who will first have his fare paid him before he will carry the souls over the river in his patched boat. Hereby you may see that avarice reigneth even amongst the dead; neither Charon nor Pluto will do anything for nought: for if it be a poor man that is near to die, and lacketh money in his hand, none will allow him to give up the ghost. Wherefore deliver to the foul old man one of the halfpence which thou bearest for thy passage, but make him receive it with his own hand out of thy mouth. And it shall come to pass as thou sittest in the boat, thou shalt see an old man swimming on the top of the river holding up his deadly hands, and desiring thee to receive him into the bark; but have no regard to his piteous cry, for it is not lawful to do so. When thou art past over the flood thou shalt espy certain old women weaving who will desire thee to help them, but beware thou do not consent unto them in any case, for these and like baits and traps will Venus set, to make thee let fall but one of thy sops: and think not that the keeping of thy sops is a light matter, for if thou lose one of them thou shalt be assured never to return again to this world. For there is a great and marvellous dog with three heads, huge and horrid, barking continually at the souls of such as enter in, to frighten them with vain fear, by reason he can now do them no harm; he lieth day and night before the gate of Proserpina, and keepeth the desolate house of Pluto with great diligence: to whom, if thou cast one of thy sops thou mayest have access to Proserpina without all danger: she will make thee good cheer, and bid thee sit soft, and entertain thee with delicate meat and drink, but sit thou upon the ground and desire brown bread and eat it, and then declare thy message unto her, and when thou hast received what she giveth, in thy return appease the rage of the dog with the other sop, and give thy other halfpenny to covetous Charon, and crossing his river come the same way again as thou wentest in to the upper world of the heavenly stars: but above all things have a regard that thou look not in the box, neither be not too curious about the treasure of the divine beauty."

'In this manner the high tower prophetically spake unto Psyche, and advertised her what she should do: and immediately she took two halfpence, two sops, and all things necessary and went unto Taenarus to go towards Hell, and thence passing down in silence by the lame ass, she paid her halfpenny for passage, neglected the desire of the dead old man in the river, denied to help the wily prayers of the women weaving, and filled the ravenous mouth of the dog with a sop, and came to the chamber of Proserpina. There Psyche would not sit in any royal seat, nor eat any delicate meats, but sitting lowly at the feet of Proserpina, only contented with coarse bread, declared the message of Venus, and after she had received a mystical secret in the box she departed, and stopped the mouth of the dog with the other sop, and paid the boatman the other halfpenny. Then returning more nimbly than before from Hell, and worshipping the white light of day, though she was much in haste to come to the end of her task, she was ravished with great desire, saying: "Am not I a fool, that knowing that I carry here the divine beauty, will not take a little thereof to garnish my face, to please my lover withal?" And by and by she opened the box, where she could perceive no beauty nor anything else, save only an infernal and deadly sleep, which immediately invaded all her members as soon as the box was covered, covering her with its dense cloud in such sort that she fell down on the ground, and lay there in her very steps on that same path as a sleeping corpse. But Cupid being now healed of his wound and malady, not able to endure the long absence of Psyche, got him secretly out at a high window of the chamber where he was enclosed, and (his wings refreshed by a little repose) took his flight toward his loving wife; whom when he had found, he wiped away the sleep from her face, and put it again into the box, and awaked her with an harmless prick of the tip of one of his arrows, saying: "O wretched captive, behold thou wert well nigh perished again with thy overmuch curiosity; well, go thou, and do bravely thy message to my mother, and in the mean season I will provide all things accordingly"; wherewithal he took his flight into the air, and Psyche brought to Venus the present of Proserpina.

'Now Cupid being more in love with Psyche, and fearing the sudden austerity of his mother, returned again to his tricks, and did pierce on swift wings into the heavens, and arrived before Jupiter to declare his cause: then Jupiter after that he had eftsoons embraced his dear face and kissed his hand, began to say in this manner: "O my lord and son, although thou hast not given due reverence and honour unto me as thou oughtest to do, but hast rather soiled and wounded this my breast (whereby the laws and order of the elements and planets be disposed) with continual assaults of terrene luxury and against all laws, yea even the Julian* law, and the utility of the public weal, hurting my fame and name by wicked adulteries, and transforming my divine beauty into serpents, fire, savage beasts, birds and bulls.† Howbeit remembering my modesty, and that I have nourished thee with mine own proper hands, I will do and accomplish all thy desire. But still thou shouldest beware of spiteful and envious persons, and if there be any excellent maiden of comely beauty in the world, remember yet the benefit which I shall show unto thee, by

---

* The law of Augustus against adultery. See the commentators to Juvenal, II, 37.

† The various forms assumed by Jupiter in his love-affairs with earthly women. *Cf.* Ovid, *Metamorphoses*, II, 103:

> The Lydian maiden in her web did portray to the full
> How Europe was by royal Jove beguiled in shape of Bull . . .
> She portrayed also there
> Asterie struggling with an Erne which did away her bear.
> And over Leda she made a Swan his wings to splay.
> She added also how by Jove in shape of Satyr gay
> The fair Antiope with a pair of children was besped . . .
> And now he also came
> To Danae like a shower of gold, to Aegine like a flame,
> A shepherd to Mnemosyne, and like a Serpent sly
> To Proserpine.

recompense of her love towards me again.''

'When he had spoken these words, he commanded Mercury to call all the gods to counsel, and if any of the celestial powers did fail of appearance, he should be condemned in ten thousand pounds: which sentence was such a terror unto all the gods, that the high theatre was replenished with them, and Jupiter began to speak in this sort: "O ye Gods, registered in the books of the Muses, you all doubtless know this young man Cupid, whom I have nourished with mine own hand, whose raging flames of his first youth I have thought best to bridle and restrain. It sufficeth in that he is defamed in every place for his adulterous living and all manner of vice; wherefore all such occasion ought to be taken away and his boyish wantonness tied up in the bonds of marriage: he hath chosen a maiden that favoureth him well, and hath bereaved her of her virginity; let him have her still and possess her, and in the embrace of Psyche take his own pleasure.'' Then he turned unto Venus, and said: "And you, my daughter, take you no care, neither fear the dishonour of your progeny and estate, neither have regard in that it is a mortal marriage, for I will see to it that this marriage be not unequal, but just, lawful, and legitimate by the law civil.'' Incontinently after, Jupiter commanded Mercury to bring up Psyche into the palace of heaven. And then he took a pot of immortality, and said: "Hold, Psyche, and drink to the end thou mayest be immortal, and that Cupid may never depart from thee, but be thine everlasting husband.''

'By and by the great banquet and marriage feast was sumptuously prepared. Cupid sat down in the uppermost seat with his dear spouse between his arms: Juno likewise with Jupiter and all the other gods in order: Ganymedes, the rustic boy, his own butler, filled the pot of Jupiter, and Bacchus served the rest: their drink was nectar, the wine of the gods. Vulcanus prepared supper, the Hours decked up the house with roses and other sweet flowers, the Graces threw about balm, the Muses sang with sweet harmony, Apollo turned pleasantly to the harp, fair Venus danced finely to the music, and the entertainment was so ordained that while the Muses sang in quire, Satyrus and Paniscus played on their pipes: and thus Psyche was married to Cupid, and after in due time was delivered of a child, whom we call Pleasure.'

This the trifling and drunken old woman declared to the captive maiden, but I, poor ass, not standing far off, was not a little sorry in that I lacked pen and book to write so worthy a tale; when by and by the thieves came home laden with treasure, and many of them which were of strongest courage being wounded: then (leaving behind such as were lame and hurt to heal and air themselves) said they would return back again to fetch the rest of their pillage which they had hidden in a certain cave. So they snatched up their dinner greedily, and brought forth me and my horse into the way to carry those goods, and beat us before them with staves, and about night (after that we were weary by passing over many hills and dales) we came to a great cave, where they laded us with mighty burdens, and would not suffer us to refresh ourselves any season, but brought us again in our way, and hied very fast homeward; and what with their haste and cruel stripes wherewith they did belabour and drive me, I fell down upon a stone by the highway side. Then they beat me pitifully in lifting me up, hurting my right thigh and my left hoof; and one of them said: 'How long shall we continue to feed this evil-favoured ass that is now also lame?' Another said: 'Since the time we had him first he never did any good, and I think he came into our house with evil luck; for we have had great wounds since, and loss of our valiant captains.' Another said: 'As soon as he has brought unwillingly home his burden, I will surely throw him out upon the mountain to be a prey for vultures.'

While these gentle men reasoned together of my death, we fortuned to come home, for the fear that I was in caused my feet to turn into wings. After that we were discharged of our burdens, they took no account of our needs, nor even of my slaying; they fetched their fellows that lay wounded, and returned again to bring the rest of the things, by reason (as they said) of our great tardiness and slowness by the way. Then was I brought into no small anguish, when I perceived my death prepared before my face, and I communed with myself: 'Why standest thou still, Lucius? Why dost thou look for thy death? Knowest thou not that the thieves have cruelly ordained to slay thee, and they shall find it easy enough? Seest thou not these sharp precipices and pointed flints which shall bruise and tear thee in pieces or ever thou comest to the bottom of them? Thy gentle magician hath not only given thee the shape and travail of an ass, but also a skin so soft and tender as it were of a leech. Why dost thou not take a man's courage and run away to save thy life? Now hast thou the best occasion of flight while the thieves are from home. Art thou afraid of the old woman, which is more than half dead, whom with a stripe of thy heel, though lame, thou mayest easily dispatch? But whither shall I fly? What lodging shall I seek? Behold an assy cogitation of mine; for who is he that passes by the way and will not gladly take up a beast to carry him?'

Then while I devised these things, I broke suddenly the halter wherewith I was tied, and ran away with all my four feet:* howbeit I could not escape the kite's eyes of the old woman, for when she saw me loose she ran after me, and with more audacity than becometh her kind and age, caught me by the halter and thought to pull me home; but I, not forgetting the cruel purposes of the thieves, was moved with small pity, for I kicked her with my hinder heels to the ground. I had well nigh slain her, who (although she were thrown and hurled down) yet held still the halter and would not let me go, but was for some time dragged along the ground by me in my flight. Then she cried with a loud voice and called for succour of some stronger hand, but she little prevailed because there was no person to bring her help, save only the captive gentlewoman, who, hearing the voice of the old woman, came out to see what the matter was and perceived a scene worth telling, a new Dirce† hanging, not to a bull, but to an ass. Then she took a good courage and performed a deed worthy of a man: she wrested the halter out of her hands, and (entreating me with gentle words) stopped me in my flight and got upon my back and drove me to my running again. Then I began to run, both that I might escape and to save the maiden, and she gently kicked me forward, in so much that beneath her frequent urging I seemed to scour away like a horse, galloping with my four feet upon the ground. And when the gentlewoman did speak I would answer her with my braying, and oftentimes (under colour to rub my back) I would turn back my neck and sweetly kiss her tender feet.

Then she, fetching a sigh from the bottom of her heart, lifted up her eyes unto the heavens, saying: 'O sovereign gods, deliver me, if it be your pleasure, from these present dangers; and thou, cruel fortune, cease thy wrath; let the sorrow suffice thee which I have already

* *Quadripedi cursu* seems to be a phrase for galloping, as in modern Greek στὰ τέσσερα.

† Dirce was killed by being tied by her hair to a wild bull in revenge for her similar cruelty to her rival Antiope.

sustained. And thou, little ass, that art the occasion of my safety and liberty, if thou canst once render me safe and sound to my parents, and to that comely one that so greatly desireth to have me to his wife, thou shalt see what thanks I will give thee, with what honour I will reward thee, and how I will feed thee. First I will finely comb thy mane and adorn it with my maiden necklaces, and then I will bravely dress the hair of thy forehead, and tie up thy rugged tail trimly, whose bristles are now ragged and matted by want of care: I will deck thee round about with golden trappings and tassels, in such sort that thou shalt glitter like the stars of the sky, and shalt go in triumph amid the applause of the people: I will bring thee every day in my silken apron the kernels of nuts, and will pamper thee up with dainty delights; I will set store by thee, as by one that is the preserver of my life. Finally, thou shalt lack no manner of thing, and amongst thy glorious fare, thy great ease, and the bliss of thy life, thou shalt not be destitute of dignity, for thou shalt be chronicled perpetually in memory of my present fortune, and the providence divine. All the whole history of this our present flight shall be painted upon the wall of our house: thou shalt be renowned throughout all the world, and this tale (though rude) shall be registered in the books of doctors, how an ass saved the life of a young maiden, a princess, that was a captive amongst thieves. Thou shalt be numbered amongst the ancient miracles: we shall believe by the example of this truth that Phrixus saved himself from drowning upon a ram, Arion escaped upon a dolphin, and that Europa rode upon a bull. If Jupiter transformed himself into a lowing bull, why may it not be that under shape of this ass is hidden the figure of a man, or some power divine?'

While that the virgin did thus mix sorrowful sighs with her hopes and prayers we fortuned to come to a place where three ways did meet, and she took me by the halter and would have me turn on the right hand to her father's house, but I (knowing that the thieves were gone that way to fetch the residue of their pillage) resisted with my head as much as I might, saying within myself: 'What wilt thou do, unhappy maiden? Why wouldest thou go so willingly to Hell? Why wilt thou run into destruction in despite of my feet? Why dost thou seek thine own harm and mine likewise?' And while we two strove together like men striving at law about the division of land, or rather about some right of way, the thieves returned laden with their prey, and perceived us afar off by the light of the moon: and after they had known us they laughed despitefully, and one of them began to say: 'Whither go you so hastily? Be you not afraid of spirits and ghosts of the night? And you (you harlot) do you go to see your parents? Come on, we will bear you company for safety's sake and show you the way to your parents.' And therewithal one took me by the halter and drove me back again, beating me cruelly with a great staff that he had, full of knobs; then I returning against my will to my ready destruction, and remembering the grief of my hoof, began to shake my head and to wax lame, but he that led me by the halter said: 'What, dost thou stumble? Canst thou not go? These rotten feet of thine can run well enough, but they cannot walk; thou couldst mince it finely even now with the gentlewoman, so that thou didst seem to pass the horse Pegasus in swiftness.' In jesting and saying these kindly words they beat me again with a great staff, and when we were come almost home we saw the old woman hanging by a noose upon a bough of a cypress-tree; then one of them cut her down where she hanged, together with her rope, and cast her into the bottom of a great ditch. After this they bound the maiden in chains and fell greedily to their victuals which the miserable old woman had provided for them to eat after she was dead.

Now while they devoured all very gluttonously they began to devise with themselves of our death and how they might be revenged. Divers were the opinions of this divers number, such as might well be in a turbulent company: the first said that he thought best the maid should be burned alive; the second said she should be thrown out to wild beasts; the third said she should be hanged upon a gibbet; the fourth said she should be flayed alive with tortures: certainly was the death of the poor maiden decided by the vote of them all. But one of the thieves did make them all to be silent, and then very quietly speak in this manner: 'It is not convenient unto the oath of our company, nor to the clemency of each person, nor indeed to my own gentleness, to suffer you to wax more cruel than the quality of the offence doth merit; for I would that she should not be hanged, nor burned, nor thrown to wild beasts, nor even that she die any sudden death; but hearken to my counsel, and grant her life, but life according to her desert. You know well what you have determined already of this dull ass, that always eateth more than he is worth, and now who feigneth lameness, and that was the cause and helper of the flying away of the maid. My mind is that he shall be slain tomorrow, and when all the guts and entrails of his body are taken out let the maid, whom he hath preferred to us, be stript and sewn into his belly, so that only her head be without, but the rest of her body be enclosed within the beast. Then let us lay this stuffed ass upon a great stone against the broiling heat of the sun; so they shall both sustain all the punishments which you have ordained: for first the ass shall be slain as he hath deserved; and she shall have her members torn and gnawed with beasts, when she is bitten and rent with worms; she shall endure the pain of the fire, when the broiling heat of the sun shall scorch and parch the belly of the ass; she shall abide the gallows, when the dogs and vultures shall drag out her innermost bowels. I pray you number all the torments which she shall suffer: first, she shall dwell alive within the paunch of the ass; secondly, her nostrils shall receive the carrion stink of the beast; thirdly, she shall die for heat and hunger, and she shall find no means to rid herself from her pains by slaying herself, for her hands shall be sewn up within the skin of the ass.' This being said, all the thieves consented not by their votes* only, but with their whole hearts to the sentence; and when I (poor ass) heard with my great ears and understood all their device I did nothing else save bewail and lament my dead carcass, which should be handled in such sort on the next morrow.

---

* *Lit.* 'by the feet' – a technical term taken from the voting-lobbies of the Senate.

BOOK SEVEN

As soon as the day shone bright and night was past, and the clear chariot of the sun had spread his bright beams on every coast, came one of the company of the thieves (for so his and their greeting did declare); who at his first entry into the cave (after he had breathed himself and was able to speak) told these tidings unto his companions in this sort: 'Sirs, as touching the house of Milo of Hypata, which we forcibly entered and ransacked the last day, we may put away all fear, and doubt nothing at all; for after that you by force and arms had spoiled and taken away all things in the house, and so returned hither unto our cave, I (thrusting in amongst the press of the people and showing myself as though I were sad and sorrowful for the mischance) consulted with them for the bolting out of the matter, whether and how far they would devise for the apprehension of the thieves, to the intent I might learn and see all that was done to make relation thereof unto you, as you willed me. The whole fact at length by manifest and evident proofs, as also by the common opinion and judgement of all the people, was laid to one Lucius' charge, as manifest author of this committed robbery, who, a few days before, by false and forged letters and coloured honesty, had feigned himself to be a true man and had gotten himself so far in favour with this Milo that he entertained him into his house and received him as chief of his familiar friends; which Lucius, after that he had sojourned there a good space, and won the heart of Milo's maid by feigned love, did thoroughly learn the ways and doors of all the house, and curiously viewed the coffers and chests, wherein was laid the whole substance of Milo. Neither was there small cause to judge him culpable, since as the very same night as this robbery was done, he fled away, and could be found in no place, and to the intent he might clean escape and better prevent such as made hue and cry after him, he took his white horse and galloped away. After this his servant was found in the house, who was taken as able to give an information of the felony and escape of his master, and was committed to the common gaol, and the next day following was cruelly scourged and tormented till he was well nigh dead, but he would confess nothing of the matter; and when they could wrest or learn no such thing of him, yet sent they many persons after towards Lucius' country to enquire him out, and so take him prisoner to pay the punishment of that crime.'

As he declared these things, I did greatly lament with myself to think of mine old and pristine estate, and what felicity I was sometimes in, in comparison to the misery that I presently sustained, being changed into a miserable ass. Then had I no small occasion to remember how the old and ancient writers did feign and affirm that fortune was stark blind and without eyes, because she always bestoweth her riches upon evil persons and fools, and chooseth and favoureth no mortal person by judgement, but is always conversant especially with such whom if she could see, she would more shun and forsake; yea, and which is worse, she soweth such diverse or rather contrary opinions in men, that the wicked do glory with the name of good, and contrary the good and innocent be detracted and slandered as evil. Furthermore I, who by her great cruelty was turned into a four-footed ass in most vile and abject manner, yea, and whose estate seemed worthy to be lamented and pitied of the most hard and stony hearts, was accused of theft and robbing of my dear host Milo. This villainy might rather be called parricide than theft, yet might I not defend mine own cause, or deny the fact by any one word, by reason I could not speak; howbeit lest my conscience should seem to accuse me of so base a crime by reason of silence, and again being enforced by impatience, I endeavoured to speak, and fain would have said: 'Never did I do that deed.' And verily the first words, 'Never,' I cried out once or twice somewhat handsomely, but the residue I could in no wise pronounce, but still remaining in one voice cried 'Never; never, never;' though I settled my hanging lips as round as I could to speak the rest of it. But why should I further complain of the cruelty of fortune, since she was not much ashamed to make me a fellow-slave and partner with my servant and my own horse?

While I pondered tempestuously with myself all these things, a greater care came to my remembrance, touching the death which the thieves had devised for me to be an offering to the ghost of the maiden, and still as I looked down to my belly, I thought of the poor gentlewoman that should be closed within me. Then the thief which a little before had brought the false news against me, drew out of the skirt of his coat a thousand gold crowns, which he had rifled away from such as he met, and cast it very honestly, as he said, into the common treasury. Then he carefully enquired how the residue of his companions did, and to him it was declared that the most valiant were murdered and slain in divers manners, but very bravely; whereupon he persuaded them to remit all their affairs a certain season, leaving the highways in peace, and to seek for other fellows to be in their places, that by the exercise of new lads the terror of their martial band might be brought again to the old number; and he assured them that such as were unwilling might be compelled by menaces and threatenings, and such as were willing might be encouraged forward with reward: further, he said that there were some which (seeing the profit which they had) would forsake their base and servile estate and rather be contented to live like tyrants amongst them. Moreover, he declared that for his part he had spoken with a certain tall man, a valiant companion, but of young age, stout in body, and courageous in fight, whom he had advised and at last fully persuaded to exercise his idle hands, dull with long slothfulness, to his greater profit, and, while he might, to receive the bliss of better fortune, and not to hold out his sturdy arms to beg for a penny, but rather to take as much gold and silver as he would. Then everyone consented that he that seemed so worthy to be their companion should be one of their company, and that they would search for others to make up the residue of the number: whereupon he went out, and by and by returning again brought in a tall young man, as he promised, to whom none of the residue might be compared, for he was higher than they by the head, and of more bigness in body, though the down of his beard had but now begun to spread over his cheeks; but he was poorly apparelled with rags of divers clothes sewn ill together, in so much that you might see all his breast and strong belly naked.

As soon as he was entered in, he said: 'God speed ye, soldiers of Mars, and my faithful companions, I pray you make me welcome as one of your band, and I will ensure you that you shall have a man of singular courage and lively audacity, for I had rather receive wounds upon my body than money or gold in my hands; and as for death (which other men do fear) I care nothing at all for it. Yet think you not that I am an abject or a beggar, neither judge you my virtue and prowess by my ragged clothes, for I have been a captain of a great company, and wasted all the country of Macedonia; I am the renowned thief Haemus the Thracian, whose name whole countries and nations do greatly fear: I am the son of Theron the notable thief, nourished with human blood, brought up amongst the stoutest of such a band, and finally I am inheritor and follower of my father's virtues. Yet I lost in a short time all my ancient company and all my riches by one assault which I made, to my hurt, upon a factor of the Prince, which sometime had received a wage of two hundred pounds, but then had been cast down from his rank by fortune. Hearken, and I will tell you the whole matter in order.

'There was a certain man in the Court of the Emperor which had many offices and high renown, and in great favour with the Prince himself, who at last by the envy and cunning of divers persons was banished away and compelled to forsake the Court: but his wife Plotina, a woman of rare faith and singular shamefastness, having borne ten children to her husband to be the foundation of his house, despised all worldly pomp and delicacy of living in cities, and determined to follow her husband, and to be a partaker of all his perils and dangers: wherefore she cut off her hair, disguised herself like a man, and sewed into her girdle much jewellery and treasure, passing through the bands of the soldiers that guarded him and the naked swords without any fear; whereby she shared all his dangers and endured many miseries with the spirit of a man, not of a woman, and was partaker of much affliction to save the life of her husband. And when they had escaped many perilous dangers as well by land as by sea, they went towards Zacynthus to continue there for a time according as fortune had appointed. But when they arrived on the sea-coast of Actium (where we in our return from Macedonia were roving about) when deep night was come they turned into a house, not far distant from the shore and their ship, where they lay all night to escape the tossing of the waves. Then we entered in and took away all their substance, but verily we were in great danger, for the good matron, perceiving us incontinently by the noise of the gate, went into the chamber, and aroused all by her cries, calling up soldiers and servants, every man by his name, and likewise the neighbours that dwelt round about; and it was but by reason of the fear that everyone was in, each one hiding himself, that we hardly escaped away. But this most holy woman, faithful and true to her husband (as the truth must be declared) and a favourite of all for her great worth, returned to Caesar desiring his aid and puissance, and obtained for her husband his soon return and vengeance for the injury done to him. Then willed Caesar that the company of Haemus should not any longer be, and straightway it went to wrack: so great was the authority and word of the Prince. Howbeit when all my band was lost and cut up by search of the Emperor's army, I only stole away and hardly delivered myself from the very jaws of death, in this manner: I clothed myself in a woman's gaudy attire, that flowed into loose and free folds, covering my head with a woven cap, and placing the white and thin shoes of women upon my feet: and thus hidden and changed into the similitude of the worser sex, and mounted upon an ass that carried barley sheaves, passing through the middle of them all, I escaped away, because everyone deemed I was a woman that drove asses, by reason at that time I lacked a beard and my cheeks shone with the colour and smoothness of a boy's. Howbeit I left not off for all this, nor did degenerate from the glory of my father or mine own virtue, though somewhat fearful among the drawn martial swords, yet disguised like a woman I invaded towns and castles alone to get some prey.' And therewithal he pulled out two thousand crowns, by ripping up his ragged coat, saying: 'Hold here this gift, or rather this dowry which I present unto your brotherhood; hold eke my person, which you shall always find trusty and faithful if you shall willingly receive me to be your captain: and I will ensure you that in so doing, within short space I will make and turn this stony house of yours into gold.'

Then by and by everyone consented to make him their captain, and so they gave him a better garment to wear and throw away his old, wherein the gold had been. When he had changed his attire, he embraced them one after another; then placed they him in the highest room of the table, and drank unto him in great cups in token of good luck: and then they began to talk, and declared unto him the going away of the gentlewoman, and how I bare her upon my back, and what horrid death was ordained for us two. Then he asked where she was, whereupon being brought to the place where the gentle-woman was fast bound, whom as soon as he beheld, he turned himself despising and wringing his nose and blamed them, saying: 'I am not so much a beast or so rash a fellow that I would drive you quite from your purpose; but my conscience will not suffer me to conceal anything that toucheth your profit, since I am careful for you; therefore give me your affiance, especially seeing that if my counsel do displease you, you may at your own liberty proceed again in your enterprise to the ass. For I doubt not but all thieves, and such as have a good judgement, will prefer their own lucre and gain above all things in the world, and above their vengeance which may purchase damage both to themselves and to divers other persons. Therefore if you put this virgin in the ass's belly, you shall but execute your indignation against her without all manner of profit: but I would advise you to carry the virgin to some town and to sell her. And such brave girl as she is, and so young, may be sold for great quantity of money: and I myself know certain bawd merchants, amongst whom peradventure someone will give us great sums of gold for her, and will lay her in a brothel equal to her good birth, when she shall not again run away: and so, as bound in slavery to a bawdy-house, you shall have vengeance enough of her. This is my true opinion touching this affair; but advise you what you intend to do, for you may rule me in this case.'

In this manner the good thief pleaded for the thieves' treasury and defended our cause, being a good patron to the hapless virgin and to me poor ass. But they stayed hereupon a good space with long deliberation, which made my heart (God wot) and spirit greatly to quail. Howbeit in the end they consented freely to his opinion, and by and by the maiden was unloosed of her bonds; who, seeing the young man, and hearing the name of brothels and bawd merchants, began to wax joyful, and smiled with herself. Then began I to deem evil of the generation of women, when I saw that the maiden (who had pretended that she had loved a young gentleman, and that she so greatly desired her chaste marriage with the same) was now delighted with the talk of a wicked and filthy brothel-house and other things dishonest. In this sort the consent and manners of all the race of women depended in the judgement of an ass. But then the young man spoke again, saying: 'Masters, why go we not about to make our prayers to Mars touching this selling of the maiden, and seeking for other companions? But as far as I see, here is no manner of beast to make sacrifice withal nor wine sufficient for us to drink. Let me have ten more with me, and we will go to the next town, whence I will bring you back a supper fit for a priest.' So he and ten more with him went their way, and in the mean season the residue made a great fire and an altar with green turfs in the honour of Mars.

By and by they came again, bringing with them bottles of wine and a great number of beasts, amongst which there was a big ram goat, fat, old, and hairy, which they killed and offered unto Mars, to help and be with them. Then supper was prepared sumptuously; and the new companion said unto the others: 'You ought to account me not only your captain in robbery and fight, but also in your pleasures and jollity.' Whereupon by and by with pleasant cheer he prepared all things very cleverly; and trimming up the house he set the table in order and cooked the meal, and brought the pottage and dainty dishes to the table; but above all, he plied them well with great pots and jugs of wine. Sometimes (feigning to fetch somewhat they required) he would go to the maiden and give her pieces of meat which he had privily taken away, and would give her cups of wine whence he had already drunken, which she willingly took in good part. Moreover, he kissed her twice or thrice, whereof she was well pleased, and would gladly kiss him in return again; but I (not well content thereat) thought in myself: 'O wretched maid, hast thou forgotten thy marriage, and thy lover whom thou didst love, thou a virgin maid, and dost esteem this stranger and bloody thief above thy dear husband which thy parents ordained for thee? Now perceive I well thou hast no remorse of conscience, but more delight to do utterly away with thy love and play the harlot here amongst so many weapons and swords. What, knowest thou not how the other thieves, if they knew thy demeanour, would put thee back to the ass's death as they had once appointed, and so work my destruction likewise? Well do now I perceive that thou dost take pleasure and sport at the risk of another's hide.'

While I did devise with myself all these things with an orator's indignation, I perceived by certain signs and tokens (which were doubtful but yet not ignorant to so wise an ass) that he was not the notable thief Haemus, but rather Tlepolemus her husband. For after much communication he began to speak more openly, not fearing any more my presence than if I were dead, and said: 'Be of good cheer, my sweet friend Charite, for thou shalt have by and by all these thy enemies captive unto thee.' Then he filled wine to the thieves more and more, mixed with no water, but a little warmed, and never ceased till they were all overcome and soaked with abundance of drink, whereas he himself abstained and bridled his own appetite: and truly, I did greatly suspect that he had mingled in their cups some deadly poison, for incontinently they all fell down asleep on the ground one after another, drowned and overcome by the wine, and lay as though they had been dead. Then did he very easily tie them all in chains and bind them as he would, and he took the maiden and set her upon my back and went homeward.

Now when we were near come home, all the people of the city (especially her parents and kinsmen, friends and family and servants) came running forth joyfully; and all they of the town of every age and sex gathered together to see this new sight and strange, a virgin in great triumph sitting upon an ass.* Then I (not willing to show less joy than the rest, as far as I might as present occasion served) set and pricked up my long ears, blew out my nostrils, and cried stoutly; nay rather I made the town to ring again with my shrilling sound. When we were come to her father's house she was received into a chamber honourably, and her parents tended her well; as for me, Tlepolemus, with a great number of other citizens, did drive me back again with other horses to the cave of the thieves, and I was not very unwilling, for I much desired to be present to see the taking of them. There we found them all asleep, lying on the ground as we left them, overcome rather by wine than by bonds: and then they first brought out all the gold and silver and other treasures of the house and laded us withal: which when they had done, they threw many of the thieves down into the bottom of deep cliffs hard by, and the residue they slew with their own swords.

After this we returned home glad and merry of so great vengeance upon them, and the riches which we carried was committed to the public treasury, and this done the maid was married to Tlepolemus, according to the law, whom by so much travail he had valiantly recovered. Then my good mistress looked about for me, calling me her saviour and deliverer, and asking for me, commanded, the very same day as her marriage, that my manger should be filled with barley, and that I should have hay and oats abundantly, as much as would be enough for a camel of Bactria. But how greatly and worthily did I curse Fotis in that she had transformed me into an ass,

* It has been supposed, perhaps without very much reason, that Apuleius intended this to be a parody of our Saviour's Palm Sunday entry into Jerusalem. See note on Book IX, ch. 14.

and not into a dog, because I saw the dogs had filled their paunches to bursting with the relics and bones of so worthy a supper as they had. The next day, after that best of nights and her learning of the secrets of Venus, this new wedded woman (my mistress) did not forget to commend me before her parents and husband for the kindness I had showed unto her, and never left off until such time as they promised to reward me with great honours. Then they called together all their friends of more dignity, to resolve in what manner it were most worthy to reward me; and thus it was concluded: one said that I should be closed in a stable and never work, but continually be fed and fatted with fine and chosen barley and beans and vetch; howbeit another prevailed, who wished my liberty, for me to run lasciviously in the fields amongst the horses, whereby I might mount the mares and engender upon them some stout mules for my mistress. Therefore the groom that kept the horses was called for, and I was delivered unto him with great care, in so much that I ran before him right pleasant and joyous, because I hoped that I should carry no more fardels or burdens: moreover I thought that when I should thus be at liberty, in the springtime of the year, when the meadows and fields were green, I should find some roses in some place; after which it came into my mind that if my master and mistress did render to me so many thanks and honours being an ass, they would much more reward me being turned into a man. But when he (to whom the charge of me was so straitly committed) had brought me a good way distant from the city I perceived no delicate meats nor any liberty which I should have, but by and by his covetous wife and most cursed quean made me a mill ass, and (beating me with a cudgel with many twigs) would wring bread for herself and her household out of my skin. Yet was she not contented to weary me and make me a drudge with carriage and grinding of her own corn, but she made me to grind for her neighbours and so earned more gain by my toil: nor would she give me such meat as it was ordained that I should have, for all my miserable labours, for my own barley which I ground in that same mill by my own goings about she would sell to the inhabitants by, and after that I had laboured all day upon this engine of toil, she would set before me at night a little filthy bran, nothing clean but caked together and full of stones.

Being crushed down by this calamity, yet cruel fortune worked me other new torments, so that (as they say) I might verily boast of a full reward for all my brave deeds done at home and abroad: for on a day I was let loose into the fields to pasture with the herds of horses by commandment of my master, who so did at last obey his lord's bidding. O how I leaped for joy, how I brayed to see myself in such liberty, but especially since I beheld so many mares, which I thought should be my easy wives and concubines! But this my joyful hope turned into utter destruction, for incontinently all the stallion horses, which were well fed and made strong for their duty by ease of pasture, terrible in any case and much more puissant than a poor ass, were jealous over me, and feared for the cuckolding of their race by a weakling, and (not having regard to the law and order of the hospitable god Jupiter) ran fiercely and terribly against me their rival; one reared up his broad chest and high head, and lifted up his fore feet and kicked me spitefully, another turned to me his strong and brawny back, and with his hinder heels spurned me cruelly, the third threatening with a malicious neighing dressed his ears, and showing his sharp and white teeth bit me on every side. In like sort have I read in histories how before the king of Thrace* would throw his miserable guests to be torn in pieces and devoured of his wild horses; so niggish was that tyrant of his provender that he nourished his hungry and starveling beasts with the bodies of men.

After the same manner I was cruelly handled by the horses, so that I longed for the mill again whereby I went round and round; but behold fortune (insatiable of my torments) had devised a new pain for me. I was appointed to bring home wood every day from a high hill, and who should drive me thither and home again but a boy that was the veriest hangman in all the world: he was not contented with the great travail I took in climbing up the steep hill, neither that my hoofs were torn and worn away by sharp flints, but he beat me cruelly and very often with a great staff, in so much that the marrow of my bones did ache for woe; for he would strike me continually in my right hip and still in one place, whereby he tare my skin and made of my wide sore a great hole or trench, or rather a window to look out at, and although it ran down of blood, yet would he not cease beating me in that place. Moreover he laded me with such great trusses and burdens of wood that you would think they had rather been prepared for

* Diomede, king of the Bistones in Thrace. His final destruction was one of the twelve labours of Hercules.

elephants than for an ass, and when he perceived that my wood hanged more of one side than another (when he should rather take away the heavy sides and so ease me, or else lift them up a little, or at least put them over to make them equal with the other) he laid great stones upon the lighter side to remedy the matter. Yet could he not be contented with this my great misery and immoderate burdens of wood, but when we came to any river by the way, he, to save his boots from water, would leap upon my loins likewise, which was no small load upon load. And if by adventure I had fallen down in any dirty or miry place by the water-side, on the slippery bank, under that load too great for me to bear, when he should have lent a hand to pull me out, or lifted me out by the bridle or by my tail, or taken off some of my load so that I might be able to rise, he would never help me, but laid me on from top to toe, yea, from my very ears, with a mighty staff, whereby I was compelled by force of the blows, as by a medicine, to stand up. The same hangman boy did invent another torment for me: he gathered a great many sharp thorns, as sharp as needles and of most poisonous prick, and bound them with knots into a bundle which he tied at my tail to prick me, so that as I walked they would swing against me and wound me sorely with their accursed spikes. Then was I afflicted on either side; for when I endeavoured to run away from his bitter onslaughts the thorns pricked me more vehemently, and if I stood still to rest from the pain the boy beat me until I ran again, whereby I perceived that the hangman did devise nothing else save to kill me by some manner of means, and even so he would often swear and threaten to do. And in truth there was some occasion to stir his malicious mind into worse attempts; for upon a day (after my patience had been altogether overcome by his wickedness) I lifted up my heels and spurned him well-favouredly. Then he invented this vengeance against me: after he had well laded me with tow and flax, and had trussed it round safely with ropes upon my back, he brought me out into the way: then he stole a burning coal out of a man's house of the next village and put it into the middle of the load, and soon the fire caught and increased in the dry and light matter and burst into flames, and the fierce heat thereof did burn me on every side; and I could see no remedy for my utter destruction, nor how I might save myself, and in such a burning it was not possible for me to stand still, and there was no time to advise better; but fortune was favourable towards me in my misfortune, perhaps to reserve me for more dangers; at least she saved me from the present death thus devised, for I espied a great hole full of muddy rain-water that fell the day before; thither I ran hastily and plunged myself therein, in such sort that I quenched the fire and was delivered both from my load and from that peril. But the vile boy turned even this his most wicked deed upon me, and declared to all the shepherds about that I willingly leaped over a fire of the neighbours and tumbled in it and set myself afire. Then he laughed upon me, saying: 'How long shall we keep this fiery ass in vain?'

A few days after, this boy invented another mischief much worse than the former: for when he had sold all the wood which I bare to certain men dwelling in a village by, he led me homeward unladen. And then he cried that he was not able to rule me, for that he was unequal to my naughtiness, and that he would not drive me to the hill any longer for wood, saying: 'Do you see this slow and dull beast, too much an ass? Now, besides all the mischiefs that he hath wrought already, he inventeth daily more and more. For when he espieth any passing by the way, whether it be a fair woman or a maid ready for marriage, or a young boy, he will throw his burden from his back, yea, and often break his very girths, and runneth fiercely upon them and, a lover of such sort as you see, he assails humans. And after that he hath thrown them down, he casts desirous eyes upon them and essays forbidden and unheard of acts of bestial lust and invites them to a union from which love's goddess is averse. Moreover, he will feign as though he would kiss them with his great and wicked mouth, but he will bite their faces cruelly, which thing may work us great displeasure, or rather be imputed unto us as a crime; and even now, when he espied an honest maiden passing by the highway, he by and by threw down his wood in a heap and aimed upon her a frenzied assault; and when this jolly lover had thrown her upon the ground, he would have ravished her before the face of all the world, had it not been that by reason of her crying out with shrieks and loud lamentations, she was succoured of those that passed by, and pulled from his heels and so delivered. And if it had so come to pass that this fearful maiden had been slain by him by a painful death, what danger had we not been in?'

By these and like lies, he provoked the shepherds earnestly to my destruction, which grieved me (God wot) full sore that I could say nothing to defend my chastity. Then one of the shepherds said: 'Why

do we not make sacrifice of this common adulterous ass as his horrid
doings deserve? My son,' quoth he, 'Let us kill him and throw his
guts to the dogs, and reserve his flesh for the labourers' supper. Then
let us cast dust upon his skin, and carry it home to our master, and
easily feign that the wolves have devoured him.' The boy that was
my evil accuser made no delay, but prepared himself to execute the
sentence of the shepherd, rejoicing at my present danger, and
thinking upon the kick which I gave him; but oh how greatly did I
then repent that the stripe of my heel had not killed him! Then he
drew out his sword, and made it sharp upon a whetstone to slay me,
but another of the shepherds began to say: 'Verily it is a great offence
to kill so fair an ass, and go (by accusation of luxury and lascivious
wantonness) to lack so necessary his labour and service, where
otherwise if you would cut off his stones, he might not only be
deprived of the prick of his lust, but also become gentle, and that we
should be delivered from all fear of danger. Moreover, he would be
thereby more fat and better in flesh. For I know myself as well many
slow asses, as also most fierce horses, that by reason of their
wantonness have been most mad and terrible, but (when they were
gelded and cut) they have become very gentle and tame, and tractable
both to bearing burdens and to all other use. Wherefore I would
counsel you to geld him; and if you consent thereto, I will by and by,
when I have gone to the next market, fetch from my house mine
irons and tools for the purpose: and I will thence immediately return,
and I assure you that after I have gelded and cut off his stones, I will
deliver this fierce and rude lover unto you as tame as a lamb.'

When I did perceive that I was delivered from death, but reserved
for the pain of gelding, I wept that with the hinder part of my body I
should perish altogether, but I sought about to kill myself by some
manner of means, whether by fasting continually or by throwing
myself down some crag or precipice, to the end if I should die, I
would die with unperished members: and while I devised with
myself in what manner I might end my life, the rope-ripe boy my
destroyer on the next morrow led me to the hill again, and tied me to
a bough of a great oak, and in the mean season he took his hatchet
and went a little way up and cut wood to load me withal. But behold
there crept out of a cave by a marvellous great bear holding out his
mighty head; whom when I saw, I was suddenly stricken in fear with
the sudden sight and (throwing all the strength of my body into my

hinder heels) lifted up my strained head and broke the halter wherewith I was tied. Then there was no need to bid me run away, for I scoured not only on foot, but tumbled over the stones and rocks with my body, till I came into the open fields beneath, to the intent I would escape away from the terrible bear, but especially from the boy that was worse than the bear.

Then a certain stranger that passed by the way (espying me alone as a stray ass) took me up quickly and rode upon my back, beating me with a staff which he bare in his hand through a blind and unknown lane: whereat I was little displeased, but willingly went forward to avoid the cruel pain of gelding which the shepherds had ordained for me, but as for the stripes I was nothing moved, since I was accustomed to be beaten so every day. But fortune, ever bent on my ruin, would not suffer me to continue in such estate long, but with wondrous quickness undid my timely escape and set a new snare for me: for the shepherds (looking about for a cow that they had lost), after they had sought in divers places, fortuned to come upon us unawares; who when they espied and knew me, they would have taken me by the halter, but he that rode upon my back valiantly resisted them, saying: 'Good Lord, masters, what intend you to do? Will you rob me?' Then said the shepherds: 'What, thinkest thou that we handle thee otherwise than thou deservest, which art stealing away our ass? Why dost thou not rather tell us where thou hast hidden the boy that led him, whom thou hast doubtless slain?' And therewithal they pulled him down to the ground, beating him with their fists and spurning him with their feet. Then he swore unto them saying that he saw no manner of boy, but only found the ass loose and straying abroad, which he took up to the intent he might have some reward for the finding of him, and to restore him again to his master. 'And I would to God,' quoth he, 'That this ass (which I would verily I had never seen) could speak as a man, to give witness of my innocence: then would you be ashamed of the injury which you have done to me.'

Thus reasoning for himself, he nothing prevailed, for those angry shepherds tied a rope about his neck and led him back again through the trees of the hill to the place where the boy accustomed to resort for wood. And after that they could discover him in no place, at length they found his body rent and torn in pieces, and his members dispersed in divers places, which I well knew was done by the cruel bear, and verily I would have told it if I might have spoken; but (which I could only do) I greatly rejoiced at the vengeance of his death, although it came too late. Then they gathered the pieces of his body and hardly joined them together and buried them, and straightway they laid all the fault to him that was my Bellerophon,* charging him that it was he that took me up by the way, and had assaulted and slain the boy, and (bringing him home fast bound to their houses) purposed on the next morrow to accuse him of murder, and to lead him before the justices to have judgement of death. In the mean season, while the parents of the boy did lament and weep for the death of their son, the shepherd (according to his promise) came with his instruments and tools to geld me, and then one of them said: 'Tush, our present mischief is not of his doing, but now we are contented that tomorrow not only this vile ass's stones shall be cut off, but also his head, and you shall not lack helpers.'

So was it brought to pass that my death was delayed till the next morrow; but what thanks did I give to that good boy who at least (being so slain) was the cause of my pardon for one short day! Howbeit I had no time then to rest myself, for the mother of the boy, weeping and lamenting for his cruel death, attired in mourning vesture, tore her hair and threw ashes upon it, and beat her breast, crying and howling very bitterly, and came presently into the stable, saying: 'Is it reason that this careless beast should do nothing all day but hold his head in the manger, filling and bolling his guts with meat, without compassion of my great misery or remembrance of his slain master? Surely, contemning my age and infirmity, he thinketh that I am unable to revenge his great mischiefs. Moreover he would persuade me that he were not culpable; indeed it agreeth with the manner of malefactors to hope for safety, even when as the conscience doth confess the offence: but, O good Lord, thou cursed beast, if thou couldest for the nonce utter the contents of thine own mind, whom (if he were the veriest fool in all the world) mightest thou persuade that this murder was void or without thy fault, when it lay in thy power either to keep off the thieves from this poor boy with thy heels or else to bite and tear them with thy teeth? Couldest not thou (that so oft in his lifetime didst spurn and kick him) defend

---

* By calling his rider Bellerophon (which Adlington merely translated 'my new master'), the ass implies that he was a very Pegasus.

him now from his death by like means? Yet at least thou shouldest have taken him upon thy back, and so brought him from the cruel hands of thieves, where contrary thou rannest away alone, having forsaken and cast down thy fellow-servant, thy good master, thy pastor and conductor. Knowest thou not that even such as deny their wholesome help and aid to them which are in danger of death, are wont to be punished because they have offended against good manners and the law natural? But I promise thee that thou shalt not long rejoice at my harms, thou murderer; I will ensure thee thou shalt feel the smart of my grief, and I will see what nature can do.' Therewithal she unloosed her apron, and bound all my feet together to the end I might not help myself in my punishment: then she took a great bar which accustomed to bar the stable door, and never ceased beating of me till she was so exceeding weary and tired that the bar fell out of her hands: whereupon she (complaining of the soon faintness of her arms) ran to the fire and brought a glowing firebrand and thrust it under my tail, burning me continually till such time as (having but one remedy) I all bewrayed her face and eyes with my dirty dung; whereby, what with the stink thereof, and what with the filthiness that fell in her eyes, she was well nigh blind, and so I enforced the quean to leave off; otherwise I had died as an ass as Meleager did by the stick, which his mad mother Althea* cast into the fire.

* Ovid, *Metamorphoses*, viii, 451:

> There was a certain firebrand which, when Oeneus' wife did lie
> In childbed of Meleager, she chanced to espy
> The Destinies putting in the fire: and, in the putting in,
> She heard them speak these words, as they his fatal thread did spin:
> 'O lately born, like time we give to thee and to this brand':
> And when they so had spoken, they departed out of hand.
> Immediately the mother caught the blazing bough away
> And quenched it. This bough she kept full charily many a day:
> And in the keeping of the same she kept her son alive.

But when she heard that Meleager had killed her brothers as the result of a quarrel about the spoils of the Calydonian boar, she threw the brand on the fire, thus causing his death.

BOOK EIGHT

About the cockcrow of night came a young man from the next city, which seemed to be one of the family of the good woman Charite which sometime endured so much misery and calamity with me amongst the thieves; who, after that he had taken a stool and sat down by the fireside in the company of the servants, began to declare many terrible things that had happened unto Charite and unto her house, saying: 'O ye horsekeepers, shepherds, and cowherds, you shall understand that we have lost our good mistress Charite miserably and by evil adventure, but not alone did she go down to the ghosts. But to the end you may learn and know the whole matter, I purpose to tell you the circumstance of every point, whereby such as are more learned than I, to whom fortune has ministered more copious style, may paint it out in paper in form of an history.

'There was a young gentleman dwelling in the next city, born of good parentage, valiant in prowess, and rich in substance, but very much given and addict to whore-hunting and continual revelling by broad day: whereby he fell in company with thieves, and had his hand ready to the effusion of human blood; and his name was Thrasyllus. The matter was this according to the report of every man: when Charite had come to an age ripe for marriage, he was among the chiefest of her suitors and very ardently sought her hand; but although he were a man more comely than the residue that wooed her, and also had riches abundantly to persuade her parents, yet because he was of evil fame, and a man of wicked manners and conversation, he had the repulse and was put off by Charite. And so our master's daughter married with Tlepolemus; howbeit this young man secretly cherished his downfallen love, and moved somewhat at her refusal, he busily searched some means to work his damnable intent: and so (having found occasion and opportunity to present himself there) he girt himself for the evil purpose which he had long time concealed; and so he brought it to pass, that the same day that

Charite was delivered by the subtle means and valiant audacity of her husband from the puissance of the thieves, he mingled himself amongst the assembly, feigning with a notable show that he was glad above all others of the new marriage and of the hope of future offspring. Hereby (by reason that he came of so noble parents) he was received and entertained into the house as a chief guest, and falsely coloured himself to be one of their most principal friends: and so, under cloak of a faithful well-wisher, he dissimuled his mischievous mind and intent. In continuance of time, by much familiarity and often conversation and banqueting together, he was taken more and more in favour: then did he fall little by little and unawares into the deeper gulf of lust and desire. What wonder indeed? Like as we see it fortuneth to lovers, who are at first delighted by the flame of cruel love, when as it is small, until by continual feeding of it with the fuel of use and wont, it gloweth and flameth and altogether burneth them up.

'Thrasyllus had long pondered within himself, perceiving that it was a hard matter to break his mind secretly to Charite, and that he was wholly barred from accomplishment of his luxurious appetite both by the multitude of her guards and servitors, and because the love of her and her husband was so strongly linked together that the bond between them might in no wise be dissevered; and moreover it was a thing impossible to ravish her, because even if she would, although she would not, she knew nothing of the arts of deceiving a spouse. Yet was he still provoked forward by an obstinate madness to that very thing which he could not, as though he could. At length the thing which seemeth so hard and difficult, when love has been fortified through time, doth ever at last appear easy and facile; but mark, I pray you, diligently, to what end the furious force of his inordinate desire came.

On a day Tlepolemus went to the chase with Thrasyllus to hunt for wild beasts, but only for goats – if indeed goats be wild beasts – for his wife Charite desired him earnestly to meddle with no other beasts which were of more fierce and wild nature, armed with tusk or horn. When they were come within the chase to a great thicket on a hill, fortressed about with briars and thorns, they compassed round the goats, which had been spied out by trackers; and by and by warning was given to let loose the dogs, that had been bred of a noble stock, to rout up the beasts from their lairs. They, remembering all their careful teaching, spread out and covered every entry; and first they did not give tongue, but when on a sudden the signal was given they rushed in with such a cry that all the forest rang again with the noise; but behold there leaped out no goat, nor timid deer, nor hind, most gentle of all beasts, but an horrible and dangerous wild boar, such as no one had seen before, thick with muscles and brawn, with a filthy and hairy hide, his bristles rising along his pelt, foaming at the mouth, grinding his teeth; looking direfully with fiery eyes, and rushing like lightning as he charged with his furious jaws. The dogs that first set upon him he tare and rent with his tusks, and rifled them up and hurled them away on every side, and then he ran quite through the nets that had checked his first charges and escaped away. When we saw the fury of this beast, we were all greatly stricken with fear, and because we never accustomed to chase such dreadful boars, and further because we were unarmed and without weapons, we got and hid ourselves under bushes and trees.

'Then Thrasyllus, having found opportunity to work his treason, said to Tlepolemus: "What, stand we here amazed? Why show we ourselves like these slaves of ours, or why leave we so worthy a prey to go forth from our very hands, despairing like some timid woman? Let us mount upon our horses and pursue him incontinently: take you a hunting javelin, and I will take a spear"; and by and by they leaped upon their horses and followed the beast earnestly. But he, forgetting not his natural strength, returned against them burning with the fire of his wild nature, and gnashing his teeth, pried with his eyes on whom he might first assail with his tusks: and Tlepolemus struck the beast first on the back with his javelin. But Thrasyllus attacked not the beast, but came behind and cut the hamstrings of the hinder legs of Tlepolemus' horse, in such sort that he fell down in much blood to the ground and threw despite his will his master: then suddenly the boar came upon Tlepolemus, and furiously tare and rent first his garments and then him with his teeth as he would rise. Howbeit, his friend Thrasyllus did not repent of his wicked deed to see him thus wounded, nor was it enough for his cruelty only to look: but when he was gored and essayed to protect his fresh wounds from the heavy blows, and desired his friendly help, he thrust Tlepolemus through the right thigh with his spear, the more boldly because he thought the wound of the spear would be taken for a wound of the boar's teeth: then he easily killed the beast likewise.

And when the young man was thus miserably slain, every one of us came out of our holes, and went sorrowfully towards our slain master. But although that Thrasyllus was joyful of the death of Tlepolemus, whom he did greatly hate, yet he cloaked the matter with a sorrowful countenance, he feigned a dolorous face, he often embraced the body which he himself slew, he played all the parts of a mourning person, saving there fell no tears from his eyes. Thus he resembled us in each point (who verily, and not without occasion, had cause to lament for our master) laying all the blame of this homicide unto the boar.

'Incontinently after, the sorrowful news of the death of Tlepolemus came to the ears of all the family, but especially to unhappy Charite, who, when she had heard such pitiful tidings, as a mad and raging woman ran up and down the streets and the country fields, crying and howling lamentably. All the citizens gathered together, and such as met her bare her company running towards the chase, so that all the city was emptied to see the sight. When they met the slain body of Tlepolemus, Charite threw herself upon him, weeping and lamenting grievously for his death, in such sort that she would have presently ended her life upon the corpse of her slain husband, whom she so entirely loved, had it not been that her parents and friends did comfort her, and hardly pulled her away. Then the body was taken up, and in funeral pomp brought to the city, and buried.

'In the mean season Thrasyllus feigned much sorrow for the death of Tlepolemus, crying and beating his breast beyond all measure, but in his heart he was well pleased and joyful, and the tears that he had not for his former grief were ready to come now for his gladness. And to counterfeit very truth by words of kindness, he would come to Charite and say: "O what a loss have I had, by the death of my friend, my fellow, my companion, my brother Tlepolemus" (adding the name in a melancholy voice). "O Charite, comfort yourself, pacify your dolour, refrain your weeping, beat not your breasts." And so saying, he would hold her hands and restrain them, so that she might not beat her bosom: with soft words he would blunt the sting of her sorrow, and with divers examples of evil fortune he endeavoured to comfort her; but he spake and did not this for any other intent but that in guise of friendship he might closely handle the woman, and so nourish his odious love with filthy delight. Howbeit, Charite, after the burial of her husband, sought the means to follow him, and tried every way, but especially that which is most gentle and easy, nor requireth any weapon, but is most like to quiet sleep: for she purposed to finish her life with starvation and neglecting herself, she buried herself deep in the darkness and had done with the light for good and all. But Thrasyllus was very importunate, and at length brought to pass that at the intercession both of himself and of the friends and familiars, and last of the parents of Charite, she somewhat refreshed her body, that was all befouled and well nigh broken, with refection of meat and bathing. Howbeit, she did it unwillingly, more at the commandment of her parents and the duty she owed to them, than for anything else: and she wore a calmer, but yet not a merry face, while she went about the duties of the living, but inwardly she tormented herself very greatly with grief and mourning: she spent whole days and nights in miserable longing, and there was an image of her husband, which she had made like unto Bacchus, unto which she rendered divine honours and services, so that she grieved herself even by her consolation.

'In the mean season Thrasyllus, not being able to refrain any longer, a man bold and impatient according to the signification of his name,* before Charite had assuaged her dolours with tears, before her troubled mind had pacified her fury, before her grief had become less from its own abundance and long continuance, while she wept for her husband, while she tare her garments and rent her hair, doubted not to demand her in marriage, and so very rashly detected the secrets and unspeakable deceits of his heart. But Charite detested and abhorred his demand, and as she had been stricken with some clap of thunder, with some storm, or with the lightning of Jupiter, she presently fell down to the ground all amazed with a cloud. Howbeit in the end, when her spirits were revived and that she returned to herself crying and shrieking like some beast, remembering all that had passed with the wicked Thrasyllus, she demanded respite to deliberate and to take advice on the matter.

'In the mean season of delay the shape of Tlepolemus that was slain so miserably appeared to Charite as she chastely slept, with a pale and bloody face, saying: "O my sweet wife (a name which no other person shall say but I), even if the memory of me in thy heart groweth dim, or the remembrance faileth of my pitiful death, in so

---

* Thrasyllus is derived from the Greek θρασύς, venturous, bold, rash.

much that our bond of love hath been severed, marry happily with any other person, so that you marry not with the traitor Thrasyllus; have no conference with him, eat not with him, lie not with him; avoid the bloody hand of mine enemy, let not thy marriage be begun with parricide.* For those wounds, the blood whereof thy tears did wash away, were not all the wounds of the teeth of the boar, but the spear of wicked Thrasyllus parted me from thee.' Thus spoke Tlepolemus unto his loving wife, and declared the whole residue of the damnable fact. But Charite lay as she had first fallen asleep, with her face buried in her pillow; now she wetted her cheeks with her welling tears: and now aroused as by some new anguish, she began to cry aloud as if she renewed her dolour, to tear her garments, and to beat her comely arms with her furious hands: howbeit she revealed the vision which she saw to no manner of person, but dissembling that she knew the truth of the mischief, devised silently with herself how she might be revenged on the wicked murderer, and finish her own life, to end and knit up all sorrow. Again came Thrasyllus the detestable demander of the pleasure that should betray him, and wearied the closed ears of Charite with talk of marriage; but she, gently refusing his communication, and colouring the matter with passing craft in the midst of his earnest desires and humble prayers, began to say: "Thrasyllus, you shall understand that yet the comely face of your brother† and my husband is always before mine eyes; I smell yet the cinnamon scent of his precious body, I yet feel Tlepolemus alive in my heart: wherefore you shall do well if you grant to me, miserable woman, necessary time to bewail his death, until after the residue of a few months the whole year may be expired, which thing toucheth as well my shame as your wholesome profit, lest peradventure by our speedy and quick marriage we should justly raise and provoke the resentful spirit of my husband to work your destruction."

'Howbeit Thrasyllus was not contented with this speech, nor even cheered by her hopeful promise, but more and more was earnest

---

* Parricide had in Roman legal phraseology a much wider sense than the English word. The murder of a free man, or any assassination or treachery, was called parricidal; and a woman's marriage with her husband's murderer would be in the same category.

† Brother-in-arms, fellow, comrade, as in ch. 7 above.

upon her, to whisper wickedly in her ear with his busy tongue, in so much that she was enforced to seem conquered by him, and to speak to him in this manner: "My friend Thrasyllus, this one thing must thou grant to my earnest prayers, that we should take our pleasure in such sort and so secret, that no servant of the house may perceive it until the whole year be complete and finished." Then Thrasyllus, trusting the false promises of the woman, consented gladly to her secret embraces, and was joyful in his heart and looked for night, when as he might have his purpose, preferring his inordinate pleasure above all things in the world. "But come you quietly about midnight," said Charite, "Covered up and disguised without all company. And do but hiss at my chamber-door, and await; my nurse shall attend sitting before the barrier for thy coming. Then shall she let thee in, and bring thee without any light, that might betray us, to my sleeping-room."

'This counsel of fatal marriage pleased Thrasyllus marvellously; who, suspecting no harm, and in a turmoil of expectation, did always complain that the day was long and the evening came not: but when at last the sun gave way to the night, according to Charite's commandment he disguised himself and went straight, full of hope, to her chamber, where he found the nurse attending for him with feigned diligence. She (by the appointment of her mistress) fed him with flattering talk, brought silently cups and a flagon, and gave him drink mingled and doled with sleepy drugs, excusing the absence of her mistress Charite by reason that she attended on her father being sick, until such time that with sweet talk and operation of the wine (for he drank greedily and suspected nothing) he fell in a sound sleep. Now when he lay prostrate on the ground ready to all attack, Charite (being called for) came in, and with manly courage and bold force stood over this sleeping murderer, saying: "Behold the faithful companion of my husband, behold this valiant hunter, behold my dear spouse; this is the hand which shed my blood, this is the heart which hath devised so many subtle means to work my destruction, these be the eyes whom I have pleased to my ill: behold how in a manner they foreshowed their own destined punishment when they prayed for the darkness to come. Sleep careless, dream that thou art in the hands of the merciful, for I will not hurt thee with thy sword or with any other weapon; God forbid that I should make thee equal to my husband by a like death. But thy eyes shall fail thee still living, and

thou shalt see no more save when thou dreamest: I will see to it that
thou shalt think the death of thine enemy more sweet than thy life: of
a surety thou shalt have no delight, thou shalt lack the aid of a leader,
thou shalt not have me as thou hopest, thou shalt have no delight of
my marriage, thou shalt have no rest in the quiet of death, and yet
living thou shalt have no joy, but wander between the light of day
and the darkness of hell as an unsure image: thou shalt seek the hand
that pricked out thy eyes, yet shalt thou not know (the most grievous
part in all calamity) of whom thou shouldst complain: I will make
libation with the blood of thine eyes upon the grave of my husband, I
will pacify his holy shade with these eyes of thine. But why dost thou
gain respite of thy due torment through my delay? Perhaps thou
dreamest that thou embracest me in thine arms to thine own ruin:
leave off the darkness of sleep, and awake thou to receive a penal
deprivation of light: lift up thy sightless face, regard thy vengeance
and evil fortune, reckon thy misery: so pleaseth thine eyes to a chaste
woman, so have the nuptial torches lightened thy couch, that thou
shalt have the Furies to be women of thy bedchamber, blindness to
be thy companion, and an everlasting prick of remorse to thy
miserable conscience."

'When she had prophesied in these words, she took a great needle
from her head and pricked out both his eyes: which done, leaving
him blind and waking in great pain (though he knew not whence it
came) from his drunkenness and sleep, she by and by caught the
naked sword which her husband Tlepolemus accustomed to wear,
and ran throughout all the city like a mad woman towards the
sepulchre of her husband, doubtless bent on some wild purpose.
Then we with all the citizens left our houses and ran incontinently
after her, exhorting each other to take the sword out of her furious
hands; but she, clasping about the tomb of Tlepolemus, kept us off
with her naked weapon, and when she perceived that every one of us
wept and lamented, she spake in this sort: "I pray you, my friends, let
there be no unasked tears for me nor laments unworthy of my
courage, for I am revenged of the death of my husband, I have
punished deservedly the wicked breaker of our marriage;* now is it

* The Latin can also (and perhaps better) bear the meaning of 'the robber
of my marriage' in the sense of one who would force her to marry him by
fraud or violence.

time to seek out with this sword the way to my sweet Tlepolemus."
And therewithal, after she had made relation of the whole matter
which was declared unto her by the vision of her husband which she
saw, and told by what means she deceived Thrasyllus, thrusting the
sword under her right breast and wallowing in her own blood, she
babbled some uncertain words and at length with manly courage
yielded up the ghost. Then immediately the friends of miserable
Charite did wash carefully her body and bury her within the same
sepulchre with Tlepolemus to be his spouse for ever. Thrasyllus,
hearing all the matter, and knowing that by no death he could fitly
atone for this present ruin, for he thought his sword was not sufficient
to revenge so great a crime, at length went of himself to the same
sepulchre, and cried with a loud voice, saying: "O ye dead spirits
whom I have so highly offended, receive me; behold I make sacrifice
unto you with my body": which said he closed the doors of the
sepulchre upon him, purposing to famish himself, and so finish his life
there and yield up his accursed ghost in sorrow.'

These things the young man with pitiful sighs and tears declared
unto the cowherds and shepherds, which caused them all to weep;
but they, fearing to become subject unto new masters, and pitying
deeply the misery of their master's house, prepared themselves to
depart away; but by and by the horsekeeper, to whom the charge of
me so carefully had been committed, brought forth all the precious
things that were stored in his cottage, and laded me and other horses
withal, and so departed thence from his former place: we bare
women, children, pullets, geese, kids, whelps, and other things which
were not able to keep pace with us, which so travelled upon our feet.
As for that which I bare upon my back, although it was a mighty
burden, yet seemed it but light because I was very glad to depart and
leave him that most terribly had appointed to geld me.

When we had passed over a great mountain full of trees and were
come again into the open fields, behold we approached nigh to a fair
and rich castle, where it was told unto us that we were not able to
pass in our journey that night, nay, nor in the early morning either,
by reason of the great number of terrible wolves which were in the
country about, besieging all the roads; so great in their body and
fierce and cruel, that they put every man in fear, in such sort that they
would invade and set upon such which passed by like thieves, and
devour them and their beasts: and sometimes they would be mad

with hunger and would attack the country-farms that lay hard by, and that the same death as of the peaceful cattle would await the men therein. Moreover, we were advertised that there lay in the way where we should pass many dead bodies, half eaten and torn with wolves, and their inward flesh was all torn away and the white of their bones was everywhere to be seen. Wherefore we were willed to use all caution in our going, and to observe this above all, that in broad light, when the day was well on and the sun was high, and the fierceness of such horrible beasts was constrained by the light, to go close and round together, avoiding all hidden lairs, whereby we might pass and escape all perils and dangers. But (notwithstanding this good counsel) our caitiff drivers were so covetous to go forward, being rash in their blind haste, and so fearful of pursuit, that they never heeded the advice nor stayed till the morning: but being not long past midnight, they made us be laden and trudge in our way apace. Then I, fearing the great danger which was foretold, ran amongst the middle of the other horses and hid there as deep as I could, to the end I might defend and save my poor buttocks from the wolves: whereat every man much marvelled to see that I scoured away swifter than the other horses: but such my agility was not to get me any praise for speed, but rather a sign of fear. At that time I remembered with myself that the valiant horse Pegasus did fly rather for fear and for that was deservedly called winged, that he did leap up in the air and skip up to the very sky, more to avoid the dangerous bite of fiery Chimaera than for anything else. For the very shepherds which drove us before them were well armed like warriors for battle: one had a spear, another had a hunting lance, some had darts, some clubs, some also gathered up great stones, of which there were many upon that rough road, some held up sharpened stakes, and most feared away the wolves with light firebrands: finally we lacked nothing to make up an army but only trumpets. But when we had passed these dangers not without small fear, though it was vain and empty, all was in vain, for we fortuned to fall into a snare much worse; for the wolves came not upon us, either because of the great noise and multitude of our company, or else because of our firebrands, or peradventure they were gone to some other place, for we could see none, even afar off. But the inhabitants of the next village (supposing that we were thieves by reason of our great multitude) for the defence of their own substance, and for the fear they were in, set great and mighty mastiffs upon us, worse than any wolves or bears, which they had kept and nourished for the safety of their houses; who were both by nature very fierce and were urged on by their masters, holloing after their wont and driving them with all manner of cries; they, compassing us round about, leaped on every side, tearing us with their teeth, both man and beast, in such sort that they wounded and pulled many of us to the ground. Verily, it was a famous but a pitiful sight to see so many dogs all mad with fury, some following such as fled, some invading such as stood still, some leaping upon those which lay prostrate, and going throughout the whole of our company with savage biting. Behold, upon this, another worse danger ensued; the inhabiters of the town stood upon their roofs and the hills hard by, throwing great stones upon our heads, so that we could not tell whether it were best for us to avoid the gaping mouths of the dogs at hand, or the peril of the stones afar. Amongst whom there was one that hurled a great flint upon the head of a woman which sat upon my back; who cried out piteously, desiring her husband, the shepherd, to help her. Then he (coming to wipe off the blood from his wife) began to complain in this sort, calling upon God's name: 'Alas, masters, what mean you to trouble us poor labouring men and wayfarers and so cruelly to overcome us? What think you to gain by us? What mean you to revenge yourselves upon us, that do you no harm? You dwell not in caves or dens, you are no people barbarous that you should delight in effusion of human blood.' At these words the tempest of stones did cease, and the storm of the dogs was called back and vanished away. Then one (standing on the top of a great cypress-tree) spake unto us, saying: 'Think you not, masters, that we do this to the intent to rifle or take away any of your goods, but for the safeguard of ourselves and family from a like slaughter at your hands; now in God's name you may depart away.' So we went forward, some wounded with stones, some bitten with dogs, but generally there was none which escaped free.

When we had gone a good part of our way we came to a certain wood environed with great trees, and compassed about with pleasant meadows, where the shepherds, our guides, appointed to continue a certain space for rest, to cure their divers wounds and sores. Then they sat down on the ground to refresh their weary minds, and afterwards they sought for medicines to heal their bodies: some washed away their blood with the water of the running river, some laid upon their bruises sponges steeped with vinegar, some stopped their wounds with clouts; in this manner everyone provided for his own safety.

In the mean season we perceived an old man that looked from the top of an hill, who seemed to be a shepherd by reason of the goats and sheep that fed round about him: then one of our company demanded whether he had any milk to sell, whether new drawn or freshly made into cheese. To whom he made answer, shaking his head, saying: 'Do you think now of any meat or drink, or any other refection here? Know none of you in what place you be?' And therewithal he took his sheep and drove them away as fast as he might possible. This answer and his fleeing away made our shepherds greatly to fear, so that they thought of nothing else but to enquire what country they were in: howbeit, they saw no manner of person of whom they might demand. At length, as they were thus in doubt, they perceived another old man very tall and heavy with years, with a staff in his hand and very weary footsteps, who, approaching nigh to our company, began to weep greatly and complain, embracing the knees of every one and saying:

'Alas, masters, I pray you by your fates and lucky spirits, may you come to the years of old age strong and joyful, as you shall succour me, miserable caitiff, and restore my little one from Hell to my white hairs again. For he, my grandson, the dear companion of my path, by following a sparrow that sang upon an hedge, is fallen into a ditch hereby that lay open at the root of the shrubs, and verily I think he is in danger of death. As for me, though I know from his own voice, crying oft upon his grandsire, that he yet liveth, I am not able to help him by reason of old age, but you, that are so valiant and lusty, may easily help me herein a miserable old man, and deliver me my boy, last of my heirs and single offspring of my race that is yet left alive.'

These words and his tearing of his white and aged hair made us all to pity him: and the youngest and stoutest of heart in our company, and strongest of body, who alone escaped unhurt from the late skirmish of dogs and stones, rose up quickly, demanding in what ditch the boy was fallen. 'Marry,' said he, 'Yonder,' and pointing with his finger, brought him to a great thicket of bushes and thorn, where they both entered in. In the mean season, after that we had well refreshed ourselves with our grazing and they had cured their wounds, each took up his packs, purposing to depart away. And because we would not go away without the young man our fellow, the shepherds whistled and called for him by his name; but when he gave no answer they feared because of his long absence and sent one of their company to seek him out, and to tell him that it was now time to set forth on the journey with us. But he after a while returned again with an ashen-pale face, trembling, with strange and sorrowful news of his fellow, saying that he saw him lying upon his back and a terrible dragon eating and devouring him: and as for the miserable old man, he could see him in no place. When they heard this (remembering likewise the words of the first old man that had warned them of this and no other habitant of the place) they ran away, beating us before them, to fly from this desert and pestilent country. Then after we had very quickly passed a great part of our journey we came to a certain village, where we lay all night. But hearken, and I will tell you a great and notable mischief that happened there.

You shall understand that there was a servant to whom his master had committed the whole government of his house, and he was bailiff of the great lodging where we lay: this servant had married a maiden, a fellow-slave of the same house, howbeit he burned greatly for love of a free woman of another house. Therewith was his wife so highly displeased and became so jealous, that she gathered together all her husband's substance, with his tallies and books of accounts, and burned them with fire. She was not contented with this damage, nor thought that she had so averaged the wrong done to her bed, but she took a cord, and now raging against her own bowels, she bound her child which she had by her husband about her middle and cast herself headlong into a deep pit, carrying her babe with her. The master, taking in evil part the death of these twain, took his servant which had made for his wife the cause of this murder, and after that he had first put off all his apparel, he anointed his body with honey, and then bound him sure to a fig-tree, where in a rotten stock a great number of pismires or ants had built their nests, and ran always about in great multitudes like sprinkling water. The pismires, after they had felt the savour and sweetness of the honey, came upon his body, and by little and little but unfailing gnawing, in continuance of time with long torturing devoured all his flesh and his vitals, in such sort that there remained on the fatal tree nothing of his flesh but only his shining white bones.

This was declared unto us by the inhabitants of the village there, who greatly sorrowed for this servant: then we, avoiding likewise from this dreadful lodging, incontinently departed away, and for a whole day travelled through the plain country, and then we came very tired to a fair city very populous, where our shepherds determined to make their home and continue, by reason that it seemed a place where they might live unknown, far from such as should pursue them, and because it was a country very plentiful of corn and other victuals. There when we had remained the space of three days, and that I, poor ass, and the other horses were fed and kept in the stable to the intent we might seem more saleable, we were brought out at length to the market, and by and by a crier sounded with his horn to notify that we were to be sold. All my companion horses and the other asses were bought up by gentlemen, but as for me I stood still forsaken, for that most men passed me by with despight. And when many buyers came by and handled me and looked at my teeth in my mouth to know my age, I was so weary with opening my jaws that at length (unable to endure any longer) when one came with a stinking pair of hands and grated my gums often with his filthy fingers, I seized them and well nigh bit them clean off, which thing caused the standers-by to forsake buying me, as being a fierce and cruel beast. The crier when he had gotten a hoarse voice and was well nigh burst with crying, and saw that no man would buy me, began very scurrilously to mock my evil fortune, saying: 'To what end stand we here to offer for sale this vile ass, this old feeble beast, this slow jade with worn hoofs, made hideous by his labours, idle save when he is vicious, and good for nothing but to make sieves of his skin? Why do we not give him to somebody, if there be any that it shall irk not to find him his hay?'

In this manner the crier made all the standers-by to laugh exceedingly; but my evil fortune, which was ever so cruel against me, whom I, by travel of so many countries, could in no wise escape nor appease the envy thereof by all the woes I had undergone, did more and more cast its blind and evil eyes upon me, with invention of new means to afflict my poor body, in giving me another master very fit for my hard fate. Listen what man he was. There was an old naughty man, somewhat bald, with long and grey hair, one of the number of those of the lewdest dregs of the people which go from door to door throughout all the villages, bearing the image of the Syrian goddess, and playing with cymbals and bones, to get the alms of good and charitable folks. This old man came hastily towards the crier, and demanded where I was bred. 'Marry,' quoth he, 'In Cappadocia: and he is very strong.' Then he enquired what age I was of, and the crier, jesting, answered: 'A mathematician, which disposed to me his planets, said that he was five years old; yet this doth he know best himself from his own register public. For I would not willingly incur the penalty of the law Cornelia in selling a free citizen for a servile slave, yet if you shall buy him you shall have a good and useful chattel both at home and about the country.' But this cursed buyer did never stint to question of my qualities, and at length he demanded whether I were gentle or no: 'Gentle!' quoth the crier, 'As gentle as a lamb, tractable to all use: he will never bite, he will never kick, but you would rather think that under the shape of the ass there were some well-advised man, which verily you may easily conject; for if you would thrust your nose in his tail you shall perceive how patient he is.'

Thus the crier wittily mocked the old rascal; but he, perceiving his taunts and jests, waxed very angry, saying: 'Away, doting crier, thou deaf and dumb carrion, I pray the omnipotent and omniparent Syrian goddess, Saint Sabadius, Bellona with the Idaean mother, and Venus with her Adonis to strike out both thine eyes that with taunting mocks hast scoffed me in this sort. Dost thou think that I will put a goddess upon the back of any fierce beast, whereby her divine image should be thrown down on the ground, and so I, poor wretch, should be compelled (tearing my hair) to look for some physician to help her as she lies fallen?' When I heard him speak this, I thought with myself suddenly to leap up like a mad ass, to the intent he should not buy me, thinking me very fierce; but incontinently, like an eager buyer, he prevented my thought, and would lay down my price for me, even seventeen pence: then my master was glad, being weary of me, and receiving the money, delivered me by mine halter of straw to my new master, who was called Philebus. He carried his new servant home, and when he came to the door of the house, he called out his troop, saying: 'Behold, my daughters,* what a gentle servant I have bought for you.' Yet were these daughters a band of lewd and

---

* The feminine is ironically used for the effeminate crew of priests. So in the Attis poem of Catullus (LXIII) the hero, after his emasculation, speaks of himself in the feminine gender.

naughty fellows, and at first they were marvellous glad, prattling and shouting for joy with their broken and harsh voices, like a troop of women, in discordant sounds, and thought verily that he had brought home a fit and convenient servant for their purpose. But when they perceived that it was not even an hind* instead of a maiden, but rather a makeshift ass for a man, they began to reprove him with great scorn, saying that he had not brought a servant for them, but rather a stalling ass for himself. 'Howbeit,' quoth they, 'Keep this pretty beast not wholly for your own delight, but let us, your darling doves, likewise have him at commandment.'

Therewithal babbling in this wise, they led me into the stable, and tied me to the manger; and there was a certain stout young man with a mighty body, well skilled in playing on flutes, whom they had bought in a market with the money they had collected; and he walked before their procession, playing the horn when they carried round their goddess, and at home he shared in all their labours and they made great use of him. Now he, as soon as he espied me, entertained me very well, for he filled my rack and manger with meat, and spake merrily, saying: 'O master ass, you are welcome; now you shall take my office in hand: you are come to supply my room, and to ease me of my miserable labour: I pray God thou mayest long live and please my master well, to the end thou mayest continually deliver my weary sides from so great pain and labour.' When I heard his words, I did prognosticate my new misery to come. The day following I saw them apparelled in divers colours, and hideously tricked out, having their faces ruddled with paint, and their eyes tricked out with grease, mitres on their heads, vestments coloured like saffron, surplices of silk and linen; and some ware white tunics painted with purple stripes that pointed every way like spears, girt with belts, and on their feet were yellow shoes; and they attired the goddess in silken robe, and put her upon my back. Then they went forth with their arms naked to their shoulders, bearing with them great swords and mighty axes, shouting and dancing like mad persons to the sound of the pipe. After that we had passed many small villages, we fortuned to come to a certain rich man's house, where at our first entry they began to howl all out of tune and hurl themselves hither and thither, as though they were mad. They made a thousand

* The usual reference to the story of Iphigenia.

guests with their feet and their heads; they would bend down their
necks and spin round so that their hair flew out in a circle; they
would bite their own flesh; finally, everyone took his twy-edged
weapon and wounded his arms in divers places. Meanwhile there was
one more mad than the rest, that fetched many deep sighs from the
bottom of his heart, as though he had been ravished in spirit, or
replenished with divine power, and he feigned a swoon and frenzy, as
if (forsooth) the presence of the gods were not wont to make men
better than before, but weak and sickly. Mark then how by divine
providence he found a just and worthy recompense: after that he had
somewhat returned to himself, he invented and forged a great lie,
noisily prophesying and accusing and charging himself, saying that he
had displeased the divine majesty of the goddess by doing of
something which was not convenable to the order of their holy
religion, wherefore he prayed that vengeance might be done of
himself. And therewithal he took a whip, such as is naturally borne by
these womanish men, with many twisted knots and tassels of wool,
and strung with sheep's knuckle-bones, and with the knotted thongs
scourged his own body very strong to bear the pain of the blows, so
that you might see the ground to be wet and defiled with the
womanish blood that issued out abundantly with the cutting of the
swords and the blows of the scourge: which thing caused me greatly
to fear to see such wounds and effusion of blood, lest the same foreign
goddess should likewise desire the blood of an ass for her stomach, as
some men long for ass's milk. After they at last were weary, or at least
satisfied with rending themselves, they ceased from this bloody
business: and, behold, they received from the inhabitants, who
offered eagerly, into their open bosoms copper coins, nay silver too,
vessels of wine, milk, cheese, flour and wheat; and amongst them
there were some that brought barley to the ass that carried the
goddess: but the greedy whoresons thrust all into their sacks which
they brought for the purpose, and put them upon my back, to the
end I might serve for two purposes, that is to say: for the barn by
reason of my corn, and for the temple by reason of the goddess that I
bare.

In this sort they went from place to place robbing all the country
over; at length they came to a certain town, purposing to make good
cheer there, being glad at a great gain they had gotten, where, under
colour of divination, they brought to pass that they obtained a fat ram

of a poor husbandman for the goddess' supper, and to make sacrifice
withal. After that the banquet was richly prepared, they washed their
bodies, and brought in to sup with them a lusty young man of the
village, muscular of body and not a wit ill endowed in the groin; and
when he had scarce tasted a few herbs, before the very table, these
most filthy wretches waxed bestial, their unspeakable itch urging
them to the extreme basenesss of their illicit lust. For they stripped the
young man, flung him naked on his back, compassed him round
about and beset him with their accursed mouths. But when my eyes
would not long bear to behold this horrible fact, I could not but
attempt to utter my mind and say, 'O masters,' but I could
pronounce no more but the first letter 'O,' which I roared out very
clearly and valiantly and like an ass; but at a time inopportune, for
some young men of the town, seeking for a stray ass that they had lost
the same night, and searching diligently all the inns, heard my voice
within the house, whereby they judged that I had been theirs, but
concealed in a hidden place, and resolving to manage their own
business, they entered altogether unawares, and found these persons
committing their vile abomination. This when they saw they called
all the neighbouring inhabitants and declared to them their unnatural
villainy, mocking and laughing at this the pure and clean chastity of
these priests. Then they, ashamed at the report which was dispersed
throughout all the region there of their beastly wickedness, so that
they were justly hated and despised of all, about midnight brought
together all their trumpery and departed away from the town. When
we had passed a good part of our journey before the rising of the sun,
and were now come into a wide desert in the broad day, they
conspired much together to slay me. For after they had taken the
goddess from my back and set her gingerly upon the ground, they
likewise took off all my harness and bound me surely to an oak, and
then beat me with that whip which was knotted with sheep's bones,
in such sort that they had well nigh killed me. Amongst them there
was one that threatened to cut my hamstrings with his hatchet,
because by my noise I had so famously hurt his pure chastity; but the
others, regarding more the image that lay upon the ground than my
safety, thought best to spare my life; and so they laded me again,
driving me before them with their naked swords till they came to a
noble city. There the principal patron, who was in every way a man
very religious, and especially bearing high reverence unto the

goddess, came in great devotion to meet us when he heard our tinkling cymbals and tapping drums and the soft strain of the Phrygian music, and received her and all our company as a pious host into his great house, and he hastened with much sacrifice and veneration to appease her godhead.

But there, I remember, I thought myself in most danger of all my life; for there was one that brought venison to the master of the house, a side of a fat buck, for a present; which being hanged carelessly behind the kitchen door, not far from the ground, was clean eaten up by a hunting greyhound that came in, who, joyful to have gotten his prey, escaped the eyes of them that watched. The cook, when he saw the venison devoured, reproving his own negligence, lamented and wept to no purpose, and because supper-time approached nigh, when his master should now call for the meat, he sorrowed and feared greatly; and bidding farewell to his little child, he took a halter to hang himself; but his good wife, perceiving whereabout he went, ran incontinently to him, and taking the deadly halter in both her hands stopped him of his purpose, saying: 'O husband, are you out of your wits with this present trouble? What intend you to do? See you not a chance remedy before your eyes ministered unto you by divine providence? I pray you, husband, if you have any sense left in this storm of fortune, listen attentively to my counsel: carry this strange ass out into some secret place and kill him; which done, cut off one of his sides, and sauce it well like the side of the buck, and set it before your master in place thereof.' Then the naughty rascal, the cook, was well pleased to slay me, to save himself, and praised greatly the shrewd counsel of his wife; and to bring his purpose to pass, he went to the whetstone to sharp his tools accordingly for the butchery he had promised.

BOOK NINE

In this manner the traitorous cook prepared himself to slay me: and when he was ready with his knives to do his feat, I devised with myself how I might escape the present peril, and I did not long delay, for incontinently I brake the halter wherewith I was tied, I dashed forth at full speed, and flinging my heels hither and thither, at length to save myself I ran hastily through a passage that was near, burst into a parlour where the master of the house was feasting after the sacrifice with the priests, and disquieted all the company, throwing down their meats and drinks and even the table itself. The master of the house, dismayed at my great disorder, strictly commanded one of his servants to take me up as a savage and wanton ass, and lock me in some strong place to the end I might disturb them no more; but I regarded my imprisonment as my safety, considering that by my clever colouring and deceit I was happily delivered from the hands of the traitorous cook.

Howbeit, if fortune be opposite, nothing may prosper a man, nor may the fatal disposition of the divine providence be avoided or changed by wise counsel, nor by any wholesome remedy: for that very deceit, which seemed to have found for me safety for the moment, brought upon me a grievous danger, nay well nigh utter destruction: for by and by, as they were familiarly whispering together, a lad came running into the parlour, all trembling and fearful in his countenance, and declared to the master of the house that a mad dog had run in from the next lane and had rushed furiously into the back gate; which had done much harm, for he had bitten many greyhounds and thence had entered the stable and had with like savagery attacked most of the beasts; nor finally had he spared men, for there was one Myrtilus a muleteer, Hephaestion a cook, Hypatarius a chamberlain, and Apollonius a physician, nay many more, who (thinking to chase away the mad dog) were cruelly bitten by him; and, indeed, many horses and other beasts had been infected with the venom of his poisonous teeth and become mad likewise. This thing caused them all at the table greatly to fear, and thinking that I had been made mad by being bitten and was mad in like sort, they snatched up all manner of weapons and came out exhorting one another so to keep off the common destruction of all, themselves rather a prey to the same disease of madness. Verily, with their spears, clubs, and pitchforks, which their servants easily found for them, they had torn me limb from limb, had I not by and by observed the storm of sudden danger and crept into a chamber, where my masters intended to lodge that night. Then they closed and locked fast the doors about me, and kept the chamber round, till such time as they thought that they would not have to meet me in battle and the pestilent rage of madness should have killed me. Now when I was thus shut in the chamber, I had at last gained my liberty, and taking the gift that fortune had sent me, to be alone, I laid me down upon the bed to sleep, considering it was long time past since I lay and took my rest as a man doth.

When morning was come, and that I was well reposed by the softness of the bed, I rose up lustily. In the mean season I heard them which watched about the chamber all night reason with themselves in this sort: 'Verily,' quoth one, 'I think the ass be still raving.' 'So think not,' quoth another, 'For the outrageous poison of madness hath killed him.' But being thus in divers opinions, they determined to put them to the test and looked through a crevice, and espied me standing still, sober and quiet, in the middle of the chamber; and then they opened the doors and came towards me to prove whether I were gentle or no. Amongst whom there was one, which in my opinion was sent from heaven to save my life, that put forward a proof to see whether I were sane: and he willed the others to set a basin of fair water before me, and thereby they should know whether I were mad or no, for if I did drink without fear, as I accustomed to do, it was a sign that I was whole and free of all disease, where contrary if I did fly and abhor the sight and taste of the water, it was an evident proof of my continued madness; which thing he said that he had read in ancient and credible books. Whereupon they agreed thereto and took a basin of clear water from a spring hard by and presented it before me, hesitating and delaying still; but I, as soon as I perceived the wholesome water of my salvation, ran incontinently and, thrusting my head into the basin, drank all that water, that was truly water of salvation to me, as though I had been greatly athirst. Then did I suffer them to stroke me with their hands, and to bow my ears, and to take me by the halter and aught else that they dared, so that I might, by taking each thing in good part, disprove their mad presumption* by my meekness and gentle behaviour. When I was thus delivered from this double danger, the next day I was laded again with the trappings of the goddess and other trumpery, and was brought out into the way with rattles and cymbals, to beg in the villages which we passed by according to our custom. And after that we had gone through a few hamlets and castles, we fortuned to come to a certain village, which was builded (as the inhabitants there affirmed) among the ruined foundations of a famous and ancient city. And after that we had turned into the next inn, we heard of a pretty jest committed in the town there, in the matter of the cuckoldry of a certain poor man, which I would that you should know likewise.

There was a man dwelling in the town, very poor, that had naught to live upon but that which he got by his labour as a smith and the travail of his hands: his wife too was very poor, but known to be lascivious and exceeding given to the desire of the flesh. Now it fortuned on a day that while this man was gone betimes in the morning about his business, according as he accustomed to do, his wife's lover secretly came into his house to have his pleasure with her. And so it chanced that during the time that he and she were busking together too much off their guard, her husband, suspecting no such matter, returned suddenly home praising the chaste continency of his wife, in that he found his doors fast locked and closed; wherefore, as his custom was, he whistled to declare his coming home. Then his crafty wife, ready with present shifts, loosed her lover from her embrace and hid him in a great tub standing in a corner, and it was very ruinous and dirty, but empty withal; and then she opened the door, blaming her husband in this sort: 'Comest thou home so every day empty with thy hands wrapped in thy cloke? And bringest nothing by thy accustomed labour to maintain our house? Thou hast no regard for our profit, neither providest for any meat or

* *Vesana praesumptio* has a double meaning which it is not easy to render into English. Lucius had stated above (ch. 2) that his pursuers were so much excited that they seemed mad themselves, but it also has the idea of 'their presumption of my madness'.

drink, whereas I, poor wretch, do nothing day and night but wear my sinews with spinning, and yet my travail will scarce find the candles to lighten our hut. O how much more happy is my neighbour Daphne, that eateth and drinketh at her pleasure, and well foxed passeth the time with her amorous lovers according to her desire.' 'What is the matter?' quoth her husband, much grieved at that she said, 'Though our master hath business in the market and hath made holiday for us, yet think not but that I have made provision for our supper this day; dost thou not see this tub that keepeth a place here in our house in vain, and doth us no service save to hinder us in our coming and going? Behold I have sold it to a good fellow (that now cometh) for five pence, and he will pay the money and carry it away. Wherefore I pray thee lend me thy hand that I may mend it and take it up and deliver him the tub.' His wife (having invented a present shift) laughed boldly on her husband, saying: 'What a notable and goodly merchant have I gotten in you, to fetch away my tub for so little for which I, poor woman that sit all day alone in my house, have been proffered long ago seven pence!' Her husband, being well pleased at the greater price, demanded what he was that would give so much. 'Look, fool,' quoth she, 'He is gone under to see where it be sound or no.'

Then her lover, which was under the tub, began to stir that his words might agree to the words of the woman, and said: 'Dame, will you have me tell the truth? This tub is old and rotten and cracked as meseemeth on every side.' And then he turned himself to her husband, colouring the matter and saying: 'I pray, honest man, whoever you be, light a candle that I may make the tub clean within, to see if it be for my purpose or no, for I do not mind to cast away my money wilfully.' This clever husband by and by, suspecting nothing, delayed not to light a candle, saying: 'I pray you, good brother, put not yourself to so much pain, but stand by and let me make the tub clean and ready for you'; whereupon he put off his coat and took the light and crept under the tub to rub away the old filth from the sides. In the mean season the minion lover cast his wife on the bottom of the tub, and had his pleasure with her over his head, and she, like the very harlot that she was, played a merry prank upon her husband; for as she was in the midst of her pastime, she turned her head on this side and that side, showing now this and now that to be cleansed, till as they had both ended their business, and then he delivered seven pence for the tub: and then the poor smith must himself carry it on his back to the lover's lodging.

After that we had tarried there a few days at the cost and charges of the whole village, and had gotten much money by our divination and prognostication of things to come, those good priests invented a new mean to pick men's purses; for they had one lot whereon was written this cheating answer, which they gave for every enquiry; and it was: '*The oxen tied and yoked together: do plough the ground to the intent it may bring forth her increase.*'* And by these kind of lots they deceived many of the simple sort: for if one had demanded whether he should have a good wife or no, they would say that his lot did testify the same, that he should be tied and yoked to a good woman and have increase of children: if one demanded whether he should buy lands and possessions, they said that there was much reason in the mentioning of the oxen and the yoke, which foretold that he should have much ground that should yield his increase: if one demanded the advice of heaven whether he should have a good and prosperous voyage, they said he should have good success because that now these gentlest of beasts were joined together and ready to go, and that of the increase of the soil should be his profit: if one demanded whether he should vanquish his enemies, or prevail in pursuit of thieves, they said that the oracle foretold victory, for that his enemies' necks should be brought under the yoke, and that a rich and fertile gain should be gotten from the thieves' booty.

Thus by the telling of fortunes so cleverly and cunningly they gathered a great quantity of money; but when they were weary with giving of answers, they drove me away before them the next night, through a lane which was more dangerous and stony than the way which we had gone before; for it was full of deep and gaping holes, sometimes wet with quagmires and foggy marshes, and sometimes very slippery with mud and filth, whereby my legs failed me with often stumbling and falling, in such sort that I could scarce come

---

* Adlington has here a marginal note, 'So used feigned Egyptians of late years in England,' and the practice of the trade has not varied since his time. Adlington did not attempt a poetical version of the lines. I may perhaps quote that of the late Dean Farrar:

> The patient oxen plough the soil,
> And harvests rich repay their toil.

wearily and with bruised legs to the plain field-paths. And behold by and by from behind a great company of the inhabitants of the town, armed with weapons and on horseback, overtook us, hardly pulling up the horses of their car, for they galloped furiously, they incontinently arrested Philebus and his priests, and tied them by the necks and beat them cruelly, calling them sacrilegious thieves and vile robbers, and after that they had manacled their hands they urged them furiously again and again: 'Show us,' quoth they, 'The cup of gold, the temptation of your crime, which you have taken privily away from the very shrine of the Mother of the gods, under the colour of your solemn religion, which you must needs perform secretly shut up in her temple; and now you think to escape in the night without punishment for your deed, leaving the boundaries of town and setting secretly forth before it be yet light.' By and by one came towards me, and thrusting his hand into the bosom of the goddess which I bare, found and brought out before them all the cup which they had stole: howbeit, for all their robbery which appeared evident and plain, those accursed and vile creatures would not be confounded or abashed, but, jesting and laughing out the matter, began to say: 'Is it reason, masters, that you should thus rigorously entreat us, as often befalls innocent men, and threaten to bring the faithful priests of religion into danger of death for a small trifling cup, which the Mother of the gods determined to give to her sister for a present?' Howbeit, for all their lies and cavillations, they were carried back to the town and put in prison by the inhabitants, who, taking the cup of gold and the image of the goddess which I bare, did put and consecrate them amongst the treasure of the temple. The next day I was carried to the market to be sold by the voice of the crier, and again my price was set; but I was sold at seven pence more than Philebus gave for me. There fortuned to pass by a baker of the next village, who, after that he had bought a great deal of corn, bought me likewise to carry it home, and when he had well laded me therewith, he drove me through a stony and dangerous way to his bakehouse.

There I saw a great company of horses that went round and round in the mill turning the stones and grinding of corn: and not day only, but at night also they must needs still work at the mill and make flour in those engines that never stood still: but lest I should be discouraged at the first, my master entertained me well in a luxurious place; for the first day I had a holiday and did nothing but fare daintily at a full manger. Howbeit, such mine ease and felicity did not long endure; for the next day following I was tied to the greatest mill (as it seemed to me) betimes in the morning with my face covered, and placed in a small path of a circle to the end in turning and winding so often one way I might keep a certain course and tread in my own path again and again. But I forgot not my wisdom and careful prudence so as to lend myself too easily to the new labour, for although when I was a man I had seen many such horse-mills, and knew well enough how they should be turned, yet feigning myself ignorant of such kind of toil I stood still and would not go, whereby I thought I should be taken from the mill as an ass unapt, and put to some other lighter labour, or else to be driven into the fields to pasture: but my subtlety did me small profit, for by and by when the mill stood still, the many servants came about me armed with sticks, whereas I suspected nothing, mine eyes being covered, and suddenly when a sign was given they cried out and plentifully beat me forward, in such sort that I could not stay to advise myself, because of the sudden attack and noise, but leaned sturdily against my rope and went briskly on my appointed path; whereby all the company laughed to see so sudden a change.

When a good part of the day was past, so that I was not able to endure any longer, they took off my harness, and tied me to the manger; but although my bones were weary, and that I needed to refresh myself with rest and provender, being utterly dead with hunger, yet I was so curious and anxious also, that I did greatly delight to behold the horrible fashion of the baker's mill, in so much that I could not eat nor drink while I looked on, although there was food in plenty. O good Lord, what a sort of poor slaves were there; some had their skin bruised all over black and blue, some had their backs striped with lashes and were but covered rather than clothed with torn rags, some had their members only hidden by a narrow cloth, all wore such ragged clouts that you might perceive through them all their naked bodies, some were marked and burned in the forehead with hot irons, some had their hair half clipped, some had shackles on their legs, ugly and evil favoured, some could scarce see, their eyes and faces were so black and dim with smoke, their eyelids all cankered with the darkness of that reeking place, half blind and sprinkled black and white with dirty flour like boxers which fight together befouled with sand. But how should I speak of the horses my companions, how they, being old mules or weak horses, thrust their heads into the manger and ate the heaps of straws? They had their necks all wounded and worn away with old sores, they rattled their nostrils with a continual cough, their sides were bare with continued rubbing of their harness and great travail, their ribs were broken and the bones did show with perpetual beating, their hoofs were battered very broad with endless walking, and their whole skin ragged by reason of mange and their great age. When I saw this dreadful sight, I greatly began to fear lest I should come to the like state: and considering with myself the good fortune which I was sometime in when I was a man, I greatly despaired and lamented, holding down my head, but I saw no comfort or consolation of my torments, saving that my mind and my inborn curiosity was somewhat recreated to hear and understand what every man said and did, for they neither feared nor doubted my presence. At that time I remembered how truly Homer, the divine author of ancient Poetry among the Greeks, described him to be a wise man* which had travelled divers countries and nations, and by straitly observing them all had obtained great virtue and knowledge. Wherefore I do now give great thanks to my assy form, in that by that mean I have seen the experience of many things, and am become more experienced (notwithstanding that I was then very little wise). But I will tell you a pretty and handsome jest, which cometh now to my remembrance, to the intent your ears may be delighted in hearing the same, and I do now begin it.

The baker which bought me was an honest and sober man, but his wife the most pestilent woman in all the world, in so much that he endured with her many miseries and afflictions to his bed and house, so that I myself did secretly pity his estate and bewail his evil fortune: for there was not one single fault that was lacking to her, but all the mischiefs that could be devised had flowed into her heart as into some filthy privy; she was crabbed, cruel, cursed, drunken, obstinate, niggish, covetous in base robberies, riotous in filthy expenses, an enemy to faith and chastity, a despiser of all the gods whom others did honour, one that affirmed that she had instead of our sure

* The description of Ulysses in the opening lines of the *Odyssey*.

religion an only god by herself,* whereby, inventing empty rites and
ceremonies, she deceived all men, but especially her poor husband,
delighting in drinking wine, yea, early in the morning, and
abandoning her body to continual whoredom. This mischievous
quean hated me in such wonderful sort that she commanded every
day, before she was up, that I, the new ass, should be put in the mill
to grind: and the first thing which she would do in the morning,
when she had left her chamber, was to see me cruelly beaten, and
that I should grind and be kept from the manger long after the other
beasts did feed and take rest. When I saw that I was so cruelly
handled, she gave me great desire to learn her conversation and her
life; for I saw oftentimes a young man, which would privily go into
her chamber, whose face I did greatly desire to see, but I could not,
by reason mine eyes were covered every day: and verily, if I had
been free and at liberty, I would have discovered all her abomination. She had an old woman, a bawd, a messenger of mischief, that
daily haunted to her house, and made good cheer with her at
breakfast, and then they would drink wine unmixed, and after this
first skirmish they would contrive and plot to the utter undoing and
impoverishment of her husband: but I, that was greatly offended
with the negligence of Fotis, who made me an ass instead of a bird,
did yet comfort myself for the miserable deformity of my shape by
this only mean, in that I had long ears, whereby I might hear all
things that were done even afar off.

On a day I heard the shameless old bawd say to the baker's wife:
'Dame, you have chosen (notwithstanding my counsel) a young man
to your lover, who as meseemeth is dull, fearful, without any grace,
and dastardly coucheth at the frowning looks of your odious
husband, whereby you have no delight nor pleasure with him. How
far better is the young man Philesitherus, who is comely, beautiful,
in the flower of his youth, liberal, courteous, valiant, and stout
against the diligent pryings and watches of husbands, alone worthy to
embrace the worthiest dames of this country, and alone worthy to
wear a crown of gold, be it for one part alone that he played with
clever wit to one that was jealous over his wife. Hearken how it was,
and then judge the diversity of these two lovers.

* It is supposed that Apuleius represents this abandoned woman as a
Christian, and so expresses his dislike and contempt of the new religion.

'Know you one Barbarus, a senator of our town, whom the vulgar people call likewise Scorpion for his peevish manners? This Barbarus had a gentlewoman to his wife, of exceeding beauty, whom he caused daily to be enclosed within his house with diligent custody.' Then the baker's wife said: 'I know her very well, for her name is Arete, and we two dwelled together at one school.' 'Then you know,' quoth the old woman, 'The whole tale of Philesitherus?' 'No, verily,' said she, 'But I greatly desire to know it: therefore I pray you, mother, tell me the whole story.' By and by the old woman, which knew well to babble, began to tell as followeth:

'You shall understand that on a day this Barbarus, preparing himself to ride abroad, and willing to keep the chastity of his wife (whom he so well loved) alone to himself, called his man Myrmex (whose faith he had tried and proved in many things) and secretly committed to him the custody of his wife, threatening him, that if any man did but touch her with his finger as he passed by, he would not only put him in prison, and bind him hand and foot, but also cause him to be put to death cruelly and shamefully; which words he confirmed by oath of all the gods in heaven, and so he departed careless away, leaving Myrmex to follow his wife with all diligence. When Barbarus was gone Myrmex, being greatly astonished and afraid at his master's threatenings, was exceeding constant and fixed in his purpose, and would not suffer his mistress to go abroad, but as she sat all day a-spinning, he was so careful that he sat by her; and when night came he went with her to the baths, holding her by the garment, so faithful he was to fulfil the commandment of his master. Howbeit, the beauty of this noble matron could not be hidden from the burning eyes of Philesitherus, who considering her great chastity, and how she was diligently kept by Myrmex, was greatly set afire, and ready to do or suffer aught to gain her; and so he endeavoured by all kind of means to enterprise the matter, and to break through the serene guard of her house, and remembered the fragility of man, that might be enticed and corrupted with money, since by gold even adamant gates may be opened. On a day when he found Myrmex alone, he discovered his love, desiring him to show his favour to heal him thereof (otherwise he intended and should certainly die unless he soon obtained his desire) with assurance that he need not fear, as he might privily be let in alone and under the covering of the night, without knowledge of any person, and in a moment come out again.

To these, and other gentle words, he added a wedge which might violently split the hard tenacity of Myrmex; for he showed him glittering new gold pieces in his hand, saying that he would give his mistress twenty crowns, and him ten.

'Now Myrmex, hearing these words, was greatly troubled, abhorring in his mind to commit so wicked a mischief; wherefore he stopped his ears, and turning his head departed away. Howbeit, although far apart and having now speedily gotten him home, the glittering hue of these crowns could never out of his mind, but he seemed to see the money, which was so worthy a prey, before his eyes. Wherefore, poor Myrmex was tossed on the waves of opinions and was utterly distracted and could not tell what to do; for on the one side, he considered the promise which he made to his master, and the punishment which should ensue if he did contrary, while on the other side, he thought of the gain and passing pleasure of the crowns of gold. In the end the desire of the money did more prevail than the fear of death, for the desire of the flourishing crowns was not abated by distance of space, but it did even invade his dreams in the night time, and where the menaces of his master compelled him to tarry at home, the pestilent avarice of the gold egged him out of doors wherefore, putting all shame aside without further delay, he declared the whole matter to his mistress; who, according to the light nature of women, when she heard him speak of so great a sum, put her chastity in pawn to the vile money. Myrmex, seeing the intent of his mistress, was very glad, and hastened to the ruin and breaking of his faith, and for great desire that the gold should not only be his, but that he might handle the same instantly, ran hastily to Philesitherus, declaring that his mistress had consented to his mind, wherefore he demanded the gold which he promised; and then incontinently Philesitherus delivered him ten golden crowns, who had never before possessed even money of copper. When night came, Myrmex brought him disguised and covered into his mistress' chamber; but, about midnight, when with their first embraces they were making sacrifices to their budding love, naked soldiers fighting in Venus's army, behold, her husband (contrary to their expectation) came and knocked at the door, calling with a loud voice and beating upon it with a stone. Their long tarrying increased the suspicion of the master, in such sort that he threatened to beat Myrmex cruelly: but he, being troubled with fear, and driven to his latter shifts, excused the matter as best he could, saying that he could not find the key, by reason it had been hidden curiously away and that the night was so dark. In the mean season Philesitherus, hearing the noise at the door, slipped on his coat (yet barefoot, because of his great confusion) and privily ran out of the chamber. When at last Myrmex had fitted the key into the lock and opened the door to his master that still threatened terribly by all the gods, and had let him in, he went into the chamber to his wife; in the mean while Myrmex let out Philesitherus, and when he had seen him pass the threshold, he barred the doors safe, and went to bed, fearing nothing.

'The next morning, when Barbarus was about leaving his chamber, he perceived two unknown slippers lying under his bed, in the which Philesitherus had entered the night before. Then he conceived a great suspicion and jealousy in his mind: howbeit, he would not discover his heart's sorrow to his wife, neither to any other of his household, but putting secretly the slippers in his bosom, commanded his other servants to bind Myrmex incontinently, and to bring him quickly bound to the justice after him, groaning and wailing inwardly within himself, and thinking verily that by the means of the slippers he might track out the matter. It fortuned that while Barbarus went through the street towards the justice with a countenance of fury and rage, and Myrmex fast bound followed him weeping, not yet because he was found guilty before the master, but by reason he knew his own conscience guilty and therefore he cried bitterly and called upon the mercy which availed him nothing, behold, by adventure Philesitherus (going about other earnest business) fortuned to meet them by the way; who, fearing the matter which he so suddenly saw, yet not utterly dismayed, remembering that which he had forgotten in his haste, and conjecturing the rest, did suddenly invent a mean, for that he was of great confidence and present mind, to excuse Myrmex; for he thrust away the slaves and ran upon him and beat him wildly about the head with his fists, saying: "Ah, mischievous varlet that thou art, and perjured knave, it were a good deed if thy master here would put thee to death, and all the gods whom thou hast hastily swallowed down with thy false swearing, for thou art worthy to be imprisoned in a dark dungeon, and to wear out these irons, that stolest my slippers away when thou wert at the baths yesternight." Barbarus, hearing these words, was utterly convinced and deceived by the timely subtlety of that clever

youth, and returned incontinently home, and calling his servant
Myrmex, forgave him and commanded him to deliver the slippers
again to the right owner, whence he had stolen the same.'

The old woman had scarce finished her tale, when the baker's wife
began to say: 'Verily she is blessed, and most blessed, that hath the
free fruition of so worthy a lover; but as for me, poor wretch, I am
fallen into the hands of a coward, who is afraid every clap of the mill,
and dares do nothing before the blind face of yonder scabbed ass.'
Then the old woman answered: 'I promise you certainly, if you will,
you shall have this young man, that is firm and constant of mind, as
well as smart and brisk, at your pleasure this very evening,' and
therewithal she departed out of the chamber, appointing to return at
night. In the mean season, the baker's chaste wife made ready a
lordly supper with abundance of wine and exquisite fare, fresh meat
and gravy, and waited for the coming of the young man as for some
god: for it happened by good fortune that her husband supped at a
fuller's that lived next door. When, therefore, the day was coming
towards its term, so that my harness should be taken off and that I
should rest myself in peace, I was not so joyful of my liberty, as that
the veil being taken from mine eyes, I should see all the abomination
of this mischievous quean. When night was come and the sun gone
down beneath the sea to lighten the under part of the earth, behold
the old bawd and the young lover at her side came to the door; and
he seemed to me but a boy, by reason that his cheeks were yet
smooth and bright, and very pleasant: then the baker's wife kissed
him a thousand times, and receiving him courteously, placed him
down at the table. But he had scarce taken any first draught nor eaten
the first morsel, when the good man (contrary to his wife's
expectation) returned home, for she thought he would not have
come so soon; but, Lord, how she cursed him, good woman,
praying God that he might break his legs at the first entry in. In the
mean season she caught her lover, that was now very pale and
trembling, and thrust him into the bin that lay near by some chance,
where she accustomed to sift her flour, and dissembling her
wickedness by her wonted craft, put on a firm countenance and
asked of her husband why he came home so soon, and left the
supper of his dear friend so early. 'I could not abide,' quoth he,
deeply sighing, 'To see so great a mischief and wicked fact which my
neighbour's wife committed, but I must run away. Oh, how good

and trusty a matron she seemed, but what a harlot is she become, and how she hath dishonoured her husband! I swear by this goddess Ceres that if I had not seen it with mine eyes I would never have believed it.' His wife, made desirous by his words to know the mutter, desired him to tell what she had done; and she ceased not to urge him until he accorded to the request of his wife, and ignorant of the state of his own house, declared the mischance of another.

'You shall understand,' said he, 'That the wife of the fuller my companion, who seemed to be a wise and chaste woman, regarding her own honesty and the profit of her house, had begun secretly to love a knave, and did often meet him: and this very night, as we came back to supper from the baths, he and she were together. Then she was troubled by our sudden presence and thrust him into a mew made with twigs, built up high with rods woven in and out, and appointed to lay on clothes to make them white with the smoke and fume of brimstone: and so he being very safe hidden therein (as she thought) she sat with us at the table to colour the matter. In the mean season the young man, covered in the mew, could not forbear oft sneezing, by reason of the sharp smoke, for he was wholly surrounded and choked with the heavy fumes of this lively sublimate. The good man, thinking it had been his wife that sneezed (for the noise thereof came from behind her back) cried, as they are wont to say, "Christ help"; but when he sneezed more and more, he suspected the matter, and willing to know who it was, rose, pushing back the table, and went to the mew, where he found the young man now choked well nigh dead with smoke. When he understood the whole matter he was so inflamed with anger at this outrage that he called for a sword to kill him: and undoubtedly he had so done, had not I hardly restrained his violent hands from his purpose, that had brought danger unto us all, assuring him that his enemy would die with the force of the brimstone without any harm which he might get from it: howbeit, my words would not appease his fury, but as necessity required he took the young man well-nigh choked, and carried him out at the doors to the nearest lane. In the mean season I counselled his wife and did persuade her to leave his shop and absent herself at some neighbour's house till the choler of her husband was pacified, lest he should be moved against her, and do her some harm and to himself also. And so being weary of their supper, I forthwith returned home.'

When the baker had told this tale, his impudent and rash wife began to curse and abhor the wife of the fuller, calling her whore and shameless, and a great shame to all the sex of women, in that she had lost all modesty, broken the bond of her husband's bed, turned his house into a bawdy-house, and had lost the dignity of a spouse to become an harlot; and said that such women were worthy to be burned alive. But knowing her own guilty conscience and proper whoredom, that she might the sooner save her lover from hurt lying in the bin, she willed her husband now early to go to bed, but he, having lost his supper and eaten nothing, said gently that he would sup before he went to rest: wherefore she was compelled, though very unwilling, to set such things on the table as she had prepared for her lover. But I was much troubled in heart, as considering the past great mischief of this wicked quean and her present obstinacy and impudence, and devised with myself how I might help my master by revealing the matter, and by kicking away the cover of the bin (where like a snail the young man was couched) make her whoredom apparent and known. As I was tormented by the insult put upon my master, at length I was aided by the providence of God, for there was a lame old man to whom the custody of us was committed, that drove me, poor ass, and the other horses in a herd to the water to drink, and the time was then come; then had I good occasion ministered to my revenge, for as I passed by I perceived the fingers of the young man in the narrow space under the side of the bin, and lifting up my heels I spurned the flesh thereof with the force of my hoofs, and crushed them small, where by the great pain thereof he was compelled to cry out, and to throw down the bin on the ground, and so the whoredom of the baker's wife was known and revealed. The baker, seeing this, was little moved at the dishonesty of his wife, but he took the young man, pale and trembling for fear, by the hand, and with cold and courteous words spake in this sort: 'Fear not any trouble from me, my son, nor think that I am so barbarous or cruel or rustical a person that I would stifle thee with the smoke of sulphur, as our neighbour the fuller accustometh, nor will I punish thee accord to the rigour of the Julian law, which commandeth that adulterers should be put to death. No, no, I will not execute any cruelty against so fair and comely a young man as you be, but we will divide our pleasure between us; I will not sue thee for a division of our inheritance, but we will be equal

partners by the sharing all three of one bed. For never hath there
been any debate nor dissension between me and my wife, but both
of us may be contented, for I have always lived with her in such
tranquillity that according to the saying of the wise men, the one
hath said, that the other holdeth for law; but indeed equality will not
suffer but that the husband should bear more authority than the
wife.' With these and like smooth and jesting words he led the
young man, reluctant but still following, to his chamber, and closing
his chastest of wives in another chamber, he lay alone with the boy
and enjoyed the most delicious revenge for his corrupted marriage.
On the next morrow when the sun's rays did first usher in the day,
he called two of the most sturdiest servants of his house, who hoist
up the young man while he scourged his buttocks well-favouredly
with rods like a child. When he had well beaten him he said: 'Art
thou not ashamed, thou that art so tender and delicate a boy, to
refuse the lovers of thine own budding age, and to desire the
violation of honest marriages, and defame thyself with wicked living,
whereby thou hast gotten the name of an adulterer?' And so he
whipped him again and chased him out of his house: the young man,
the bravest of all adulterers, ran away, having won unlooked for
freedom, and did nothing else, save only bewail his white buttocks
after their battering both at night and in the day. Soon after the baker
sent one to his wife who divorced her away in his name: but she,
beside her own natural mischief (offended at this contumely, though
she had worthily deserved the same) had recourse to wicked arts and
trumpery* that women use, never ceasing till she had found out an
enchantress, who (as it was thought) could do what she would with
her sorcery and conjuration. The baker's wife began to entreat her,
promising that she would largely recompense her, if she could bring
one of these two things to pass, either to make that her husband
might be reconciled to her again, or else, if he would not agree
thereto, to send some ghost or devil into him to dispossess the spirit
of her husband. Then the witch with her abominable science began

---

* Adlington's note to the passage is worthy of transcription: 'In like sort do
many nowadays go to wise women which are witches, when they have lost
silver spoons, or have their cattle hurt to seek remedy, but to seek redress by
such means is lack of faith, when they forsake God and run for help to the
devil, with whom, as S. Augustine sayeth, they shall be damned.'

at first to conjure with the lighter arts of her wicked practice, and to make her ceremonies to turn the offended heart of the baker to the love of his wife: but all was in vain; wherefore angry with her gods, and considering on the one side that she could not bring her purpose to pass, and on the other side the loss of her gain and the little account that was made of her science, she began to aim against the life of the baker, threatening to send an ill spirit of a certain woman that had died violently to kill him by mean of her conjurations.

But peradventure some scrupulous reader may demand me a question, how I, being an ass, and tied always within the walls of the mill-house, could be so clever as to know the secrets of these women: learn then, I answer, notwithstanding my shape of an ass, yet having the sense and knowledge of a man, how I did curiously find out and know out such injuries as were done to my master. About noon there came suddenly a woman into the mill-house, very sorrowful, clothed in wretched rags, and in gloomy garb like those that are accused of a crime, half naked and with bare and unshod feet, meagre, exceeding pale and thin, ill-favoured, and her hair, which was growing towards white, mixed with cinders and scattering upon her face. This woman gently took the baker by the hand, and feigning that she had some secret matter to tell him, led him into his chamber, where they remained a good space with closed doors. But when all the corn was ground that was ready to hand, and the servants were compelled to call their master to give them more, they called very often at his chamber door, and asked that they might have further matter for their labour. But when no person gave answer to their often and loud crying, they knocked louder to none effect: then they began to mistrust, in so much that with great pushing they brake open the door, which was very closely barred; but when they were come in, they could not find the woman, but only their master hanging dead upon a rafter of the chamber. Thereupon they cried and lamented greatly, and took his body from the noose; and according to the custom, when they had mourned him much and washed the body, they performed all the funeral rites and buried him, much people attending. The next morrow the daughter of the baker, which was married but a little before to one of the next village, came crying with hair awry and beating her breast: not because she heard of the sad fortune of her house by the message of any man, but because her father's lamentable spirit, with a halter about his neck, appeared to her in the night, declaring the whole circumstance of the matter; of the wickedness of her stepmother and her whoredom, of the witchcraft and how by enchantment he was descended to hell. After that she had lamented a good space, and was then somewhat comforted by the servants of the house and had ceased therefrom, and when nine days were expired, and all was duly done at the tomb, as inheritress to her father she sold away all the substance of the house, both slaves and furniture and beasts, whereby the goods of one household chanced by the operation of fortune into divers men's hands.

There was a poor gardener amongst the rest, which bought me for the sum of fifty pence, which seemed to him a great price, but he thought to gain it again by the common travail of himself and me. The matter requireth to tell likewise, how I was handled in his service. This gardener accustomed to drive me every morning laden with herbs to the next village, and there, when he had sold his herbs, he would mount upon my back and return to the garden. Now while he digged the ground, and watered the herbs, and bent himself to his other business, I did nothing but repose myself with great ease: but when the signs of heaven were turned in their ordained courses, and the year in due order passed by days and by months from the pleasant delights of the autumn unto Capricorn, with sharp hail, rain, and wintry frosts, I had no stable, but standing always under a hedgeside, beneath the unceasing rain and the dews of night, was well nigh killed with cold; for my master was so poor that he had no lodging for himself, much less he had any litter or place to cover me withal; but he himself always lay under a little roof, shadowed and covered with boughs. In the morning when I walked, I had no shoes to my hoofs to pass upon the sharp ice and frosty mire, neither could I fill my belly with meat as I accustomed to do; for my master and I supped together and had both one fare, and it was very slender, since we had nothing else saving old and unsavoury salads, which were suffered to grow for seed, like long brooms, and all their sweet sap and juice had become bitter and stinking.

It fortuned on a day that an honest man of the next village was benighted, and constrained, by reason of the rain and that it was dark without moon, to lodge (his horse being very weary) in our garden; where although he was but meanly received, yet served well enough considering time and necessity. This honest man, to recompense our kindly entertainment, promised to give my master some corn, oil, and two bottles of wine: therefore my master, not delaying the matter, laded me with a sack and empty bottles, and sat upon my bare back and rode to the town, which was seven miles off. When we came to the honest man's farm, he entertained and feasted my master exceedingly; and it fortuned while they ate and drank together in great amity, there chanced a strange and dreadful case; for there was a hen which ran cackling about the yard, even as though she would have laid an egg; the good man of the house, perceiving her, said: 'O good and profitable pullet, that now for so long hast fed us every day with thy fruit, thou seemest as though thou wouldst give us some pittance for our dinner. Oh, boy, put the pannier in the accustomed corner that the hen may lay.' Then the boy did as his master commanded, but the hen, forsaking her accustomed litter, came towards her master, and laid at his feet an offspring too early indeed, and one that should betoken great ill to come; for it was not an egg which every man knoweth, but a chicken, with feathers, claws, and eyes, nay even with a voice, which incontinently ran peeping after his dame. By and by happened a more strange thing which would cause any man to abhor; for under the very table whereon was the rest of their meat, the ground opened, and there appeared a great well and fountain of blood, in so much that the drops thereof sprinkled about the table. At the same time, while they wondered at this dreadful sight, and feared that which the gods should presage thereby, one of the servants came running out of the cellar, and told that all the wine, which had long before been racked off, was boiled out of the vessels, as though there had been some great fire under. By and by without the house weasels were seen that drew with their teeth a dead serpent; and out of the mouth of a shepherd's dog leaped a green frog, and immediately after a ram that stood hard by leaped upon the same dog and strangled him with one bite. All these things that happened horribly astonished the good man of the house and the residue that were present, in so much they could not tell how they stood or what to do, which first and which last, which more and which less, or with what or how many sacrifices to appease the anger of the gods.

While every man was thus stricken in fear of some hideous thing that should come to pass, behold one brought word to the good man of the house of a great and terrible mishap. For he had three sons who had been brought up in good literature and endued with good manners, in whom he greatly gloried. Now they three had great acquaintance and ancient amity with a poor man, which was their neighbour and dwelled hard by them in a little cottage. And next unto that little cottage dwelled another young man very rich both in lands and goods, but using ill the pride of his high descent, very factious, and ruling himself in the town according to his own will. This young royster did mortally hate this poor man, in so much that he would kill his sheep, steal his oxen, and spoil his corn and other fruits before the time of ripeness; yet was he not contented with this spoiling of his thrift, but he burned to encroach upon the poor man's ground and by some empty quarrel of boundaries claimed all his heritage as his own. The poor man, which was very simple and fearful, seeing all his goods taken away by the avarice of the rich man, called together and assembled many of his friends to show them in much fear the metes and bounds of his land, to the end he might at least have so much ground of his father's heritage as might bury him. Amongst whom he found these three brethren as friends to help and aid him as far as they might in his adversity and tribulation. Howbeit the presence of all these honest citizens could in no wise persuade or frighten this madman to leave his power and extortion, and though at the first he did show temperance in his tongue, yet of a sudden the more they went about with gentle words to tell him his faults, the more would he fret and fume, swearing all the oaths under God, and pledging his own life and his dearest, that he little regarded the presence of the whole city, and incontinently he would command his servants to take the poor man by the ears, and carry him out of his cottage and thrust him afar off. This greatly offended all the standers-by; and then forthwith one of the brethren spake unto him somewhat boldly, saying: 'It is but folly to have such affiance in your riches, and to use your tyrannous pride to threaten, when as the law is common for the poor alike, and a redress may be had by it to suppress the insolence of the rich.'

These words made his harsh temper to burn more than oil on flames, or brimstone in a fire, or a Fury's scourge of whips, and he became furious to madness, saying that they should be all hanged and their laws too, before he would be subject to any person: and therewithal he called out his bandogs and great mastiffs that followed the sheep on his farm, which accustomed to eat the carrion and carcasses of dead beasts in the fields, and had been trained to set upon such as passed by the way. These he commanded should be put upon all the assistants to tear them in pieces; and as soon as they heard the accustomed hiss of their masters the shepherds, ran fiercely upon them, roused to madness, and barking very horridly, invading them on every side, wounding and tearing them, and not sparing even them that sought to fly, in so much that the more they fled to escape away, the more cruel and terrible were the dogs. It fortuned amongst all this fearful company, that in running the youngest of the three brethren stumbled at a stone, and bruising his toes fell down to the ground to be a prey to these wild and furious dogs, and they came upon him and tare him in pieces with their teeth, whereby he cried out bitterly: his other two brethren, hearing his lamentable voice, ran towards him to help him, casting their cloaks about their left arms, and took up stones to defend their brother and chase away the dogs. But all was in vain, for they could not make to cease nor drive away the fierce beasts, but they must see their brother dismembered in every part of his body; who, lying at the very point of death, desired his brethren to revenge his death against the cruel tyrant, and therewithal he gave up the ghost. The other two brethren, perceiving so great a murder, did not only despair of their only safety, but neglected their own lives and madly dressed themselves against the tyrant, and threw a great number of stones at him; but the bloody thief, exercised to such and like mischiefs, took a spear and thrust one of them clean through the body. Howbeit, although utterly destroyed, he fell not down to the ground: for the spear that came out at his back ran into the earth with the force of the thrust and sustained him up quivering in the air. By and by came one of this tyrant's servants, the most sturdiest of the rest, to help his master; and at his first coming, he took up a stone and threw it from afar at the third brother, and struck his left arm, but by reason the stone ran by the ends of his fingers it fell to the ground and did not hurt him, which chanced otherwise than all men's expectation was. Then did this fortunate chance give the young man, that was very wise, a hope for vengeance; for he feigned that his arm was greatly wounded, and spake these words unto the cruel bloodsucker: 'Now mayst thou, thou wretch, triumph upon the destruction of all our family; now mayst thou feed thy insatiable cruelty with the blood of three brethren; now mayst thou rejoice at the fall of thy fellow-citizens: yet think not but that how far soever thou dost remove and extend the bounds of thy land by depriving of poor men, thou shalt still have some neighbour: but how greatly am I sorry in that by the injustice of fate I have lost mine arm wherewithal I minded to cut off thy head.' When he had spoken these words, the furious thief was the more enraged and drew out his dagger, and running upon the young man thought verily to have slain him: but it chanced that he had attacked one no whit weaker than he, for the young man resisted him stoutly beyond all his expectation, and buckling together by violence seized his right hand: which done, he poised the weapon, and oft striking made the rich thief to give up his guilty ghost, and to the intent the young man would escape the hands of the servants, which came running to assist their master, with the same dagger that dripped with his enemy's blood he cut his own throat. These things were signified by the strange and dreadful wonders which fortuned in the house of the wretched man, who, after he had heard these sorrowful tidings, could in no wise even silently weep, so far was he stricken into dolour, but presently taking the knife wherewith he had but now divided the cheese and other meat for his guests, he cut his own throat with many blows like his most unhappy son, in such sort that he fell head foremost upon the board and washed away with the streams of his blood in most miserable manner those prodigious drops which had before fallen thereon.

Hereby was my master the gardener deprived of his hope, and pitying very greatly the evil fortune of the house, which in a brief moment of time had thus fallen in ruins, and getting instead of his dinner the watery tears of his eyes, and clapping oft-times together his empty hands, mounted upon my back, and so we went homeward the same way as we came. Yet was our return not free from harm: for as we passed by the way we met with a tall soldier (for so his habit and countenance declared) which was a legionary, who with proud and arrogant words spake to my master in this sort: 'Whither lead you this ass unladen?' My master, still somewhat astonished and fearful at the strange sights which he saw before, and ignorant of the Latin tongue, rode on and spake never a word. The soldier, unable to refrain his proper insolence and offended at his silence as it were an insult, struck him with a vinestick which he held on the shoulders, and thrust him from my back. Then my master

gently made answer that he knew not his tongue and so understood
not what he said; whereat the soldier angrily demanded again, but in
Greek, whither he rode with his ass: 'Marry,' quoth he, 'To the next
city.' 'But I,' quoth the soldier, 'Have need of his help, to carry the
trusses of our captain with the other beasts from yonder castle'; and
therewithal he took me by the halter, and would violently have
taken me away: but my master, wiping away from his head the
blood of the blow which he received of the soldier, desired him
gently and civilly to take some pity upon him, and to let him depart
with his own, conjuring him by all that he hoped of good fortune,
and affirming that his slow ass, well nigh dead with sickness, could
scarce carry a few handfuls of herbs from his garden hard by, being
very scant of breath; much less he was able to bear any greater trusses.
But when he saw the soldier would in no wise be entreated, but was
the more bent on his destruction, and ready with his staff to cleave
my master's head with its thicker part, being desperate he fell down
grovelling at his feet, under colour to touch his knees and move him
to some pity; but when he saw his time, he took the soldier by the
legs and cast him upon the ground: then straightway he buffeted
him, thumped him, bit him, and took a stone and beat his face and
his sides, so that he, being first laid along the ground, could not turn
or defend himself, but only threaten that if ever he rose he would
chop him in pieces. The gardener, when he heard him say so, was
advised and drew out his sword which he had by his side, and when
he had thrown it far away, he knocked and beat him more cruelly
than he did before, in so much that the soldier as he lay all hurt with
wounds could not tell by what means to save himself, but only by
feigning he was dead. Then my master took the sword and mounted
upon my back, riding straight in all haste to the next village; but he
had no regard to go to his garden, and when he came thither, he
turned into one of his friends' house and declared all the whole
matter, desiring him to save his life, and to hide himself and his ass
awhile in some secret place, that he might be hid for the space of two
or three days, until such time as all danger were past. Then his friend,
not forgetting the ancient amity between them, entertained him
willingly, and tying my legs drew me up a pair of stairs into a
chamber, while my master, remaining in the shop, crept into a chest
and lay hidden there with the cover closed fast.

The soldier (as I afterwards learned) rose up at last as one awakened from a drunken sleep, but he could scarce go by reason of his wounds, howbeit, at length, by little and little, through aid of his staff, he came to the town; but he would not declare the matter to any person, nor complain to any justice, but inwardly digested his injury, lest he should be accused of cowardice or dastardness. Yet in the end he told some of his companions of all the matter that happened; but they advised him that he should remain for a while closed in some secret place, thinking that beside the injury which he had received, he should be accused of the breach of his faith and soldier's oath, by reason of the loss of his sword,* and that they should diligently learn the signs and appearance of my master and me to search him out and take vengeance upon him. At last, there was an unfaithful neighbour that told them where we were: then incontinently the soldiers went to the justice, declaring that they had lost by the way a silver goblet of their captain's, very precious, and that a gardener had found it, who, refusing to render up the goblet, was hidden in one of his friends' house. By and by the magistrate, understanding the loss of the captain, and who he was, came to the doors where we were, and in a loud voice exhorted our host that it were better to deliver up my master than to incur pain of death; for most certainly he was hiding us. Howbeit, these threatenings could not enforce him to confess that he was within his doors, and he was nothing afraid, but by reason of his faithful promise, and for the safeguard of his friend, he said that he knew naught of us, nor saw he the gardener a great while. The soldiers said contrary, swearing by the deity of the Emperor that he lay there, and nowhere else. Whereby, to know the verity of the matter, the magistrates commanded their sergeants and ministers to search every corner of the house; but there they could find nobody, neither gardener nor ass. Then was there a great contention between the soldiers and our host, for they said we were within the house, calling often upon Caesar in their oaths; and he said no, and swore much and often by all the gods to the same intent. But I, that was an ass very curious and restless in my nature, when I heard so great a noise craned my neck and put my head out of a little window to learn what the stir and tumult did signify. It fortuned that one of the soldiers, spying about,

---

* A soldier's loss of his sword was considered equal to desertion, and punished with equal severity.

perceived my shadow, whereupon he began to cry, saying that he
had certainly seen me: then they were all glad and a great shouting
arose, and they brought a ladder and came up into the chamber and
pulled me down like a prisoner; and when they had found me, they
doubted nothing of the gardener, but seeking about more narrowly,
at length they found him couched in a chest. And so they brought
out the poor gardener to the justices, who was committed immediately to prison, in order that he might suffer the pain of death; but
they could never forbear laughing and jesting how I looked out from
my window: from which, and from my shadow, is risen the
common proverb of the peeping and shadow of an ass.*

* Apuleius has here combined two Greek proverbs of considerably greater
antiquity than his story, ἐξ ὄνου παρακύψεως and ὑπὲρ ὄνου σκιᾶς. The first
is variously explained. There is a tale that a donkey broke some vessels in a
potter's shop by going to look out of the window; the potter sued its master
for damages, and when asked by the magistrate the subject of his complaint,
answered 'of the peeping of an ass'; or it has been explained that, frightened
by an ass looking on, some game-birds flew suddenly away and avoided or
broke a fowler's nets. The other proverb is derived from a story that a man
who hired an ass lay down to sleep in its shadow on a hot day, and the
animal's master objected that he had hired only the ass and not its shadow;
and the resulting lawsuit brought into proverbial use the expression 'about
an ass's shadow' to describe a dispute about a wholly trivial matter.

BOOK TEN

The next day how my master the gardener sped I know not, but the gentle soldier, who had been so well beaten for his exceeding cowardice, led me from my manger to his lodging (as it seemed to me) without the contradiction of any man. There he laded me well, and garnished my body for the way like an ass of arms. For on the one side I bare a helmet that shined exceedingly; on the other side a target that glittered more a thousandfold; and on the top of my burden he had put a long spear. Now these things he placed thus gallantly, not because such was the rule of arms, but to the end he might make fear those which passed by, when they saw such a similitude of war piled upon the heap of baggage. When we had gone a good part of our journey, over the plain and easy fields, we fortuned to come to a little town, where we lodged, not at an inn, but at a certain corporal's house. And there the soldier took me to one of the servants, while he himself went carefully towards his captain, who had the charge of a thousand men.

When we had remained there a few days, I understood of a wicked and mischievous deed committed there, which I have put in writing, to the end you may know the same. The master of the house had a young son instructed in good literature, and therefore endowed with virtuous manners, but especially with shamefastness, such a one as you would desire to have the like. Now his mother died a long time before, and then his father married a new wife, and had another child, that was now of the full age of twelve years. This stepdame was more excellent in beauty than honesty in her husband's house; for she loved this young man her son-in-law, either because she was unchaste by nature, or because she was enforced by fate to commit so great a mischief. Gentle reader, thou shalt not read of a fable, but rather a tragedy, and must here change from sock to buskin.* This

* The *soccus* was the low shoe of the comic actor; the *cothurnus*, the high boot of the tragedian.

woman, when little Cupid first began to do his work in her heart, could easily resist his weak strength, and pressed down in silence her desire and inordinate appetite, by reason of shame and fear; but after that Love compassed and burned with his mad fire every part of her breast, she was compelled to yield unto this raging Cupid, and under colour of disease and infirmity of her body to conceal the wound of her restless mind. Every man knoweth well the signs and tokens of love, and how that sickness is convenient to the same, working upon health and countenance; her countenance was pale, her eyes sorrowful, her knees weak, her rest disturbed, and she would sigh deeply by reason of her slow torment; there was no comfort in her, but continual weeping and sobbing, in so much you would have thought that she had some spice of an ague, saving that she wept unreasonably. The physicians knew not her disease* when they felt the beating of her veins, the intemperance of her heat, the sobbing sighs, and her often tossing on every side; no, no, the cunning physicians knew it not, but a scholar of Venus' court might easily conject the whole, seeing one burning without any bodily fire. So after that she had been long time tormented in her overmastering affection, and was no more able to keep silence, she caused her son to be called for (which word 'son' she would fain put away, that she might not be rebuked of shame). Then he, nothing disobedient to the commandment of his ailing mother, with a sad and modest countenance, wrinkled like some old grandsire, came with due obedience into the chamber of his stepdame, the mother of his brother; but she, being utterly wearied with the silence that she had kept so long to her torment, was in great doubt what she might do; for she rejected within herself every word which she had before thought most apt for this meeting, and could not tell what to say first, by reason of her shame which still trembled before its fall. This young man even then suspecting no ill, with humble courtesy and downcast countenance demanded the cause of her present disease. Then she, having found the occasion to utter her wicked intent, put on boldness, and with weeping eyes and covered face began with trembling voice to speak unto him in this manner: 'Thou, thou art the original cause of my present dolour; but thou too art my medicine and only health, for those thy comely eyes have so pierced through these eyes of mine and are so fastened within my

* Cp. *Aen.* IV, 65: 'Heu vatum ignarae mentes!'

breast, that they have kindled therein a raging and a roaring fire. Have pity therefore upon me that die by thy fault, neither let thy conscience reclaim to offend thy father, when as thou mayest save his wife for him from death. Moreover, since as thou dost resemble thy father's shape in every point, I do justly fancy thee, seeing his image in thy face. Now is ministered unto thee time and place; now hast thou occasion to work thy will, seeing that we are alone. And it is a common saying: "Never known, never done." '

This young man, troubled in his mind at so sudden an ill, although he abhorred to commit so great a crime, yet he would not be rashly stern to undo her yet more with a present denial, but warily pacified her mind with delay of promise. Wherefore with long speech he promised her to do all according to her desire: and in the mean season, he willed his mother to be of good cheer, and comfort herself and look to her health, till as he might find some convenient time to come unto her, when his father was ridden forth: wherewithal he got him away from the pestilent sight of his stepdame. And knowing that this matter touching the ruin of all the whole house needed the counsel of wise and grave persons, he went incontinently to a sage old man, a tutor, and declared the whole circumstance. The old man, after long deliberation, thought there was no better mean to avoid the storm of cruel fortune to come than to run away. In the mean season this wicked woman, impatient of any delay how little soever, egged her husband to ride abroad to visit some far lands that he had: then she, maddened by the hope that had now (as she thought) grown rife, asked the young man the accomplishment of his promise; but he, to avoid the sight of her whom he hated, would find always excuses from appearing before her, till in the end she understood by the various colour of the messages which he sent her that he nothing regarded her. Then she, in her fickle mood, by how much she wickedly loved him before, by so much and more she hated him now. And by and by she called one of her servants who had come with her among her dowry, the worst of all and ready to all mischiefs, to whom she declared all her treacherous secrets. And there it was concluded between them two, that the surest way was to kill the young man: whereupon this varlet went incontinently to buy poison, which he mingled with wine, to the intent he would give it the innocent young man to drink, and thereby presently to kill him.

But while the guilty ones were in deliberation how they might offer it unto him, behold, here happened a strange adventure. For the young son of that evil woman that came from school at noon (being very thirsty after his dinner) took the pot wherein the poison was mingled, and ignorant of the hidden venom drank a good draught thereof, which was prepared to kill his brother: whereby he presently fell down to the ground dead. His schoolmaster,* annoyed by this sudden chance, called his mother and all the servants of the house with a loud voice. Incontinently when the poisoned cup was known every man declared his opinion touching the death of the child; but the cruel woman, the signal example of stepmother's malice, was nothing moved by the bitter death of her son, or by her own conscience of parricide, or by the misfortune of her house, or by the dolour of her husband, or by the affliction of this death, but rather devised the destruction of all her family to fulfil her desire to be avenged. For by and by she sent a messenger after her husband to tell him the great misfortune which happened after his departure. And when he came home the wicked woman, putting on a bold face beyond all reason, declared that her son had been taken off with his brother's poison. And so far she spoke no lie, inasmuch as the boy had forestalled the death that was prepared for the young man; but she feigned that he had been for this reason murdered by his brother's crime, because she would not consent to his evil will which he had had towards her, and told him divers other leasings, adding in the end that he threatened with his sword to kill her likewise, because she discovered the fact. Then the unhappy father was stricken with a double storm of dolour at the death of his two children, for on the one side he saw his younger slain before his eyes, on the other side he seemed to see the elder condemned to die for his offences both of incest and of parricide, and where he beheld his dear wife lament in such sort, it gave him further occasion to hate his son more deadly.

But the funerals of his younger son were scarce finished, when the old man the father, even at the return from the grave, with weeping eyes and his white hair befouled with ashes went apace to the justice and worked with all his might for the destruction of his remaining son, accusing him of the incest that he had attempted, of the slaughter of his brother, and how he threatened to slay his wife; owing naught

* The *paedagogus* was a trusted slave who conducted the boy to and from school, and had charge of him when at home.

of that wicked woman's wiles, he besought the magistrates with tears and prayers, yea, even embracing their knees, for this son's death. Hereby with weeping and lamentation he inflamed all the elders and the people as well to pity and indignation, in so much that without any delay of trial or further inquisition or the careful pleading of defenders they cried all that he should be stoned to death, to the end that this public crime might be publicly revenged; but the justices, fearing lest a farther inconvenience might arise to themselves by a particular vengeance, and to the end there might fortune from a little beginning no sedition amongst the people with public riot, prayed the decurions and the people of the city to proceed by examination of witnesses on both sides, like good citizens, and with order of justice according to the ancient custom; for the giving of any hasty sentence or judgement without hearing of the contrary part, such as the barbarous and cruel tyrants accustom to use, would give an ill example in time of peace to their successors.

This safe opinion pleased every man; wherefore the senators and counsellors were called by an herald, who, being placed in order according to their dignity, caused first the accuser and then only the defender (again by the voice of the herald) to be brought forth, and by the example of the Athenian law, and judgement of Mars' hill, their advocates were commanded to plead their causes briefly, without preambles or motions of the people to pity. (And if you demand how I understand all this matter, you shall understand that I heard many declare the same in talking among themselves, but to recite what words the accuser used in his invective, what answer and excuses the defender made, in fine the orations and pleadings of each party, verily this I am not able to do, for I was fast bound at the manger; but as I learned and knew by others, I will, God willing, declare unto you.) So it was ordered that after the pleadings of both sides was ended, they thought best to try and bolt out the verity of the charges by witnesses, all presumptions and likelihoods set apart in so great a case, and to call in chiefly the servant, who only was reported to know all the matter. By and by this rope-ripe slave came in, who, nothing abashed at the fear of so great a judgement, or at the presence of the judges in conclave, or at his own guilty conscience, began to tell and to swear as true all those lies which he so finely feigned. With a bold countenance he presented himself before the justices, and confirmed the accusation against the young man, saying:

'O ye judges, on a day when this young man loathed and hated his stepmother he called me, desiring me to poison his brother, whereby he might revenge himself, and if I would do it, and keep the matter secret, he promised to give me a good reward for my pains; but when the young man perceived that I would not accord to his will, he threatened to slay me: whereupon he went himself and bought poison, and after tempered it with wine, and then gave it me to give to the child; but when he thought that I did it not, but kept it to be a witness of his crime, he offered it to his brother with his own hands.' When the varlet with a feigned and trembling countenance had ended these words, which seemed a likelihood of truth, the judgement was ended: neither was there found any judge or counsellor so merciful to the young man accused as would not judge him culpable, but rather gave sentence that he should be put and sewn in the leather sack for parricides.* Wherefore, since the sentences of all were alike, and all did agree to the same verdict, there wanted nothing but (as the ancient custom was) to put the sentences into a brazen pot, and when once they were cast thither, the decision of fate being finally taken, it should remain a thing irrevocable, but he would be delivered to the hands of the executioner. Then there arose a sage ancient of the court, a physician of good conscience and credit throughout all the city, that stopped the mouth of the pot that none might rashly cast his stone therein, saying thus before the assembly:

'I am right glad, ye reverend judges, that I am a man of name and estimation amongst you all the days of my life, whereby I am accounted such a one as will not suffer any person to be put to death by false and untrue accusations, neither you (being sworn to judge uprightly) to be misinformed and abused by invented lies and tales of a slave. For I cannot but declare and open my conscience, lest I should be found to bear small honour and faith to the gods: wherefore I pray you give ear, and I will show you the whole truth of the matter. You shall understand that this servant, which hath merited to be hanged, came one of these days to speak with me, promising to give me a hundred crowns if I would give him a present poison, which would cause a man to die suddenly, saying that he would have it for one that was sick of an incurable disease, to the end he might be

* The parricide was sewn up in a sack with a dog, a cock, a snake and an ape, and thrown into a river or the sea.

delivered from all his torment. But I, perceiving that the varlet was talking foolishness and telling a clumsy tale, and fearing lest he would work some mischief withal, gave him a potion, yea, I gave it; but to the intent I might clear myself from all danger that might happen, I would not presently take the money which he offered: but lest any one of the crowns should lack weight or be found counterfeit, I willed him to seal the purse wherein they were put with his manual ring, whereby the next day we might go together to the goldsmith to try them. This he did, and sealed up the money; wherefore understanding that he was brought present before you this day, I hastily commanded one of my servants to fetch the purse from my house, and here I bring it unto you to see whether he shall deny his own sign or no: and you may easily conject that his words are untrue, which he alleged against the young man touching the buying of the poison, considering he bought the poison himself.'

When the physician had spoken these words, you might perceive how the traitorous knave changed his colour, becoming deathly pale from the natural complexion of a man, how he sweated cold for fear, how he trembled in every part of his body, how he set one leg uncertainly before another, scratching now this, now that part of his head, and began to stammer forth some foolish trifles, his lips but half open, whereby there was no person but would judge him culpable. In the end when he was somewhat returned to his former subtlety, he began to deny all that was said, and stoutly affirmed that the physician did lie. But the physician, besides the oath which he had sworn to give true judgement, perceiving that he was railed at and his words denied, did never cease to confirm his sayings and to disprove the varlet, till such time as the officers, by the commandment of the judges, seized his hands and took the ring wherewith he had sealed the purse, and laid it by the seal thereon: and this augmented the suspicion which was conceived of him first. Howbeit neither the wheel nor the rack nor any other torment (according to the use of the Grecians) which were done unto him nor stripes, no nor yet the fire, could enforce him to confess the matter, so obstinate and grounded was he in his mischievous mind.

But the physician, perceiving that those torments did nothing prevail, began to say: 'I cannot suffer or abide that this young man who is innocent should against all law and conscience be punished and condemned to die, and the other which is culpable should escape so easily, and after mock and flout at your judgement: for I will give you an evident proof and argument of this present crime. You shall understand that when this caitiff demanded of me a present and strong poison, I considered that it was not the part of my calling to give occasion of any other's death, but rather to cure and save sick persons by mean of medicines.* And on the other side I feared lest if I should deny his request I might by my untimely refusing minister a further cause of his mischief by some other way, either that he would buy poison of some other, or else return and work his wicked intent with a sword or some dangerous weapon. Wherefore I gave him no poison, but a soothing drink of mandragora, which is of such force that it will cause any man to sleep as though he were dead. Neither is it any marvel if this most desperate man, who is certainly assured to be put to that death which is ordained by our ancient custom, can suffer or abide these facile and easy torments. But if it be so that the child hath received the drink as I tempered it with mine own hands, he is yet alive and doth but rest and sleep, and after his sleep he shall return to life again; but if he hath been murdered, if he be dead indeed, then may you further enquire of the causes of his death.'

The opinion of this ancient physician was found good, and every man had a desire to go to the sepulchre where the child was laid: there was none of the justices, none of any reputation of the town, nor any indeed of the common people, but went to see this strange sight. Amongst them all the father of the child removed with his own hands the cover of the coffin, and found his son rising up after his dead and soporiferous sleep: and when he beheld him as one risen from the dead he embraced him in his arms; and he could speak never a word for his present gladness, but presented him before the people with great joy and consolation, and as he was wrapped and bound in the clothes of his grave, so he brought him before the judges. Hereupon the wickedness of the servant and the treason of the stepdame were plainly discovered, and the verity of the matter nakedly revealed: whereby the woman was perpetually exiled, the servant hanged on a gallows, and by the consent of all the physician had the crowns to be a reward for the timely sleep which he had

---

* Adlington's marginal note is worth transcribing: 'The office of a physician is to cure and not to kill, as I have heard tell many physicians of speculation have done, before they have come to practice.'

prepared for the child. Behold how the great and wonderful fortune of the old man brought by the providence of God to an happy end, who, thinking to be deprived of all his race and posterity, was quickly, nay in the twinkling of an eye, made the father of two children.

But as for me I was ruled and handled by fortune, according to her pleasure: for the soldier which got me without a seller and paid never a penny for me by the commandment of his captain was sent unto Rome in course of his duty to carry letters to the great Prince, and before he went he sold me for eleven pence to two of his companions, brothers, being servants to a man of worship and wealth, whereof one was a baker, that baked sweet bread and delicates; the other a cook, which dressed with rich sauces fine and excellent meats for his master. These two lived in common, and would drive me from place to place to carry such vessels as were necessary for their master when he travelled through divers countries. In this sort I was received by these two as a third brother and companion, and I thought I was never better placed than with them: for when night came and the lord's supper was done, which was always exceedingly rich and splendid, my masters would bring many good morsels into their chamber for themselves: one would bring large rests of pigs, chickens, fish, and other good meats; the other fine bread, pastries, tarts, custards, and other delicate junkets dipped in honey. And when before meat they had shut their chamber door and went to the baths; O Lord, how I would fill my guts with those goodly dishes: neither was I so much a fool, or so very an ass, as to leave the dainty meats and grind my teeth upon hard hay. In this sort I continued a great space in my artful thieving, for I played the honest ass, taking but a little of one dish and a little of another, whereby no man mistrusted me. In the end I was more hardier and more sure that I should not be discovered, and began to devour the whole messes of the sweetest delicates, which caused the baker and the cook to suspect not a little; howbeit they never mistrusted me, but searched about to apprehend the daily thief. At length they began to accuse one another of base theft, and to keep and guard the dishes more diligently, and to number and set them in order, one by another, because they would learn what was taken away: and at last one of them was compelled to throw aside all doubting and to say thus to his fellow: 'Is it right or reason to break promise and faith in this sort, by stealing away the best meat and selling to augment thy private good, and yet nevertheless to have thy equal part of the residue that is left? If our partnership do displease thee, we will be partners and brothers in other things, but in this we will break off: for I perceive that the great loss which I sustain will at length grow from complaining to be a cause of great discord between us.' Then answered the other: 'Verily I praise thy great constancy and subtleness, in that thou (when thou hast secretly taken away the meat) dost begin to complain first; whereas I by long space of time have silently suffered thee, because I would not seem to accuse my brother of a scurvy theft. But I am right glad in that we are fallen into communication of this matter, to seek a remedy for it, lest by our silence like contention might arise between us as fortuned between Eteocles* and his brother.' When they had reasoned and striven together in this sort, they sware both earnestly that neither of them stole or took away any jot of the meat, but that they must conclude to search out the thief by all kind of means in common. For they could not imagine or think that the ass, who stood alone there, would fancy any such meats, and yet every day the best parts thereof would utterly disappear; neither could they think that flies were so great or ravenous as to devour whole dishes of meat, like the birds harpies which carried away the meats of Phineus, king of Arcadia.

In the mean season, while I was fed with dainty morsels, and fattened with food fit for men, I gathered together my flesh, my skin waxed soft and juicy, my hair began to shine, and I was gallant on every part; but such fair and comely shape of my body was cause of my dishonour, for the baker and the cook marvelled to see me so sleek and fine, considering that my hay was every day left untouched. Wherefore they turned all their minds towards me, and on a time when at their accustomed hour they made as they would go to the baths and locked their chamber door, it fortuned that ere they departed away they espied me through a little hole how I fell roundly to my victuals that lay spread abroad. Then they marvelled greatly, and little esteeming the loss of their meat laughed exceedingly at the marvellous daintiness of an ass, calling the servants of the house, one by one and then more together, to show them the greedy gorge and

* Eteocles and Polynices were the two sons of Oedipus who killed one another in the internecine strife at Thebes.

wonderful appetite of a slow beast. The laughing of them all was so immoderate that the master of the house passing by heard them, and demanded the cause of their laughter; and when he understood all the matter, he looked through the hole likewise, wherewith he took such a delectation that he had well nigh burst his guts with laughing and commanded the door to be opened, that he might see me at his pleasure. Then I, beholding the face of fortune altogether smiling upon me, was nothing abashed, but rather more bold for joy, whereby I never rested eating till such time as the master of the house commanded me to be brought out as a novelty, nay he led me into his own parlour with his own hands, and there caused all kinds of meats, which had been never before touched, to be set on the table; and these (although I had eaten sufficiently before, yet to win the further favour of the master of the house) I did greedily devour, and made a clean riddance of the delicate meats. And to prove my mild and docile nature wholly, they gave me such meat as every ass doth greatly abhor, for they put before me beef and vinegar, birds and pepper, fish and sharp sauce. In the mean season, they that beheld me at the table did nothing but laugh; then one of the wits that was there said to his master: 'I pray you, sir, give this feaster some drink to his supper.' 'Marry,' quoth he, 'I think thou sayest true, rascal; for so it may be that to his meat this our dinner-fellow would drink likewise a cup of wine. Oh, boy, wash yonder golden pot, and fill it with wine; which done, carry it to my guest, and say that I have drank to him.' Then all the standers-by looked on, looking eagerly to see what would come to pass; but I (as soon as I beheld the cup) stayed not long, but at my leisure, like a good companion, gathering my lips together to the fashion of a man's tongue, supped up all the wine at one draught, while all who were there present shouted very loudly and wished me good health.

The master, being right joyful hereat, caused the baker and the cook which had bought me to come before him; to whom he delivered four times as much for me as they paid. Then he committed me to one of his most favourite freedmen, that was very rich, and charged him to look well to me, and that I should lack nothing. He obeyed his master's commandment in every point, feeding me with kindness and civility; and to the end he would creep further into his favour, he taught me a thousand qualities and tricks for his pleasure. First he instructed me to sit at the table upon my tail,* and then how I should wrestle and dance holding up my fore feet; moreover he taught me (which was much more wonderful) how I should answer when anybody spake unto me, with lifting† my head if I would not anything, but bowing it if I would; and if I did lack drink, I should look still upon the minister of drink, winking first with one eye and then with the other. All which things I did willingly bring to pass, and obeyed his doctrine; howbeit I could have done all these things without his teaching, but I feared greatly lest in showing myself cunning to do all like a man, without a master, I should portend some great and strange wonder, and as a prodigy thereby be slain and thrown out to wild vultures. But my fame was spread about in every place, and the qualities which I could do, in so much that my master was renowned throughout all the country by reason of me. For every man would say: 'Behold the gentleman that hath an ass that will eat and drink with him, an ass that will box, an ass that will dance, an ass that understandeth what is said to him and will show his fantasy by signs.'

But first I will tell you (which I should have done before) who my master was, and of what country. His name was Thiasus; he was born at Corinth, which is the principal town of all the province of Achaea; he had passed all offices of honour in due course according as his birth and dignity required, and he should now take upon him the degree Quinquennial‡ and now to show his worthiness to enter upon that office, and to purchase the benevolence of every person, he appointed and promised public joys and triumphs of gladiators, to endure the space of three days. To bring his endeavour for the public favour to pass, he came into Thessaly to buy excellent beasts and valiant fighters for the purpose, and now when he had bought such things as were necessary, and was about returning home, he would not journey into his country in his fine chariots or splendid wagons, which travelled behind him in the rear, some covered and some open, neither would he ride upon Thessalian horses, or gennets of France, which be most excellent (by reason of their long descent) that can be found; but caused me to be garnished and trimmed with

* *Lit.* 'to recline upon my elbow'.
† The single toss of the head backwards, which is still the regular gesture of refusal in Italy.
‡ The quinquennial magistracy, or chief office of provincial towns.

trappings of gold, with brave harness, with purple coverings, with a bridle of silver, with pictured clothes, and with shrilling bells, and in this manner he rode upon me lovingly, speaking and entreating me with gentle words, but above all things he did greatly rejoice, in that I was at once his servant to bear him upon my back, and his companion to feed with him at the table. After a long time when we had travelled as well by sea as land, and fortuned to arrive at Corinth, the people of the town came about us on every side, not so much to do honour unto Thiasus as to see me: for my fame was so greatly spread there, that I gained my master much money: for when the people was desirous to see me play pranks, he caused the gates to be shut, and such as entered in should pay money; by means whereof I was a profitable companion to him every day.

There fortuned to be amongst the assembly a noble and rich matron, that after that she had paid her due to behold me was greatly delighted with all my tricks and qualities, in so much that she fell marvellously in love with me, and could find no remedy to her passions and disordinate appetite, but continually desired to have her pleasure with me, like a new Pasiphae, but with an ass. In the end she promised a great reward to my keeper for the custody of me one night, who cared for naught but for gain of a little money, and accorded to her desire. When therefore I had supped in a parlour with my master, we departed away and went into our chamber, where we found the fair matron, who had tarried a great space for our coming. Good God, how nobly all things there were prepared! there were four eunuchs that laid a bed of billowing down on the ground with bolsters accordingly for us to lie on; the coverlet was of cloth of gold and Tyrian dye, and the pillows small, but soft and tender, as whereon delicate matrons accustom to lay their heads. Then the eunuchs, not minding to delay any longer the pleasure of their mistress, closed the doors of the chamber and departed away; and within the chamber were wax candles that made light the darkness of the night all the place over. Then she put off all her garments to her naked skin, yea even the veil of her lovely bosom, and standing next the lamp began to anoint all her body with balm, and mine likewise, but especially my nose; which done, she kissed me with gentle pressure, not as they accustom to do at the stews or in brothel-houses, or in the courtesan schools for gain of money though their clients would deny it them, but purely, sincerely, and with great affection, casting out these and like loving words: 'Thou art he whom I love,' 'Thou art he whom I only desire,' 'Without thee I cannot live,' and other like preamble of talk, as women can use well enough when they mind to show or declare their burning passions and great affection of love. Then she took me by the halter and cast me upon the bed, which was nothing strange unto me, considering that she was so beautiful a matron, and I so well blown out with wine, and perfumed with balm whereby I had aroused the prick of lust. But nothing grieved me so much as to think how I should with my huge and great legs mount so fair a matron, or how I should touch her fine, dainty, and silken skin made of milk and honey with my hard hoofs, or how it was possible to kiss her soft, her pretty and ruddy lips with my monstrous great mouth and stony teeth, or how she, although she itched with lust all over, could as a woman receive so vast a member. And I verily thought if I should hurt the woman by any kind of means, I should be thrown out to the wild beasts: but in the mean season she spoke gently to me, kissing me oft, and looked on me with burning eyes, saying: 'I hold thee my cony, I hold thee my nops, my sparrow,' and therewithal she shewed me that all my fear was vain, for she embraced me very tightly and took all of me inside her, yea all of me. And as often as in consideration of her I withdrew my buttocks, so often did she draw close with hungry striving and, laying hold of my back, she cleaved to me the more fast intertwined so that, by Hercules, I believed that I might fall somewhat short of sating her lust and thought the mother of Minotaurus did not causeless quench her inordinate desire with a bull. When night was passed, with much joy and small sleep, the matron went away, avoiding the light of day, so that she might not be seen, and bargained with my keeper for another night: which he willingly granted, partly for gain of money, and partly to find new pastime for my master. He, after he was informed of all the history of my luxury, was right glad, and rewarded my keeper well for his pains, minding to show in the public theatre what I could do; but because they would not suffer that noble wife of mine to abide such shame, by reason of her dignity, and because they could find no other that would suffer even for a great reward so great a reproach at length they obtained for money an evil woman, which was condemned to be eaten of wild beasts, with whom I should be set in a cage before the people. But first I will tell you what a tale I heard concerning her.

This woman had a husband whose father, minding to ride forth, commanded his wife, the young man's mother, which he left at home great with child, that if she were delivered of a daughter, it should incontinently be killed. Now when the time of her delivery came, it fortuned that she had a daughter born while her husband was still abroad, whom she would not suffer to be slain, by reason of the natural affection which she bare unto her child, but declined from the command of her husband and secretly committed her to one of her neighbours to nurse. And when her husband returned home, she declared unto him that she was delivered of a daughter, whom, as he commanded, she had caused to be put to death. But when this child came to the flower of her age, and was ready to be married, the mother knew not by what means she should endow her daughter without that her husband should understand and perceive it. Wherefore she could do naught but discover the matter to her son,* as a secret greatly to be hidden and kept dark; for she greatly feared lest he should unawares be urged by the natural heat of youth and fancy or fall in love with his own sister. The young man understanding the whole matter did (according to his known and proved piety) perform both his duty to his mother and his natural obligation towards his sister; for he kept the matter utterly secret in his heart, feigning that he had towards her no more than common human kindness, and so performed the due offices of kinship and blood that he feigned that she was a neighbour's daughter desolate both of father and mother, that he would take her into the protection of his own house, and incontinently after endowed her largely with part of his own goods, and would have married her to one of his especial and trusty friends. But although he brought this to pass very religiously and sagely, yet in the end none of them could avoid the decree of cruel and envious fortune, which sowed great sedition in his house. For his wife (who was now for this condemned to beasts) waxed jealous of her husband, and began to suspect and then to hate the young woman as a harlot and common quean, in so much that she invented all manner of cruel snares to dispatch her out of the way: and in the end she invented this kind of mischief.

* Adlington here inserts in his text an explanation which is not in the Latin, but is convenient for following the thread of the story – that the son 'was the husband of this woman condemned to be eaten of wild beasts'.

She privily stole away her husband's ring, and went into the country, whereas she commanded one of her servants that was trusty to her, but otherwise a faithless varlet, to take the ring and to carry it to the maiden: to whom he should declare that her brother did pray her to come into the country to him, and that she should come alone, as soon as she might, without any other person, And to the end she should not delay, but come with all speed, he did deliver her the ring, to be a sufficient testimony of his message. The maiden, being very willing and desirous to obey his commandment (for she alone knew that he was her brother) and out of respect also for his signet, went in all haste alone as the messenger willed her to do. But when she was fallen into the snare and engine which was prepared for her with such infinite cunning, the mischievous woman, like one that were mad and possessed with some ill spirit, did strip her husband's sister and scourge her first with rods from top to toe; and when the poor maiden called for help with a loud voice and declared the truth of the matter, declaring oft that he was her brother, the wicked harlot (boiling with jealousy and weening that she had invented and feigned the matter) took a burning firebrand and thrust it betwixt her thighs, whereby she died miserably.

He that should be the husband of this maiden, but especially her brother, advertised of her cruel death, came to the place where she was slain, and after great lamentation and weeping they caused her to be buried honourably. The young man, her brother, taking in ill part the miserable death of his sister, and especially the unnatural source whence it came, as it was convenient he should, conceived so great dolour within his mind, and was stricken with so pestilent fury of bitter anguish, that he fell into the burning passions of a dangerous ague; whereby he seemed in such necessity that he needed to have some speedy remedy to save his life. The woman that slew the maiden, having lost the name of wife together with her faith, went to a certain traitorous physician, who could number many such triumphs as the work of his hands, and promised him fifty pieces of gold if he would sell her a present poison that she might buy the death of her husband out of hand. This done, in presence of her husband she feigned that it was necessary for him to receive a certain kind of drink, which the masters and doctors of physic do call a sacred potion, to the intent he might purge colour and scour the interior parts of his body. But the physician, instead of that healthy drink, had prepared a mortal and deadly poison, that was rather sacred to the healing of the goddess of death, and when he had tempered it accordingly, he took the pot in presence of all the family and other neighbours and friends of the sick young man, and offered it unto the patient. But the bold and hardy woman, to the end she might destroy him that was privy to her wicked intent, and also gain the money which she had promised the physician, stayed the pot with her hand, saying: 'I pray you, master physician, minister not this drink unto my dear husband until such time as you have drank some good part thereof yourself. For what know I, whether you have mingled any poison in the drink or no? Wherein I pray you not to be offended, for I know that you are a man of wisdom and learning, but this I do to the intent the conscience and love that I bear to the health and safeguard of my husband may be apparent.' The physician, being greatly troubled at the marvellous and stubborn wickedness of the mischievous woman, was void of all counsel and leisure to consider on the matter, and lest he might give any cause of suspicion to the standers-by, or show any scruple of his guilty conscience, by reason of long delay, he took the pot in his hand and presently drank a good draught thereof: which done, the young man, having now no mistrust by this example, drank up the residue. When all this was finished the physician would have gone immediately home to receive a counter-poison or antidote, to expel and drive out the first poison; but the wicked woman, persevering in the constant mischief wherein she had begun, would not suffer him to depart one foot until such time (as she said) as the potion should have begun to work, and its healthy effect be apparent; and then by much prayer and intercession she licensed him to go home. By the way the poison invaded the entrails and bowels of the whole body of the physician, in such sort that with great pain and growing heaviness he came to his own house: where he had scarce time to tell all to his wife, and to will her at least to receive the promised salary of the death of two persons, but this notable physician was violently convulsed and yielded up the ghost.

The young man also lived not long after, but likewise died, amongst the feigned and deceitful tears of his cursed wife. A few days after, when the young man was buried and the accustomed funerals and dirges ended, the physician's wife demanded of her the fifty pieces of gold which she promised for the double murder; whereat

the ill-disposed woman, keeping still that same constancy in wickedness, with resemblance of honesty (for all real honesty she had cast
away) answered her with gentle words, and made her large promises,
particularly that she would presently give her the fifty pieces of gold,
if she would fetch her a little of that same drink to proceed and make
an end of all her enterprise. Then, in short, the physician's wife was
caught in the snare of these wicked deceits, and to win the further
favour of this rich woman ran incontinently home, and brought her
the whole pot of poison; which when she saw, having now occasion
to execute her further malice, she began to stretch out farther her
bloody hands to murder. She had a little young daughter by her
husband that was poisoned, who, according to order of law, was
appointed heir of all the lands and goods of her father; but this she
bore very hard, and lusting after all the child's heritage, she
determined to slay it. So knowing that mothers succeed their children
after such a crime, and receive all their goods after their death, she
purposed to show herself a like parent to her child as she was a wife to
her husband. Whereupon at a convenient season she prepared a
dinner with her own hands, and poisoned both the wife of the
physician and her own daughter. The child, being young and tender,
died incontinently by the deadly force of the drink; but the
physician's wife, being stout and of strong complexion, feeling the
strong poison creep down into her body and wander through her
vitals, at first doubted the matter; and then, by her labouring breath
knowing of certainty that she had received her bane, ran forthwith to
the judge's house, and what with her cries as she called upon him and
all her exclamations, she raised up the people of the town, and
promising them to reveal and show divers wicked and mischievous
acts, caused that both the doors and ears of the judge were opened.
When she came in, she declared from the beginning to the end the
abomination of this woman; but she had scarce ended her tale, when
a whirling cloud and giddiness seized upon her mind in a fit, and
shutting fast her falling lips, and grinding her teeth together, she fell
down dead before the face of the judge. He, that was a ready and
prudent man, incontinently would try the truth of the matter, and
would not suffer the crime of this wicked woman, more venomous
than any serpent, by long delays to remain hidden and unpunished,
but caused the cursed woman's servants to be pulled out of the house
and enforced by pain of torment to confess the verity; which being

known, this mischievous woman, far less than she deserved, but because there could be no more cruel death invented for the quality of her offence, was condemned by him to be eaten of wild beasts.

Behold with this woman was I appointed to have to do in wedlock before the face of all the people; but I, being wrapped in great anguish, and fearing the day of the triumph, when we two should so abandon ourselves together, devised rather to slay myself than pollute my body with this mischievous harlot, and so be defamed as a public sight and spectacle. But it was impossible for me to do this, considering that I lacked human hands, I lacked fingers, and I was not able to draw a sword with my hoofs being round and short; howbeit I did console myself for this utter misfortune with a small ray of hope, for I rejoiced in myself that springtime was come and was now making all things bright with flourishing buds, and clothing the meadows very brightly, so that I was in good hope to find some roses now bursting through from their thorny coats and breathing forth their fragrant odours, to render me to my human shape that I had before as Lucius.

When the day of the triumph came, I was led with great pomp and magnificence to the theatre, whither when I was brought, I first saw the preamble of the triumph, dedicated with dances and merry taunting jests. In the mean season I was placed before the gate of the theatre, where on the one side I saw the green and fresh grass growing before the entry thereof, whereon I did gladly feed; and sometimes I conceived a great delectation when I saw, when the theatre gates were opened, how all things were finely prepared and set forth; for there I might see young boys and maidens in the flower of their youth, of excellent beauty and attired gorgeously, dancing and moving in comely order, according to the disposition of the Grecian Pyrrhic dance; for sometime they would trip round together, sometime in length obliquely, sometime divide themselves in four parts, and sometime loose hands and group them on every side. But when the last sound of the trumpet gave warning that every man should retire to his place from those knots and circlings about, then was the curtain taken away and all the hangings rolled apart, and then began the triumph to appear.

First there was a hill of wood, not much unlike that famous hill which the poet Homer called Ida, reared up exceeding high and garnished about with all sort of green verdures and lively trees, from the top whereof ran down a clear and fresh fountain, made by the skilful hands of the artificer, distilling out waters below. There were there a few young and tender goats, plucking and feeding daintily on the budding grass, and then came a young man, a shepherd representing Paris, richly arrayed with vestments of barbary,* having a mitre of gold upon his head, and seeming as though he kept the goats. After him ensued another fair youth all naked, saving that his left shoulder was covered with a rich cloak such as young men do wear, and his head shining with golden hair, and as it hung down you might perceive through it two little wings of gold; and him the rod called Caduceus and the wand did show to be Mercury. He bare in his right hand an apple of gold, and with a seemly and dancing gait went towards him that represented Paris, and after that he had delivered him the apple, he made a sign signifying that Jupiter had commanded him so to do, and when he had done his message, he departed very gracefully away. By and by behold there approached a fair and comely maiden, not much unlike to Juno; for she had a white diadem upon her head, and in her hand she bare a regal sceptre; then followed another resembling Minerva, for she had on her head a shining helmet, whereon was bound a garland made of olive-branches, having in one hand a target or shield, and in the other shaking a spear as when she would fight. Then came another, which passed the others in beauty, and represented the goddess Venus with the colour of ambrosia: but Venus when she was a maiden, and to the end she would show her perfect beauty, she appeared all naked, saving that her fine and comely privates were lightly covered with a thin silken smock, and this the wanton wind blew hither and thither, sometime lifting it to testify the youth and flower of her age, and sometime making it to cling close to her to show clearly the form and figure of her members; her colour was of two sorts, for her body was white, as descended from heaven, and her smock was bluish, as returning† to

---

* *i.e.* un-Greek. Paris would naturally be represented in Phrygian costume.
† I can hardly believe that *quod mari remeat* can mean, as has usually been suggested, 'because she came from the sea'. A preposition would surely be required before *mari*, and the contrast between *demeat* and *remeat* would be lost. The allusion here is not to the miraculous birth of Venus from the foam, but to the fact that her ordinary home (*cf.* Book IV, ch. 31) is in the sea: in the present instance the make-up of the girl who is taking her part suggests both her heavenly origin and her marine abiding-place.

the sea. After every one of these virgins which seemed goddesses, followed certain waiting servants; Castor and Pollux played by boys of the theatre went behind Juno, having on their heads round pointed helmets covered with stars; this virgin Juno in the Ionian manner sounded a flute which she bare in her hand, and moved herself quickly and with unaffected gait towards the shepherd Paris, showing by honest signs and tokens and promising that he should be Lord of all Asia if he would judge her the fairest of the three, and give her the apple of gold. The other maiden, which seemed by her armour to be Minerva, was accompanied with two young men, armed and brandishing their naked swords in their hands, whereof one was named Terror, and the other Fear; and behind them approached one sounding his flute in the Dorian manner, now with shrill notes and now with deep tones to provoke and stir the dancers as the trumpet stirreth men to battle: this maiden began to dance and shake her head, throwing her fierce and terrible eyes upon Paris, and promising that if it pleased him to give her the victory of beauty, she would make him by her protection the most strong and victorious man alive. Then came Venus and presented herself, smiling very sweetly, in the middle of the theatre, with much favour of all the people. She was accompanied with a great number of little boys, whereby you would have judged them to be all Cupids, so plump and fair were they, and either to have flown from heaven or else from the river of the sea, for they had little wings and little arrows, and the residue of their habit according in each point, and they bare in their hands torches lighted, as though it had been the day and feast of marriage of their lady. Then came in a great multitude of fair maidens: on the one side were the most comely Graces; on the other side the most beautiful Seasons, carrying garlands and loose flowers which they strewed before her; and they danced very nimbly therewith, making great honour to the goddess of pleasure with these flowers of the spring. The flutes and pipes with their many stops yielded out the sweet sound of the Lydian strain, whereby they pleased the minds of the standers-by exceedingly; but the more pleasing Venus moved smoothly forwards more and more with slow and lingering steps, gently bending her body and moving her head, answering by her motion and delicate gesture to the sound of the instruments: for sometimes her eyes would wink gently with soft motions to the music, sometimes threaten and look fiercely, and sometimes she seemed to dance only with her eyes. As soon as she was come before the judge, she made a sign and token that if he would prefer her above the residue of the goddesses, she would give him the fairest spouse of all the world and one like to herself in every part. Then the young Phrygian shepherd Paris with a willing mind delivered to Venus the golden apple, which was the victory of beauty.

Why then do ye marvel, if the lowest of the people, the lawyers, beasts of the courts, and advocates that are but vultures in gowns,* nay, if all our judges nowadays sell their judgements for money, when as in the beginning of the world one only bribe and favour corrupted the sentence between gods and men, and that one rustical judge and shepherd, appointed by the counsel of the great Jupiter, sold his first judgement for a little pleasure, which was the cause afterwards of the ruin of all his kin? By like manner of mean was another sentence given between the noble Greeks; for the wise and excellently learned personage Palamedes was convicted and attainted of treason by false persuasion and accusation, and Ulysses, being but of moderate valour, was preferred above great Ajax of most martial prowess. What judgement was there likewise amongst the Athenian lawyers, sage and expert in all sciences? Was not the old man Socrates of divine wisdom, who was preferred by the god of Delphi above all the wise men of the world, by envy and malice of wicked persons empoisoned with the herb hemlock, as one that corrupted the youth of the country, whom in truth always he bridled and kept under by correction? Thus did he leave to the men of Athens a stain and dishonour that shall never fade, for we see nowadays many excellent philosophers greatly desire to follow his sect, and for their perpetual study for happiness to swear by his name. But to the end I may not be reproved of indignation, by anyone that might say: 'What, shall we suffer an ass to play the philosopher to us?' I will return to my former purpose.

After the judgement of Paris was ended, Juno and Pallas departed away sadly and angrily, showing by their gesture that they were very wroth and would revenge themselves on Paris; but Venus, that was right pleased and glad in her heart, danced about the theatre with much joy, together with all her train. This done, from the top of the hill through a privy spout ran a flood of wine coloured with saffron, which fell upon the goats in a sweet-scented stream, and changed

---

* Apuleius seems to have entertained but a poor opinion of lawyers, perhaps as a result of the lawsuit which he describes in his *Apologia*.

their white hair into yellow more fair: and then with a sweet odour to all them of the theatre, by certain engines the ground opened and swallowed up the hill of wood. Then behold there came a man of arms through the middle of the space, demanding by the commandment of the people the woman who for her manifold crimes was condemned to the beasts, and appointed for me to do in wedlock withal. Now was our bed finely and bravely prepared, shining with the tortoise-shell of Ind, rising with bolsters of feathers, and covered with silk and other things necessary; but I, beside the shame to commit publicly this horrible fact and to pollute my body with this wicked harlot, did greatly fear the danger of death; for I thought in myself, that when she and I were together, the savage beast appointed to devour the woman was not so instructed and taught or would so temper his greediness as that he would tear her in pieces at my side and spare me with a regard of mine innocency. Wherefore I was more careful for the safeguard of my life than for the shame that I should abide; and in the mean season, while my master diligently made ready the bed, and all the residue did prepare themselves for the spectacle of hunting and delighted in the pleasantness of the triumph, I began to think and devise for myself; and when I perceived that no man had regard to me, that was so tame and gentle an ass, I stole secretly out of the gate that was next me, and then I ran away with all my force, and came after about six miles very swiftly passed to Cenchreae, which is the most famous town of all the Corinthians, bordering upon the seas called Aegean and Saronic. There is a great and mighty haven frequented with the ships of many a sundry nation, and there because I would avoid the multitude of people, I went to a secret place of the sea-coast, hard by the sprinklings of the waves, where I laid me down upon the bosom of the sand to ease and refresh myself, for now the day was past and the chariot of the sun gone down, and I lying in this sort on the ground did fall in a sweet and sound sleep.

BOOK ELEVEN

About the first watch of the night, when as I had slept my first sleep, I awaked with sudden fear, and saw the moon shining bright as when she is at the full, and seeming as though she leaped out of the sea. Then I thought with myself that this was the most secret time, when that goddess had most puissance and force, considering that all human things be governed by her providence; and that not only all beasts private and tame, wild and savage, be made strong by the governance of her light and godhead, but also things inanimate and without life; and I considered that all bodies in the heavens, the earth, and the seas be by her increasing motions increased, and by her diminishing motions diminished: then as weary of all my cruel fortune and calamity, I found good hope and sovereign remedy, though it were very late, to be delivered of all my misery, by invocation and prayer to the excellent beauty of this powerful goddess. Wherefore shaking off my drowsy sleep I arose with a joyful face, and moved by a great affection to purify myself, I plunged my head seven times into the water of the sea, which number of seven is convenable and agreeable to holy and divine things, as the worthy and sage philosopher Pythagoras hath declared. Then very lively and joyfully, though with a weeping countenance, I made this oration to the puissant goddess:

'O blessed queen of heaven, whether Thou be the Dame Ceres which art the original and motherly nurse of all fruitful things in the earth, who, after the finding of Thy daughter Proserpine, through the great joy which Thou didst presently conceive, didst utterly take away and abolish the food of them of old time, the acorn, and madest the barren and unfruitful ground of Eleusis to be ploughed and sown, and now givest men a more better and milder food; or whether thou be the celestial Venus, who, in the beginning of the world, didst couple together male and female with an engendered love, and didst so make an eternal propagation of human kind, being now worshipped within the temples of the Isle Paphos; or whether Thou be the sister of the god Phoebus, who hast saved so many people by lightening and lessening with thy medicines the pangs of travail* and art now adored at the sacred places of Ephesus; or whether Thou be called terrible Proserpine, by reason of the deadly howlings which Thou yieldest, that hast power with triple face to stop and put away the invasion of hags and ghosts which appear unto men, and to keep them down in the closures of the Earth, which dost wander in sundry groves and art worshipped in divers manners; Thou, which dost luminate all the cities of the earth by Thy feminine light; Thou, which nourishest all the seeds of the world by Thy damp heat, giving Thy changing light according to the wanderings, near or far, of the sun: by whatsoever name or fashion or shape it is lawful to call upon Thee, I pray Thee to end my great travail and misery and raise up my fallen hopes, and deliver me from the wretched fortune which so long time pursued me. Grant peace and rest, if it please Thee, to my adversities, for I have endured enough labour and peril. Remove from me the hateful shape of mine ass, and render me to my kindred and to mine own self Lucius: and if I have offended in any point Thy divine majesty, let me rather die if I may not live.'

When I had ended this oration, discovering my plaints to the goddess, I fortuned to fall again asleep upon that same bed and by and by (for mine eyes were but newly closed) appeared to me from the midst of the sea a divine and venerable face, worshipped even of the gods themselves. Then, by little and little, I seemed to see the whole figure of her body, bright and mounting out of the sea and standing before me: wherefore I purpose to describe her divine semblance, if the poverty of my human speech will suffer me, or her divine power give me a power of eloquence rich enough to express it. First she had a great abundance of hair, flowing and curling, dispersed and scattered about her divine neck; on the crown of her head she bare many garlands interlaced with flowers, and in the middle of her forehead was a plain circlet in fashion of a mirror, or rather resembling the moon by the light that it gave forth; and this was borne up on either side by serpents that seemed to rise from the furrows of the earth, and above it were blades of corn set out. Her vestment was of finest linen yielding divers colours, somewhere white and shining, somewhere yellow like the crocus flower, somewhere rosy red, somewhere

---

* Diana was the goddess called upon by women in childbirth to help them and assuage their pains, as St Maragaret in later days.

flaming; and (which troubled my sight and spirit sore) her cloak was utterly dark and obscure covered with shining black, and being wrapped round her from under her left arm to her right shoulder in manner of a shield, part of it fell down, pleated in most subtle fashion, to the skirts of her garment so that the welts appeared comely. Here and there upon the edge thereof and throughout its surface the stars glimpsed, and in the middle of them was placed the moon in mid-month, which shone like a flame of fire; and round about the whole length of the border of that goodly robe was a crown or garland wreathing unbroken, made with all flowers and all fruits. Things quite diverse did she bear: for in her right hand she had a timbrel of brass, a fat piece of metal curved in manner of a girdle, wherein passed not many rods through the periphery of it; and when with her arm she moved these triple chords, they gave forth a shrill and clear sound.* In her left hand she bare a cup of gold like unto a boat, upon the handle whereof, in the upper part which is best seen, an asp lifted up his head with a wide-swelling throat. Her odoriferous feet were covered with shoes interlaced and wrought with victorious palm. Thus the divine shape, breathing out the pleasant spice of fertile Arabia, disdained not with her holy voice to utter these words unto me:

'Behold, Lucius, I am come; thy weeping and prayer hath moved me to succour thee. I am she that is the natural mother of all things, mistress and governess of all the elements, the initial progeny of worlds, chief of the powers divine, queen of all that are in hell, the principal of them that dwell in heaven, manifested alone and under one form of all the gods and goddesses. At my will the planets of the sky, the wholesome winds of the seas, and the lamentable silences of hell be disposed; my name, my divinity is adored throughout all the world, in divers manners, in variable customs, and by many names. For the Phrygians that are the first of all men† call me the Mother of the gods at Pessinus; the Athenians, which are sprung from their own

---

* A description of the *sistrum*. Its exact form may be seen represented on the Egyptian monuments, and Plutarch gives an elaborate explanation of its symbolism in his treatise *De Iside et Osiride*.

† 'The Egyptians [of the time of Psammetichus] were brought to think that the Phrygians were the most old and ancient people of the earth, and themselves to be next in antiquity to them.' For the reasons which induced Psammetichus and his people to form this opinion, see Herodotus, II, 2.

soil, Cecropian Minerva; the Cyprians, which are girt about by the sea, Paphian Venus; the Cretans which bear arrows, Dictynnian Diana; the Sicilians, which speak three tongues, infernal Proserpine; the Eleusians their ancient goddess Ceres; some Juno, other Bellona, other Hecate, other Rhamnusia,* and principally both sort of the Ethiopians which dwell in the Orient and are enlightened by the morning rays of the sun, and the Egyptians, which are excellent in all kind of ancient doctrine, and by their proper ceremonies accustom to worship me, do call me by my true name, Queen Isis. Behold I am come to take pity of thy fortune and tribulation; behold I am present to favour and aid thee; leave oft thy weeping and lamentation, put away all thy sorrow, for behold the healthful day which is ordained by my providence. Therefore be ready and attentive to my commandment; the day which shall come after this night is dedicate to my service by an eternal religion; my priests and ministers do accustom, after the wintry and stormy tempests of the sea be ceased and the billows of his waves are still, to offer in my name a new ship, as a first-fruit of their navigation; and for this must thou wait, and not profane or despise the sacrifice in any wise. For the great priest shall carry this day following in procession, by my exhortation, a garland of roses next to the timbrel of his right hand; delay not, but, trusting to my will, follow that my procession passing amongst the crowd of the people, and when thou comest to the priest, make as though thou wouldst kiss his hand, but snatch at the roses and thereby put away the skin and shape of an ass, which kind of beast I have long time abhorred and despised. But above all things beware thou doubt not nor fear of any of those my things as hard and difficult to be brought to pass, for in this same hour that I am come to thee, I am present there also, and I command the priest by a vision what he shall do, as here followeth: and all the people by my commandment shall be compelled to give thee place and say nothing. Moreover, think not that amongst so fair and joyful ceremonies, and in so good company, that any person shall abhor thy ill-favoured and deformed figure, or that any man shall be so hardy as to blame and reprove thy sudden restoration to human shape, whereby they should gather or conceive any sinister opinion of thee, and know thou this of certainty, that the residue of thy life until the hour of death shall be bound and subject

* An epithet of the goddess Nemesis, or Fate.

to me; and think it not an injury to be always serviceable towards me whilst thou shalt live, since as by my mean and benefit thou shalt return again to be a man. You shalt live blessed in this world, thou shalt live glorious by my guide and protection, and when after thine allotted space of life thou descendest to hell, there thou shalt see me in that subterranean firmament shining (as thou seest me now) in the darkness of Acheron, and reigning in the deep profundity of Styx, and thou shalt worship me as one that hath been favourable to thee. And if I perceive that thou art obedient to my commandment and addict to my religion, meriting by thy constant chastity my divine grace, know thou that I alone may prolong thy days above the time that the fates have appointed and ordained.'

When the invincible goddess had spoken these words and ended her holy oracle, she vanished away. By and by when I awaked, I arose, having the members of my body mixed with fear, joy, and heavy sweat, and marvelled at the clear presence of the puissant goddess, and when I had sprinkled myself with the water of the sea, I recounted orderly her admonitions and divine commandments. Soon after the darkness was chased away and the clear and golden sun rose, when behold, I saw the streets replenished with people, going in a religious sort, and in great triumph. All things seemed that day to be joyful, as well all manner of beasts and the very houses, as also even the day itself seemed to rejoice. For after the hoar frost of the night ensued the hot and temperate sun, whereby the little birds, weening that the springtime had been come, did chirp and sing melodiously, making sweet welcome with their pleasant song to the mother of the stars, the parent of times, and mistress of all the world. The fruitful trees also, both those which rejoiced in their fertility and those which, being barren and sterile, were contented at the shadow which they could give, being loosened by the breathing of the south wind, and smiling by reason of their new buds now appearing, did gently move their branches and render sweet pleasant shrills; the seas were quiet from the roaring winds and the tempests of great waves; the heaven had chased away the clouds, and appeared fair and clear with his proper light.

Behold, then more and more appeared the beginnings of the pomps and processions, everyone attired in regal manner, according to his proper habit. One was girded about the middle like a man of arms; another bare a spear, and had a cloak caught up and high shoes as a hunter; another was attired in a robe of silk, and socks of gold, with fine ornament, having long hair added and fixed upon his head, and walked delicately in form of a woman; there was another which ware leg harness and bare a target, an helmet and a spear, like unto a gladiator, as one might believe; after him marched one attired in purple, with the rods borne by vergers before him, like a magistrate; after him followed one with a mantle, a staff, a pair of pantofles, and with a beard as long as any goat's, signifying a philosopher; after him went one with reeds and lime, betokening him a fowler, and another with hooks, declaring a fisher. I saw there a meek and tame bear, which in matron habit was carried on a stool; an ape with a bonnet of woven stuff on his head, and covered with saffron lawn, resembling the Phrygian shepherd Ganymede, and bearing a cup of gold in his hand; an ass had wings glued to his back and went after an old man, whereby you would judge the one to be Pegasus and the other Bellerophon, and at both would you laugh well. Amongst these pleasures and popular delectations, which wandered hither and thither, you might see the peculiar pomp of the saving goddess triumphantly march forward. The women attired in white vestments, and rejoicing in that they bare garlands and flowers upon their heads, bespread the way with herbs, which they bare in their aprons, where this regal and devout procession should pass. Others carried shining mirrors behind them which were turned towards the goddess as she came, to show to her those which came after as though they would meet her. Others bare combs of ivory, and declared by their gesture and motions of their arms and fingers that they were ordained and ready to dress and adorn the goddess's hair. Others dropped in the ways, as they went, balm and other precious ointments. Then came a great number, as well of men as of women, with lamps, candles, torches, and other lights, doing honour thereby to her that was born of the celestial stars. After that sounded the musical harmony of instruments, pipes and flutes in most pleasant measure. Then came a fair company of youth apparelled in white vestments and festal array, singing both metre and verse with a comely grace which some studious poet had made by favour of the Muses, the words whereof did set forth the first ceremonies of this great worship. In the mean season arrived the blowers of trumpets, which were dedicate unto mighty Sarapis, who, holding the same reed sidelong towards their right ears, did give forth a ditty proper to the temple and the god: and likewise were there many officers and beadles, crying room for the goddess to pass. Then came the great company of men and women of all stations and of every age which were initiate and had taken divine orders, whose garments, being of the whitest linen, glistened all the streets over. The women had their hair anointed, and their heads covered with light linen; but the men had their crowns shaven and shining bright, as being the terrene stars of the goddess, and held in their hands timbrels of brass, silver, aye and gold, which rendered forth a shrill and pleasant sound. The principal priests, leaders of the sacred rites, which were apparelled with white surplices drawn tight about their breasts and hanging down to the ground, bare the relics of all the most puissant gods. One that was first of them carried in his hand a lantern shining forth with a clear light, not very like to those which we use in our houses and light our supper withal at evening-time, for the bowl of it was of gold and rendered from the middle thereof a more bright flame. The second, attired like the other, bare in both hands those pots to which the succouring providence of the high goddess herself had given their name. The third held up a tree of palm, with leaves cunningly wrought of gold, and the verge or rod Caduceus of Mercury. The fourth showed a token of equity, that was a left hand deformed in every place and with open palm, and because it was naturally more sluggish, and that there was no cleverness nor craft in it, it signified thereby more equity than by the right hand: the same priest carried a round vessel of gold, in form of a breast, whence milk flowed down. The fifth bare a winnowing fan, wrought with sprigs of gold, and another carried a vessel for wine.

By and by after, the gods deigned to follow afoot as men do, and specially Anubis, the messenger of the gods infernal and supernal, tall, with his face sometime black, sometime fair as gold, lifting up on high his dog's head, and bearing in his left hand his verge, and in his right hand the green branch of a palm-tree. After him straight followed a cow with an upright gait, the cow representing the great goddess that is the fruitful mother of all, and he that guided her supported her as she leaned upon his shoulder, and marched on with much gravity in happy steps. Another carried after the secrets of their glorious religion, closed in a coffer. Another was there that bare in his bosom (thrice happy he!) the venerable figure of the godhead, not formed like any beast, bird, savage thing, or human shape, but made by a new invention, and therefore much to be admired, an emblem ineffable, whereby was signified that such a religion was at once very high and should not be discovered or revealed to any person; thus was it fashioned of shining gold: it was a vessel wrought with a round bottom, and hollowed with wondrous cunning, having on the outside pictures figured like unto the manner of the Egyptians, and the mouth thereof was not very high, but made to jut out like unto a long funnel; on the other side was an ear or handle which came far out from the vessel, whereupon stood an asp holding out his swelling and scaly neck, which entwined the whole as in a knot.

Finally came he which was appointed to my good fortune, according to the promise of the most puissant goddess. For the great priest, which bare the restoration of my human shape, by the commandment of the goddess approached more and more, carrying in his right hand both the timbrel and the garland of roses to give me, which was in very deed my crown to deliver me from cruel fortune which was always mine enemy, after the sufferance of so much calamity and pain, and after the endurance of so many perils. Then I, not running hastily by reason of sudden joy, lest I should disturb the quiet procession with my beastly importunity, but going softly as a man doth step through the press of people, which gave me place by the divine command on every side, I went after the priest. Then the priest, being admonished the night before, as I might well perceive, and marvelling that now the event came opportunely to fulfil that warning, suddenly stood still, and holding out his hands thrust out the garland of roses to my mouth: which garland I (trembling and my heart beating greatly) devoured with a great affection. As soon as I had eaten them, I was not deceived of the promise made unto me: for my deform and assy face abated, and first the rugged hair of my body fell off, my thick skin waxed soft and tender, my fat belly became thin, the hoofs of my feet changed into toes, my hands were no more feet but returned again to the work of a man that walks upright, my neck grew short, my head and mouth became round, my long ears were made little, my great and stony teeth waxed less, like the teeth of men, and my tail, which before cumbered me most, appeared nowhere. Then the people began to marvel, and the religious honoured the goddess for so evident a miracle, which was foreshadowed by the visions which they saw in the night, and the facility of my reformation, whereby they lifted their hands to heaven and with one voice rendered testimony of so great a benefit which I received of the goddess.

When I saw myself in such estate, I was utterly astonied and stood still a good space and said nothing; for my mind could not contain so sudden and so great joy, and I could not tell what to say, nor what word I should first speak with my voice newly found, nor what thanks I should render to the goddess. But the great priest, understanding all my fortune and misery by divine advertisement, although he also was amazed at this notable marvel, by gestures commanded that one should give me a linen garment to cover me; for as soon as I was transformed from the vile skin of an ass to my human shape, I hid the privities of my body with my hands as far as a naked man might do. Then one of the company put off his upper robe, and put it on my back; which done, the priest, looking upon me with a sweet and benign countenance, began to say in this sort: 'O my friend Lucius, after the endurance of so many labours and the escape of so many tempests of fortune, thou art now at length come to the port and haven of rest and mercy. Neither did thy noble lineage, thy dignity, neither thy excellent doctrine anything avail thee; but because thou didst turn to servile pleasures, by a little folly of thy youthfulness, thou hast had a sinister reward of thy unprosperous curiosity. But howsoever the blindness of fortune tormented thee in divers dangers, so it is that now by her unthoughtful malice thou art come to this present felicity of religion. Let fortune go and fume with fury in another place; let her find some other matter to execute her cruelty; for fortune hath no puissance against them which have devoted their lives to serve and honour the majesty of our goddess. For what availed the thieves? The beasts savage? Thy great servitude? The ill, toilsome, and dangerous ways? The fear of death every day? What availed all those, I say, to cruel fortune? Know thou that now thou art safe, and under the protection of that fortune that is not blind but can see, who by her clear light doth lighten the other gods: wherefore rejoice, and take a convenable countenance to thy white habit, and follow with joyful steps the pomp of this devout and honourable procession; let such, which be not devout to the goddess, see and acknowledge their error: "Behold, here is Lucius that is delivered from his former so great miseries by the providence of the goddess Isis, and rejoiceth therefore and triumpheth of victory over his fortune. And to the end thou mayest live more safe and sure, make thyself one of this holy order, to which thou wast but a short time since pledged by oath, dedicate thy mind to the obeying of our religion, and take upon thee a voluntary yoke of ministry: for when thou beginnest to serve and honour the goddess, then shalt thou feel the more the fruit of thy liberty.'

After that the great priest had prophesied in this manner with often breathings, he made a conclusion of his words. Then I went amongst the company of the rest and followed the procession: everyone of the people knew me, and pointing at me with their fingers, or nodding with their heads, they said in this sort: 'Behold him who is this day transformed into a man by the puissance of the sovereign goddess; verily he is blessed and most blessed that by the innocency of his former life hath merited so great grace from heaven, and as it were by a new generation is reserved straightway to the obsequy of religion.' In the mean season, amid all these loud cries and prayers, by little and little we approached nigh unto the sea-coast, even to that place where I lay the night before being an ass. There, after the images and relics were orderly disposed, was a boat cunningly wrought and compassed about with divers pictures according to the fashion of the Egyptians, which the great priest did dedicate and consecrate with certain prayers from his holy lips and purified the same with a torch, an egg, and sulphur, dedicating it unto the name of the goddess. The sail of this blessed ship was of white linen cloth, whereon was written certain letters which should testify the navigation of the new season to be prosperous; the mast was of a great length, made of a pine-tree, round, and very excellent, with a shining top seen of all eyes; the poop was covered over with plates of gold, being in shape like unto a goose's neck, and all the ship was made of citron-tree very fair. Then all the people, as well religious as profane, took a great number of winnowing fans replenished with odours and pleasant smells, and poured libation of milk into the sea, until the ship was filled up with large gifts and prosperous devotions, when as with a pleasant wind the ropes of the anchor were let go and it launched out into the deep while a breeze blew fair for that ship alone. And when they had lost the sight of the ship, by reason that it was afar off, every man of them that bore the holy things carried again that which he brought, and went towards the temple in like pomp and order as they came to the seaside.

When we were come to the temple, the great priest and those which were deputed to carry the divine figures but specially those which had long time been initiate in the religion, went into the secret chamber of the goddess, where they put and placed the lively images according to their order. This done, one of the company which was a scribe or interpreter of letters, in form of a preacher stood up in a chair before the place of the holy college of the Pastophores* (for so are they named) and calling together their whole assembly, from his high pulpit began to read out of a book, praying for good fortune to the great Prince, the Senate, to the noble order of Chivalry, and generally to all the Roman people, and to all the sailors and ships such as be under the puissance and jurisdiction of Rome, and he pronounced to them in the Grecian tongue and manner this word following, '*Ploiaphesia*',† which signified that it was now lawful for the ships to depart; whereat all the people gave a great shout, and then replenished with much joy, bare all kind of leafy branches and herbs and garlands of flowers home to their houses, kissing and embracing the feet of a silver image of the goddess upon the steps of the temple. Howbeit I could not do as the rest, for my mind would not suffer me to depart one foot away, so earnest and attentive was I to behold the beauty of the goddess, with remembrance likewise of my great travail and misery which I had endured.

In the mean season news was carried throughout the country (which goeth as swift as the flight of birds, or as the blast of wind) of the grace and benefit which I had received of the goddess, and of my fortune worthy to be had in memory. Then my parents of close blood, friends, and servants of our house, understanding that I was not dead as they were falsely informed, laid by their grief and came towards me with great diligence to see me, bearing to me gifts, as a man raised from death to life. And I likewise, which did never think to see them again, was as joyful as they, but would receive none of the honest gifts and oblations which they gave, inasmuch as my servants had taken care to bring with them enough of such things as was necessary for my body and my charges. After that I had greeted each according to his kindness, and made relation unto them of all

---

* The 'shrine-bearers' – the highest order of the Isiac priests.
† This Greek word or words had become much corrupted in the MSS: πλοιαψέσια is Mommsen's emendation. The old printed editions had λαοῖς ἄΦεσις, which may be compared with the *Ite missa est* at the end of the Roman Mass; other commentators suggest ἁγνοὶ ἐΦ' ὅσια and other formulae of Oriental religion.

my pristine misery and present joys, I went again before the face of the goddess, and hired me a house within the cloister of the temple, since I had been set apart for the service of the goddess that hitherto had been kept private from me, so that I might ordinarily frequent the company of the priests, whereby I would wholly become devout to the goddess, and an inseparable worshipper of her divine name: nor was there any night nor sleep but that the goddess appeared to me, persuading and commanding me to take the order of her religion whereto I had been long since foreordained. But I, although I was endued with a desirous goodwill, yet the reverend fear of the same held me back, considering that as I had learned by diligent enquiry her obeisance was hard, the chastity of the priests difficult to keep, and the whole life of them, because it is set about with many chances, to be watched and guarded very carefully. Being thus in doubt, I refrained myself from all those things as seeming impossible, although in truth I was hastening towards them.

On a night the great priest appeared unto me in a dream presenting his lap full of treasure, and when I demanded what it signified, he answered that this portion was sent me from the country of Thessaly, and that a servant of mine named Candidus was thence arrived likewise. When I was awaked, I mused in myself what this vision should portend, considering I never had any servant called by that name: but whatsoever it did signify, this I verily thought, that such offering of gifts was a foreshow of gain and prosperous chance. While I was thus anxious and astonished at my coming prosperity, I went to the temple, and tarried there till the opening of the gates in the morning: then I went in, and when the white curtains were drawn aside, I began to pray before the face of the goddess, while the priest prepared and set the divine things on every altar with solemn supplications, and fetched out of the sanctuary the holy water for the libation. When all things were duly performed, the religious began to sing the matins of the morning, testifying thereby the hour of prime. By and by behold arrived my servants which I had left at Hypata, when Fotis entangled me in my maze of miserable wanderings, who had heard my tale as it seemed, and brought with them even my horse, which they had recovered through certain signs and tokens which he had upon his back. Then I perceived the interpretation of my dream, by reason that beside the promise of gain, my white horse was restored to me, which was signified by the argument of my servant Candidus.*

This done, I retired the more diligently to the service of the goddess in hope of greater benefits, considering I had received a sign and token, whereby my courage increased every day more and more to take upon me the orders and sacraments of the temple: in so much that I oftentimes communed with the priest, desiring him greatly to make me initiate in the mysteries of the holy night. But he, which was a man of gravity and well-renowned in the order of priesthood, very gently and kindly deferred my affection from day to day with comfort of better hope, as parents commonly bridle the desires of their children when they attempt or endeavour any unprofitable thing, saying that the day when anyone should be admitted into their order is appointed by the goddess, the priest which should minister the sacrifice is chosen by her providence, and the necessary charge of the ceremonies is allotted by her commandment; all of which things he willed me to attend with marvellous patience: and that I should beware both of too much forwardness, and of stubborn obstinacy, avoiding either danger, that if being called I should delay, or not called I should be hasty. Moreover he said that there was none of his company either of so desperate a mind, or so rash and hardy unto death as to enterprise receiving this mystery without the command-ment of the goddess, whereby he should commit a deadly offence: considering that it was in her power both to damn and to save all persons, and that the taking of such orders was like to a voluntary death and a difficult recovery to health: and if anywhere there were any at the point of death and at the end and limit of their life, so that they were capable to receive the dread secrets of the goddess, it was in her power by divine providence to make them as it were new-born and to reduce them to the path of health. Finally he said that I must therefore attend and wait for the celestial precept, although it were evident and plain that the goddess had already vouchsafed to call and appoint me to the happy company of her ministry, and that I must refrain from profane and unlawful meats, as those priests which were already received, to the end I might come more apt and clean to the knowledge of the secrets of the religion.

Then when he had thus spoken I was obedient unto these words,

* *Servus candidus* (according as the second word is spelt with a capital letter or no) means 'my servant Candidus' or 'my white servant'.

and fretted not my duty with lack of patience; but I was attentive with meek quietness and taciturnity to prove me. I daily served at the temple: and in the end the wholesome gentleness of the goddess did nothing deceive me, for she tormented me with a long delay, but in a dark night she appeared to me in a vision, declaring in words not dark that the day was come which I had wished for so long; she told me what provision and charges I should be at for the supplications, and how that she had appointed her principal priest Mithras, that was joined unto my destiny (as she said) by the ordering of the planets, to be a minister with me in my sacrifices. When I had heard these and the other divine commandments of the high goddess, I greatly rejoiced, and arose before day to speak with the great priest, whom I fortuned to espy coming out of his chamber. Then I saluted him, and thought with myself to ask and demand with a bold courage that I should be initiate, as a thing now due; but as soon as he perceived me, he began first to say: 'O Lucius, now know I well that thou art most happy and blessed, whom the divine goddess doth so greatly accept with mercy. Why dost thou stand idle and delay? Behold the day which thou didst desire with prayer, when as thou shalt receive at my hands the order of most secret and holy religion, according to the divine commandment of this goddess of many names.' Thereupon the old man took me by the hand, and led me courteously to the gate of the great temple, where, after that it was religiously opened, he made a solemn celebration, and after the morning sacrifice was ended, he brought out of the secret place of the temple certain books written with unknown characters, partly painted with figures of beasts declaring briefly every sentence, partly with letters whose tops and tails turned round in fashion of a wheel, joined together above like unto the tendrils of a vine, whereby they were wholly strange and impossible to be read of the profane people; thence he interpreted to me such things as were necessary to the use and preparation of mine order. This done, I diligently gave in charge to certain of my companions to buy liberally whatsoever was needful and convenient; but part thereof I bought myself. Then he brought me, when he found that the time was at hand, to the next baths, accompanied with all the religions sort, and demanding pardon of the gods, washed me and purified my body according to the custom: after this, when two parts of the day was gone, he brought me back again to the temple and presented me before the feet of the goddess, giving me a charge of certain secret things unlawful to be uttered, and commanding me generally before all the rest to fast by the space of ten continual days, without eating of any beast or drinking of any wine: which things I observed with a marvellous continency. Then behold the day approached when as the sacrifice of dedication should be done; and when the sun declined and evening came, there arrived on every coast a great multitude of priests, who according to their ancient order offered me many presents and gifts. Then was all the laity and profane people commanded to depart, and when they had put on my back a new linen robe, the priest took my hand and brought me to the most secret and sacred place of the temple. Thou wouldest peradventure demand, thou studious reader, what was said and done there: verily I would tell thee if it were lawful for me to tell, thou wouldest know if it were convenient for thee to hear; but both thy ears and my tongue should incur the like pain of rash curiosity. Howbeit I will not long torment thy mind, which peradventure is somewhat religious and given to some devotion; listen therefore, and believe it to be true. Thou shalt understand that I approached near unto hell, even to the gates of Proserpine, and after that I was ravished throughout all the elements, I returned to my proper place: about midnight I saw the sun brightly shine, I saw likewise the gods celestial and the gods infernal, before whom I presented myself and worshipped them. Behold now have I told thee, which although thou hast heard, yet it is necessary that thou conceal it; wherefore this only will I tell, which may be declared without offence for the understanding of the profane.

When morning came and that the solemnities were finished, I came forth sanctified with twelve stoles and in a religious habit, whereof I am not forbidden to speak, considering that many persons saw me at that time. There I was commanded to stand upon a pulpit of wood which stood in the middle of the temple, before the figure and remembrance of the goddess; my vestment was of fine linen, covered and embroidered with flowers; I had a precious cope upon my shoulders, hanging down behind me to the ground, whereon were beasts wrought of divers colours, as Indian dragons, and Hyperborean griffins, whom in form of birds the other part of the world doth engender: the priests commonly call such a habit an Olympian stole. In my right hand I carried a lighted torch, and a garland of flowers was upon my head, with white palm-leaves sprouting out on every side like rays; thus I was adorned like unto the sun, and made in fashion of an image, when the curtains were drawn aside and all the people compassed about to behold me. Then they began to solemnise the feast, the nativity of my holy order, with sumptuous banquets and pleasant meats: the third day was likewise celebrate with like ceremonies, with a religious dinner, and with all the consummation of the adept order. Now when I had continued there some days, conceiving a marvellous pleasure and consolation in beholding ordinarily the image of the goddess, because of the benefits, beyond all esteem or reward, which she had brought me, at length she admonished me to depart homeward, not without rendering of thanks, which although they were not sufficient, yet they were according to my power. Howbeit I could hardly be persuaded to break the chains of my most earnest devotion and to depart, before I had fallen prostrate before the face of the goddess and wiped her feet with my face, whereby I began so greatly to weep and sigh that my words were interrupted, and as devouring my prayer I began to say in this sort: 'O holy and blessed dame, the perpetual comfort of human kind, who by Thy bounty and grace nourishest all the world, and bearest a great affection to the adversities of the miserable as a loving mother, Thou takest no rest night or day, neither art Thou idle at any time in giving benefits and succouring all men as well on land as sea; Thou art she that puttest away all storms and dangers from men's life by stretching forth Thy right hand, whereby likewise Thou dost unweave even the inextricable and tangled web of fate, and appeasest the great tempests of fortune, and keepest back the harmful course of the stars. The gods supernal do honour Thee; the gods infernal have Thee in reverence; Thou dost make all the earth to turn, Thou givest light to the sun, Thou governest the world, Thou treadest down the power of hell. By Thy mean the stars give answer, the seasons return, the gods rejoice, the elements serve: at Thy commandment the winds do blow, the clouds nourish the earth, the seeds prosper, and the fruits do grow. The birds of the air, the beasts of the hill, the serpents of the den, and the fishes of the sea do tremble at Thy majesty: but my spirit is not able to give Thee sufficient praise, my patrimony is unable to satisfy Thy sacrifices; my voice hath no power to utter that which I think of Thy majesty, no, not if I had a thousand mouths and so many tongues and were able to continue for ever. Howbeit as a good religious person, and according to my poor estate, I will do what I may: I will always keep Thy divine appearance in remembrance, and close the imagination of Thy most holy godhead within my breast.'

When I had ended my oration to the great goddess, I went to embrace the great priest Mithras, now my spiritual father, clinging upon his neck and kissing him oft, and demanding his pardon, considering I was unable to recompense the good which he had done me: and after much talk and great greetings and thanks I departed from him straight to visit my parents and friends, after that I had been so long absent. And so within a short while after, by the exhortation of the goddess I made up my packet and took shipping towards the city of Rome, and I voyaged very safely and swiftly with a prosperous wind to the port of Augustus, and thence travelling by chariot, I arrived at that holy city about the twelfth day of December in the evening. And the greatest desire which I had there was daily to make my prayers to the sovereign goddess Isis, who, by reason of the place where her temple was builded, was called Campensis,* and continually is adored of the people of Rome: her minister and worshipper was I, a stranger to her church, but not unknown to her religion.

When now the sun had passed through all the signs of heaven and the year was ended, and that the goddess warned me again in my sleep to receive a new order and consecration, I marvelled greatly what it should signify and what should happen, considering that I was most fully an initiate and sacred person already. But it fortuned that while I partly reasoned with myself, and partly examined the perplexity of my conscience with the priests and bishops, there came a new and marvellous thought to my mind: that is to say, that I was only religious to the goddess Isis, but not yet sacred to the religion of great Osiris, the sovereign father of all the gods; between whom, although there was a religious concord or even unity, yet there was a great difference of order and ceremony, and so I thought that I should likewise believe myself to be called to be a minister unto Osiris. There was no long delay of doubt: for in the night after appeared unto me one of that order, covered with linen robes, holding in his hands spears wrapped in ivy, and other things not convenient to declare, which he left in my chamber, and sitting in my seat, recited to me such things as were necessary for the

* The temple of Isis was in the Campus Martius.

sumptuous banquet of my religious entry. And to the end I might know him again, he showed me a certain sign, to wit, how the heel of his left foot was somewhat maimed, which caused him a little to halt. After that I did manifestly thus know the will of the gods, and all shadow of doubtfulness was taken away, when matins was ended I went diligently from one to another to find if there were any of the priests which had the halting mark of his foot, according as I learned by my vision. At length I found it true; for I perceived one of the company of the Pastophores who had not only the token of his foot but the stature and habit of his body resembling in every point as he appeared in the night, and he was called Asinius* Marcellus, a name not much disagreeing from my transformation. By and by I went to him, which knew well enough all the matter, as being admonished by like precept to give me the orders: for it seemed to him the night before, as he dressed the flowers and garlands about the head of the great god Osiris, he understood by the mouth of his image, which told the predestinations of all men, how he did send to him a certain poor man of Madaura, to whom he should straightway minister his sacraments, whereby through his divine providence the one should receive glory for his virtuous studies, and the other, being the priest himself, a great reward. When I saw myself thus deputed and promised unto religion, my desire was stopped by reason of poverty; for I had spent a great part of my patrimony, which was not very large, in travel and peregrinations, but most of all my charges in the city of Rome were by far greater than in the provinces. Thereby my low estate withdrew me a great while, so that I was in much distress betwixt the victim and the knife† (as the old proverb hath it), and yet I was not seldom urged and pressed on by that same god. In the end, being oftentimes stirred forward and at last commanded, and not without great trouble of mind, I was constrained to sell my poor robe for a little money; howbeit, I scraped up sufficient for all my affairs. Then thus it was particularly spoken unto me, saying: 'How is it that for a little pleasure thou wouldest not be afraid to sell thy vestments,

---

* Adlington's note: 'Asinius by taking away the letter i is made Asinus.'
† The old sacrificial knife was of stone, for iron was taboo (to use the current anthropological jargon) in religious, and therefore conservative, rites. The proverb has no exact equivalent in modern English: perhaps the nearest phrase is 'between the upper and the nether millstone'.

but entering into so great ceremonies, dost fear to fall into poverty? But such poverty thou shalt never repent.' I did therefore prepare myself, and for ten other days abstain from all animal meats, and did shave my head: then was initiate into the ceremonies of the great god, which were done in the night, and I did frequent his services and sacrifices the more confidently because I did already know well the like religion of this. This thing gave me great comfort in my peregrination abroad, and likewise ministered unto me more plentiful living, considering by the favour of good fortune I gained some money in haunting to the courts of law, by reason I did plead causes in the Latin tongue.

Not very much after I was again called and admonished by the marvellous commands of gods, which I did very little expect, to receive a third order of religion. Then I was greatly astonied, and I pondered doubtfully in my mind, because I could not tell what this new vision signified, or what the intent of the celestial gods was, or how anything could remain yet lacking, seeing that twice already I had entered the holy orders. And I doubted lest the former priests had given me ill counsel or not enough, and fearing that they had not faithfully entrusted me, being in this manner as it were incensed. Then while I was in this great doubt and consideration, being driven almost unto madness, the gentle image appeared to me the night following, and giving me admonition said: 'There is no occasion why thou shouldest be afraid with so often order of religion, as though there were somewhat omitted: but thou shouldest rather rejoice because the gods have found thee so worthy, since as it hath pleased them to call thee three times, when as it is hardly given to any other person to achieve to the order but once; and from that number thou mayst think thyself ever most happy for so great benefits. And know thou that the religion which thou must now receive is right necessary, if thou do but consider that the garment of the goddess which thou tookest in the province doth still remain in the temple there, and so that thou canst not persevere in the worshipping of her in Rome and in making solemnity of the festival day with thy blessed habit. Let then this thing be a glory and blessing and health to thee, and once more, the great gods being thy helpers, be initiate with glad mind into holy orders.'

After this sort the divine majesty persuaded me in my sleep what should be to my profit. Whereupon I forgat not nor delayed the matter at all, but by and by I went towards the priest and declared all that which I had seen. Then I fasted again from all flesh according to the custom, and of mine own proper will I abstained longer than the ten days which I was commanded, and I bought at my own charges all that was necessary, considering rather the measure of my piety and zeal than that which was ordained. And verily I did nothing repent of the pain which I had taken and of the charges which I was at, considering that the divine providence had given me such an order that I gained much money in pleading of causes. Finally after a few days the great god Osiris appeared in my sleep, which is the more powerful god of the great gods, the highest of the greater, the greatest of the highest, and the ruler of the greatest, to me in the night, not disguised in any other form, but in his own essence and speaking to me with his own venerable voice, commanding me that I should now get me great glory by being an advocate in the court, and that I should not fear the slander and envy of ill persons, which bare me stomach and grudge by reason of my doctrine which I had gotten by much labour. Moreover he would not that I should serve his mysteries mixed with the rest of the number of his priests, but he chose me to enter the college of the Pastophores, nay he allotted me to be one of his decurions and quinquennial priests: wherefore I executed mine office in great joy with a shaven crown in that most ancient college which was set up in the time of Sulla, not covering or hiding the tonsure of my head, but showing it openly to all persons.

WORDSWORTH CLASSICS
OF WORLD LITERATURE